"You botched the report on the Coyote Springs–Abilene game," Renn Davis complained

"Reversed the scores," he continued.

"Well," Marlee Reid drawled a little sheepishly as she climbed down from the set, "the numbers were right there on the screen. Viewers could see it was a simple mix-up."

"And how were they supposed to know which one you screwed up?" Renn retorted with a thin smile and a raised eyebrow. "Your commentary or your graphic?"

Having no suitable comeback, Marlee sashayed toward the studio door without responding, her chin held high, a taunting smile pasted on her face to disguise her annoyance at Renn's persistent criticism.

Standing over to the side, the anchor of the sportscast clucked his tongue and cocked his head in amusement at the two younger people. Renn Davis had been sniping at Marlee Reid ever since he'd arrived at KNCS-TV six months earlier to assume his first post as news director. The games those two played. They seemed totally oblivious to the subliminal message they were sending. He was looking forward to seeing the day when the light came on.

Dear Reader,

Have you ever had a job you loved but that somehow turned to…disappointment? Marlee Reid is in that position. The only thing she's ever wanted to be is a sportscaster, and by golly, she is. But then bad things happen, people around her change and her aspirations, while never completely going away, become tarnished, and she's forced to make life-altering decisions.

Her boss, Renn Davis, the news director, is in the same boat. He's spent all his life in the media, loves the frenetic world of news and sports, of perpetually being in on the action. He's also a man of principles. One is that women don't make good sportscasters. The other is a firm rule—never get involved with a woman in the media. Recent events at the television station, however, compel him to rethink both these prejudices.

I hope you enjoy this tiny glimpse into the unique and fascinating world of television news and sports and the dilemmas that the people in this story have to face.

I enjoy hearing from readers. You can e-mail me at kncasper@kncasper.com, or write me at P.O. Box 61511, San Angelo, Texas 76904. Please also visit my Web site: www.kncasper.com.

Sincerely,

K.N. Casper

Books by K.N. Casper

HARLEQUIN SUPERROMANCE

The Woman in the News

K.N. Casper

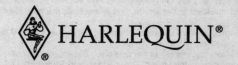

HARLEQUIN®

TORONTO • NEW YORK • LONDON
AMSTERDAM • PARIS • SYDNEY • HAMBURG
STOCKHOLM • ATHENS • TOKYO • MILAN • MADRID
PRAGUE • WARSAW • BUDAPEST • AUCKLAND

ISBN 0-373-71161-1

THE WOMAN IN THE NEWS

Copyright © 2003 by Kenneth Casper.

My thanks go first of all to my son-in-law Greg Kerr, for his insights into the world of sports and sportscasting. To Lori, who always comes through with valuable suggestions, and to Mary, who continues to inspire.

It's long past due that I offer my heartfelt thanks to Paula Eykelhof, who took a chance and gave me an opportunity for which I will always be grateful.

And a very special thanks to Beverley Sotolov, editor extraordinaire, whose patience, encouragement and friendship have guided me every step along the way.

PROLOGUE

"YOU BOTCHED the report on the Coyote Springs-Abilene game," Renn Davis complained. "Reversed the scores."

Marlee Reid glanced over at Clark Van Pelt, her boss and the anchor of the sportscast they'd just completed.

He awarded her an affectionate grin and nodded.

"Well," she drawled a little sheepishly, as she climbed down from the television set, "the numbers were right there on the screen. Viewers could see it was a simple mix-up."

"And how were they supposed to know which one you screwed up?" Renn retorted with a thin smile and a raised eyebrow. "Your commentary or your graphic?"

Having no suitable comeback, she sashayed toward the studio door without responding, her chin held high.

"You also let your ignorance of Michigan show," Renn called out to her retreating figure.

She swung around at the challenge, as he no doubt calculated she would. "I know they're going into the tournament as the favorites with a record of seventeen-three." She pasted on a taunting smile to disguise her annoyance at his persistent criticism. "Or is there something else you have in mind?"

Standing over on the side, Clark tucked his tongue in his cheek and cocked his head in amusement at the two younger people. Renn had been sniping at Marlee ever since he'd arrived at KNCS-TV six months ago to assume his first post as a news director. Clark took a kind of fierce pride in the fact that Renn always got as good as he gave. "I think he's referring to Milbrew's hometown in Michigan," he told Marlee.

"Charlotte?" she asked. "What about it?"

"It's pronounced Shallot," Renn informed her, "with the accent on the last syllable."

She pulled back and stared at Clark. "Is that true?"

He pursed his lips, his blue eyes twinkling.

"I wasn't aware of that."

"Obviously," Renn sniped. "If there are any Michiganders in the viewing area, I'm sure you'll hear about it."

Marlee snorted in frustration. "How was I supposed to know that's how they pronounced it up there? In North Carolina it's called Charlotte, just like the girl's name."

Clark started to walk away.

"Okay, wise guy," Marlee snapped at Renn. "Here's one for *you.*"

Clark turned and caught the smug, almost haughty expression on her face. The games these two played amused him, especially since they seemed totally oblivious to the subliminal messages they were sending. He was looking forward to seeing the day when the light came on.

Marlee grabbed the pen from Renn's shirt pocket, scratched a word in the margin of the top page of her broadcast notes and shoved it under his nose. "How do you pronounce the name of this town in East Texas?''

The news director grabbed the paper just before it fell to the floor, glanced at it, shrugged and said, ''Mexia?''

''Wrong,'' she said with undisguised glee. ''It's Ma-hay-ya, with the accent on the second syllable.''

This time it was Renn who looked over to Clark for confirmation. The sports anchor arched his eyebrows and nodded a *Gotcha.*

Redirecting his attention at Marlee, then at the paper in his hand, Renn let out a guffaw. ''Okay, hotshot—'' he raised a finger and stroked two marks in the air ''—Christians one, Lions one.''

She smiled sweetly at Renn and remarked, ''And we both know which side you're on.''

Clark chuckled and walked away.

CHAPTER ONE

Friday, February 7th

"WE INTERRUPT this program to bring you a special announcement," a deep, off-screen voice stated, as the news set suddenly appeared in place of the Friday-night network program. Marlee sat opposite the news anchor, both of them staring into the camera with sober expressions.

"We have just received confirmation from the Texas Department of Public Safety," Mickey Grimes said, "that about an hour ago the bus carrying the Coyote Springs High School basketball team home from Del Rio was washed off the road in a flash flood. Details are still sketchy. What we know at this point is that it happened at a low-water crossing over the dry fork of the Devil's River. A spokesman for the department informs us that the helicopter rescue squadron stationed at Laughlin Air Force Base has been deployed to the scene and is currently airlifting survivors back to Del Rio."

He turned to his left. "Our own sports director, Clark Van Pelt, was traveling with the boys after their stunning victory over the Del Rio Devils, Marlee. Have you received any word from him?"

The camera swept to her. In spite of her carefully applied makeup, she appeared pale, perhaps because ⁓ was so uncharacteristically stiff.

"I've been trying to contact him on his cell phone ever since we heard about this accident, Mickey. So far I've been unsuccessful. As soon as I do—" Her voice began to quaver.

"We'll break in with the latest developments," Grimes finished for her. "We return you now to our regularly scheduled programming."

Marlee continued to stare glassy-eyed into the camera until the red light went off and she saw the signal from the producer that they were no longer on the air.

Mickey offered her an encouraging smile. "I'm sure he's fine. Maybe a little wet, though."

She tried to return the smile and failed. While Mickey responded to a comment from the news producer, Shelley Chester, Marlee leaned over and grabbed the crutches on the floor beside her, stood up and hobbled down from the set, only vaguely aware of the sharp pain in her right ankle. Renn Davis stood by the studio door, watching her.

"Any contact yet?" she asked, though his stony expression had already given her the answer. Her insides knotted. Her stomach ached.

Renn blinked slowly and shook his head.

A heaviness settled in Marlee's chest. There were any number of reasons that Clark wasn't answering his cell phone. Atmospherics due to the storm. A tower blown down. He may have turned the phone off or forgotten to charge it—that wouldn't be the first time. Or it might have been lost or damaged.

"The highway department believes three people are missing," Renn said, then hastened to add, "but they're not sure and haven't released any names. We'll wait until we get confirmation from them and the next of kin have been notified before announcing anything on the air. No use scaring people when we don't know the facts.''

She nodded and swayed as a sudden wave of dizziness swamped her.

Renn reached out and wrapped his arm around her shoulders to steady her. ''You all right?''

The unexpected gesture and the firm strength of his touch caught her off guard. The simple contact felt reassuring enough for her to want to wallow in it. She regained her balance and straightened. He released his grip.

''I'm sure he's fine,'' Renn said, attempting to sound positive. She didn't miss the note of doubt in the words, however. He was worried, too. He walked beside her down the narrow hallway to the newsroom.

THE CAVERNOUS work center was a madhouse. The pandemonium associated with last-minute preparations for the news at ten never failed to shoot an extra spurt of adrenaline into Renn's bloodstream. He'd grown up in the media world, been lulled by the raspy chatter of teletypes when he was a kid. In spite of its downsides, erratic hours, missed weekends and holidays and occasional public hostility, the excitement hadn't completely lost its allure. Tonight there was an added throb of urgency. This wasn't just another big story, breaking news; this involved one of their own. For a few seconds he stood, watched and listened.

The telephones that people didn't have cradled against their ears as they solicited information from police, paramedics and other emergency organizations were ringing off their hooks. Stations in cities across Texas were calling for information. Against the far wall, wire-service printers clicked and buzzed, a police scanner crackled and burped, while computer sound cards beeped and chirped.

Pearl Montez, the local news reporter who handled the Hispanic beat, was hanging up the phone with one hand and jotting down notes on a steno pad with the other. A fifteen-year veteran who'd covered innumerable local accidents and tragedies, the short, round native of Coyote Springs was caring and sensitive, but she could also be aggressive.

Not far away, Darius Smith was slapping fresh labels on the stash of videotapes he carried for his camcorder. Six feet tall, rail thin, dark-skinned with a retro Afro hairdo and a diamond stud in his left ear, he was in his late twenties and had been with the station five years. He was also good with the camera.

Mickey Grimes brushed between Renn and Marlee with a barely audible "Excuse me" and raced to his desk, where he snatched up his phone. It was time for Renn to get into action.

"Pearl," he called, as he approached Montez and motioned to Darius to join them, "I want you two to take the van and drive down to the crash site. Get as close as the police will allow. Find Clark, interview him and the rest of the survivors, rescue workers and any other people on the scene. We want to know exactly what happened."

"You got it," Pearl said.

"What about the Sky-Spot?" asked Shelley. She'd just hung up the phone at the neighboring desk.

"We'll deploy it," Renn said, "at first light."

The station's helicopter was used mostly for transporting reporters to remote locations, but it had an aerial photography capability, as well. Expense of operation dictated that it be used judiciously.

"With military choppers in the area, I don't want to risk a midair collision or interfere with rescue operations. One tragedy is enough."

They nodded. No one doubted the seriousness of the situation.

"In the meantime, I want you and one of the photographers—take Wayne Prentice—to search through the archives for any footage that might fit the situation—shots of flash floods, of buses half submerged in floodwaters. We won't need them if Darius can get us something at the scene, but under the circumstances he may not be able to."

Shelley nodded and scribbled a note to herself.

"Also," Renn went on, "we'll want the most recent group pictures of the Coyote Springs High School basketball team, its coach—"

"We have Marlee's last interview with Coach Hillman after the Abilene game," Wayne Prentice offered. He'd been her photographer for about a year. Young, ambitious and enterprising, he had potential if he could learn to be more disciplined.

"Good."

Renn watched out of the corner of his eye as Marlee struggled with her crutches between the desks to join them. The pain in her foot was undoubtedly enough to cause the tight expression on her face, but he suspected it had more to do with uncertainty about Clark's fate. Not only was the sports anchor her boss and mentor, but a close personal friend.

He turned again to Wayne and Shelley. "Put together a montage of Van Pelt clips—of him interviewing famous athletes, helping with handicapped kids, the dinner where he received the National Sportscaster of the Year Award—''

''Sounds like an obit.'' Marlee cleared her throat. ''Is he dead? Have the police—''

She was close to tears, though she was fighting valiantly to hold them back. He marveled at her composure under the circumstances.

''No,'' he assured her. ''I'm putting together a tribute. Depending on what happened…if he gets hurt…or actively involved in the rescue…you have to admit it would be just like him.''

She combed her fingers nervously through her shoulder-length blond hair. He could see in her eyes that she wanted to argue with him, but she was also a professional who knew they had to plan for contingencies.

''I'll help,'' she told the others.

A surge of flowery perfume heralded the arrival of Peggy Faykus, the daytime receptionist.

''I heard what happened on the car radio after I took the grandkids home from soccer practice,'' she announced. Five-ten, with raspberry-colored big hair, she carried enough weight to intimidate a football lineman. ''Any word on Clark?''

Renn shook his head.

She looked at the familiar anarchy around her. ''I'll open the switchboard and deal with the nuisance calls.''

He was grateful for the offer. ''I don't want any information given out that hasn't already been reported on the air.''

''I'm familiar with the rules and the routine, Mr. Davis.''

He shook his head by way of apology. "Sorry, Peg. I know you're an old hand at this."

"Watch that *old* part," she retorted, forgiving him with a thin smile. At fifty-five, she'd been at the station almost thirty years, longer than anyone else.

"Thanks for doing this. We'll work out comp time or something—" He stopped when Peggy planted her right hand where Renn presumed her hip would be, frowned and peered past him. He turned.

Faye Warren, the station's vice president, stood in the reception area, the glass front door inching closed behind her. Instead of a short-skirted business suit that showed off her shapely legs, she was wearing jeans and a tank top. Several people turned to stare, unused to seeing her casually attired.

"What's going on?" she demanded of Renn without greeting him or anyone else.

He took no offense. The situation was tense. Everyone was on edge, and she wasn't the easygoing, amiable type under the best of circumstances. He led her over to the side so Peg could get behind her desk, then filled her in on the latest developments.

"Why was Van Pelt on the bus? He's the sports director, not a cub reporter. Why didn't Marlee go?"

"She sprained her ankle this morning and is using crutches. Clark's scheduled to do a feature interview with Coach Hillman next week, so he figured this trip would give him a chance to discuss it with him."

She frowned. "What are we doing to cover the story?"

Renn offered her a rundown of the assignments he'd given out. She paused, her eyes measuring him.

"I'll be in my office. Let me know as soon as you learn anything more."

He nodded. She gave another cursory glance at the busy newsroom, then entered the stairwell to the second floor. She'd barely disappeared from view when Sal Bufano, the general manager, arrived.

"What's the latest, Renn?" he asked.

Renn repeated his report.

"Why is Clark with them?"

He explained about Marlee's sprained ankle.

"This is terrible. What can I do to help?" Bufano asked.

"Renn," Peggy called out, "I have the mayor on the line."

"How about handling some of the high-profile calls? Peggy can deal with the ones from the general public, but if you could help her with—"

"Glad to. I'll take that, Peg." Sal hastily poured a cup of coffee from the machine in the corner, parked himself at the desk behind the receptionist and picked up the phone. "Good evening, Mr. Mayor."

Mickey Grimes waved from across the room. Renn hurried over. The news anchor finished scribbling a note, thanked the caller and hung up. "That was my contact in the sheriff's office. They're pretty sure there have been fatalities."

Renn pressed his fingers to his temple, as the image flashed through his mind of teenage boys' dead bodies lined up side by side on the cold, wet ground. "Any names?"

"Not yet."

"I don't want any speculation on the air, not about

life and death.'' Renn looked over at the switchboard, which was all lit up. ''The community is tense enough.''

Grimes nodded. ''The police are bringing the parents of team members to the high-school auditorium so they can all be briefed together about developments.''

''Good. We can report that in our next bulletin.'' Renn tried to imagine the agony the families of the victims must be going through. As a reporter, commentator and news anchor himself, he'd covered many tragedies over the years, but he'd never found words that made it easier to deal with the death or injury of loved ones, especially children. At least in this case, the next of kin wouldn't be alone.

''We need to get a team over there to cover the human-interest angle. Who's available?''

''Just Marlee and me.''

He peered over, not for the first time, at the editing booth where she and Wayne Prentice were reviewing tapes. She was sitting at the moment with her leg up on the end of a work table, but in a minute she'd stand and walk to another shelf of cassettes. Judging by the way she adjusted the foot, her ankle was killing her. He'd send her home if he thought she'd go, but he knew she wouldn't. Clark was more like a father than a colleague. Renn envied her that. Close friendships were exceptional in this business, which thrived on competition. To have someone you could completely trust was rare. If Clark was one of the fatalities, how would she handle it? He hoped he wouldn't have to find out.

"She's in no condition to go over there," he told Mickey. He wasn't thinking as much about her physical limitations as the emotional shape she'd be in if Clark turned out to be among the dead. "Take Wayne and file your report live from the auditorium. Marlee can handle things at this end."

The newsman nodded. "If Clark is—"

"She'll be better off here. Now, get going."

The ten o'clock broadcast was devoted almost exclusively to the mishap. Mickey Grimes, reporting from the high school, repeated the story they'd broken earlier and followed it with interviews of friends and family members assembled there, tensely waiting for word of their loved ones.

From the studio Marlee showed highlights of the game against the Del Rio Devils that Wayne Prentice had put together earlier. Coyote Springs had won, but the victory now seemed unimportant.

MARLEE COULDN'T stop trembling. Notes she wrote to herself were illegible. When she stood up on her good foot, she was so weak she nearly collapsed.

Clark would never have been on that bus if it hadn't been for her. She'd been the one scheduled to go to Del Rio to cover the game against the Devils, but on her usual three-mile run this morning she'd tripped and twisted her ankle badly enough to send her to the emergency room. Nothing broken, as she'd feared. The medics had bound the swollen joint and given her crutches, with instruction to stay off the foot for the next week. Even with the Tylenol she was taking, the pain throbbed mercilessly when she didn't keep the leg elevated.

Clark had been upset and solicitous about her when she'd hobbled in at two o'clock, her regular time. Since the basketball game was the last of the regular season and would determine if Coyote Springs got to play in the statewide finals, his first impulse had been to send Wayne Prentice, the photographer, by himself to shoot video. Not an ideal solution, especially if Coyote Springs was victorious, but at least Marlee would have something to show on the late news.

Then, at the last moment, Clark had decided to make the trip himself, saying it would give him a chance to discuss his upcoming interview with Coach Hillman. He and Wayne had taken the station's van to the border town, but Clark had sent the cameraman back after the first half, in time to edit footage for the ten o'clock broadcast. Clark himself elected to hang around and return home with the team on the school bus. If Marlee had gone as planned, she would have come back with Wayne, and Clark would still be here. Instead, because of her clumsiness, he'd been caught in a flash flood. If anything happened to him, how would she ever face his wife, Audrey, and the rest of the family?

Marlee wouldn't even be here if not for Clark. He'd been her broadcast journalism professor at Texas University at Coyote Springs and the person she naturally gravitated toward for help and encouragement, like the father she wished she had. They'd kept in touch following her graduation, after she'd moved to Austin with her new husband to start her own career. Three years later her contract as a sports producer ended about the same time a sports reporter job came open at KNCS-TV. Clark had urged her to apply for it. Coyote Springs was a smaller market than the capital city, and some people might see her coming back as a sign of failure. But, as Clark had pointed out, it was an excellent opportunity to expand her experience and get on camera. She'd learned so much under his tutelage. He'd also taken her into his family and made her feel a part of it.

She had tried to call Audrey to find out if she'd heard from Clark, but the line was always busy…except the last time. She'd gotten the answering machine, probably because, like the parents of all the team members, Audrey had gone to the school auditorium. Marlee had become angry enough to yell at Renn when she found out he'd sent Mickey Grimes there instead of her. She wanted to be with Audrey and the other families, but Renn had pointed to her injured foot and insisted she stay at the station, ready to go on the air with the next breaking news.

An excuse. That was all it was. He'd already made it abundantly clear he didn't think much of her as a sports reporter. Now he was saying she couldn't handle this situation because it was too personal. She was a professional, dammit, not some flighty schoolgirl. Even if…if Clark was one of the victims— No, she wouldn't go there. He was safe. He had to be.

IT WAS NEARLY midnight when Renn received official word and the full story could be released. Grimes was still at the assembly hall, so Marlee took his seat on the news set, while everyone, including the executives, crowded into the studio and stood behind the camera in total silence.

"Ladies and gentlemen," she began soberly, "the Texas Department of Public Safety has just informed us that three people were lost and are confirmed dead in the flash flood that capsized the bus bringing the Coyote Springs High School basketball team home from Del Rio. They are James Brookshire, seventeen, Mamoud Stone, sixteen, and—" she paused for a second "—KNCS-TV's sports director and television anchor, Clark Van Pelt."

CHAPTER TWO

FAYE WARREN CLIMBED the carpeted stairs to her office, surprised when she realized her knees were shaking. Clark's death was a shock she'd never anticipated. Life was so damn unfair. The sports director had been the one person at KNCS she'd genuinely respected and admired, the one man she felt she could trust to be true to his word. He was only a few years her senior, yet she'd looked up to him the way she'd looked up to her father. Like her father, he'd left abruptly, without a word of farewell, without ever giving her a chance to tell him how she felt about him.

That was probably part of her attraction to Taggart. He was the least likely candidate for father figure she'd ever met. More like a bad-boy kid brother, except she didn't have any brothers, and she and Tag were having sex. Very hot sex.

She crumpled into her chair, took a deep breath and picked up the phone. He answered on the third ring, his voice muffled from sleep.

"He's dead, Tag," she said. "Clark's dead. Did you see the special bulletin?"

She'd called him earlier in the evening with news of the bus accident, half expecting him to come into the station like almost everyone else who worked there. But he hadn't. Probably just as well. She suspected most people at KNCS knew about their relationship, but it wouldn't have helped her image if she'd cried on his shoulder when they'd received word of Clark's death.

"I fell back to sleep," Tag said. "He drowned?"

"Trying to save a couple of the kids. God, what must his wife be going through."

Faye's own marriage, when she was twenty-two, had lasted only four years. She'd dreamed of growing old with Clayton Abernathy, surrounded by children and grandchildren, but when he found out she couldn't have kids, he'd promptly divorced her. She'd loved Clay with all her heart, but it hadn't made any difference. Love didn't conquer anything—not in her life. It just left her vulnerable, and she was tired of being hurt by other people. Dreaming was a mistake, she'd learned, because eventually you had to wake up.

Taggart didn't respond to her comment, but then, what could he possibly say? Platitudes didn't change anything, either.

"Where are you now?" he asked after a long pause.

"Still at the office."

"Instead of going home, why don't you come on over here?"

The invitation was tempting. She wanted to be held, needed a man's body curled up against her to assure her she could feel something besides the pain of loss, the agony of loneliness. The men in her life all disappeared—her father, her husband, not to mention the guys who had followed for various lengths of time. And now Clark. Each left her to grieve and ask the unanswerable question: why? That could be another reason she'd hooked up with Taggart this time. He was young—six years her junior—and strong. Realizing she wanted to experience his virility tonight shamed her.

"You don't have to be alone," Taggart added.

He understood. Maybe what she was feeling was normal after all.

"Besides," he added, "we have to work out a strategy, start planning."

"Strategy? Plan? What are you talking about?"

"Come on, Faye. With Clark gone, the sports director job is open. I want it. You shouldn't have any problem giving it to me now."

A good man was dead and Taggart was only interested in the spoils, the opportunity it opened for him.

"You bastard," she snarled. "He hasn't even been buried yet, and already you're—"

"Whoa, sweetheart. Calm down. Sorry if that makes me sound callous—"

It's always about him, she thought, and immediately reprimanded herself. She was being unfair. He'd lost a colleague, too. To see things objectively in the face of tragedy and death was hard for anyone.

"But you can't tell me," he continued, "that you haven't thought about what you're going to do now that he's gone."

What he said was true, which only reinforced her sense of guilt. Clark had been a legend at KNCS-TV long before she got there. Ensuring his shoes were properly filled was now her responsibility. Taggart was the logical choice.

"I don't want to talk about it tonight," she told him, without denying the truth of his statement.

"Come on over anyway," he said. "You don't have to sleep alone."

Did that make her some sort of monster? A colleague had just died, and she was fixating on sex, as if it alone could prove she was still alive, still desirable. Is this what they called a midlife crisis? Maybe if she focused on work, on hiring Taggart as the new sports director...

"I'll be there in about fifteen minutes." Maybe she could make this man stay, faults and all.

Wednesday, February 12

UNLIKE THE ROOMS downstairs in the sprawling two-story TV station, the general manager's office on the second floor had windows. Also unlike the work spaces below, with their commercial-grade carpets and cheap wall paneling, the executive suites were elegantly appointed.

Sal Bufano waited until Renn and Faye had taken seats across from his massive desk. "I thought Marlee's eulogy for Clark was beautiful," he said.

Faye had suggested Taggart give it for the station, but Audrey Van Pelt had adamantly refused.

Renn wasn't quite sure how Marlee managed to keep from breaking down during her emotional tribute, one that had most of the women audibly sniffling and a few of the men tearing up, but she had, and he admired her for it.

"I hate funerals," Faye Warren muttered, as she removed a blond hair from the sleeve of her black suit—a sharp contrast to the soft colors and pastels she normally wore.

"I'm glad it's over," Renn said sympathetically.

"We're going to miss him," Sal added. "Who would ever have imagined he'd drown in a school bus. I mean—it's so unlikely. He certainly had a lot of friends and admirers. There must have been over a thousand people at the church, and the cortege to the cemetery held up traffic for miles."

"It's time to move on," Faye said, obviously uncomfortable with the discussion.

"The question now," Sal said, "is whether we bring in someone from outside to replace Clark or we promote from within."

"We move Taggart into the anchor slot," Faye said, as if the answer were obvious.

Renn cringed. As the news director, the sports department came under his immediate supervision. Theoretically, the decision was his, and there was no way he wanted the opinionated sports analyst—whose personality traits ranged from temperamental self-importance to smug condescension—taking over the sports-director job. Anyone would be better than Taggart.

"He doesn't have the journalism background," Renn offered.

Faye crossed one shapely leg over the other, not bothering to tug down the hem of her skirt, and stabbed Renn with a sharp glare. "Taggart knows more about sports than anyone we're likely to hire."

"How about Chris Berman or Al Michaels?" Renn suggested, his expression deadpan. No way would either of the two nationally known sports commentators come to modest KNCS-TV.

"Get real," she scoffed.

Sal nodded. "We also have a budget."

Renn suppressed a smile. The general manager was

an all-right guy, but he was essentially a bean counter, used to dealing with numbers rather than personalities. Subtleties of humor tended to slip past him.

"Do you have anyone else in mind?" he asked.

Renn had been mulling it over since the day after Clark was killed. Six months earlier he would have recoiled at what he was about to propose, but if nothing else, it would buy him time to find someone better qualified. "Marlee Reid."

Faye's mouth curved down in exaggerated disdain. "As I said before, get real."

"Our surveys and focus groups give her high marks for viewer recognition. Audiences identify with her. She's also got camera presence."

"I suppose Taggart doesn't?" Faye scorned. "Anyway, she's too young."

Renn crooked a brow. "I didn't know we practiced age discrimination."

Faye shot him a withering glance, while Sal shifted uncomfortably in his seat. The *D* word was an absolute no-no.

"I'm not referring to her age," Faye replied with condescending patience. "I'm referring to her years of experience."

"Actually, her credentials are better than Taggart's." Renn counted off on his fingers. "A degree in broadcast journalism with a specialty in sports, three years as a sports producer in Austin and two years here as a reporter and weekend anchor under the direct supervision of Van Pelt, not to mention her filling in for him when he hasn't been here."

"Why did she leave Austin, anyway?" Sal asked. "They're a bigger market than we are."

"She wanted airtime and couldn't get it there.

Moving to a smaller market early in a career isn't unheard of, and it's not necessarily a bad thing.'' Renn turned to Faye. ''Van Pelt was smart to hire her. She's good and she's getting better.''

''This isn't The Learning Channel. Let her hone her skills on her own. We're not a school for amateurs but a commercial television station with a responsibility to our viewers to put our best assets on display.''

An obvious comeback was on Renn's lips, but no use wasting a cheap shot or stirring up a hornet's nest with personal attacks.

''We also have an obligation to our owners,'' he said, ''to produce in the most economical way possible.''

''Are you saying if we hire Reid for the anchor slot we can pay her less?'' Sal asked, interested but leery of the proposition, especially after the spector of prejudice had been introduced.

''I'd offer her a three-year contract with a substantial initial pay raise and annual pay increases after that. Taggart, I suspect, will demand as much or more than Clark was drawing simply because he considers himself a celebrity.''

Faye worried her lips and examined her long, sculptured fingernails but said nothing.

Renn continued, ''Even if we're able to hold Taggart to Clark's compensation package, he'll end up costing us more in operating expenses.''

''How?'' Sal asked, genuinely confused. ''I don't get it.''

A glance at Faye told Renn she understood perfectly where he was going, and she wasn't pleased.

''Taggart's a reasonably good analyst, but—''

She stiffened. ''He's taken awards for his sports analysis.''

''Most of them are ten years old. The only recent one was locally generated against competition that is virtually nonexistent.''

The vice president turned her face away.

''The problem,'' Renn went on, ''is that Taggart has never written or edited a news story. He has absolutely no experience as a producer or reporter, or—''

''The anchor doesn't have to,'' Faye interjected. ''That's Marlee's job.''

''Clark had decades of experience in all aspects of media coverage,'' Renn persisted, ''and could handle any task that needed doing. That's why he went to Del Rio in the first place, to report—''

''If Marlee had done her job and gone there like she was supposed to, we wouldn't be sitting here.''

Renn went stock-still, stunned by the heartlessness of the comment. He remembered the abject horror on Marlee's face when she had found out Clark was among the dead. After the broadcast that night, which she'd handled remarkably well, she'd turned into a virtual zombie. Renn had driven her home. On the way she'd said nothing, but at her door she'd finally cracked. He'd guided her inside, then held her while she cried, feeling totally helpless the entire time because he had no words to console her.

He'd butted heads with her often enough over the past several months to know she was quite capable of taking care of herself, but seeing her vulnerable side, hearing her berate herself for the very thing Faye was now insinuating, had shifted something inside him. He couldn't stop Marlee from having those thoughts, but he could keep this coldhearted woman from voicing them.

After a brittle six seconds, he asked, "Are you blaming her for Clark's death?"

Her eyes met his. She flinched. "Of course not. I didn't mean it that way."

"Good. I recommend you never, ever make a statement like that again."

Her mouth fell open; she was shocked by the coiled threat in his tone even more than his words. The sudden tension between the two of them prompted Bufano to step in.

"Why do you think Taggart would be better?" he asked Faye.

She paused for a moment to compose her thoughts. "He's a recognized expert in his field. No one knows more about sports in the TV market than he does, and no one has more contacts, which are vital to the sports coverage."

Renn wondered if he should point out that like Taggart's awards, his contacts were ten years out-of-date, mostly retired coaches and graduated college players.

"The job demands more than a command of statistics," he said. "Yeah, Taggart's well-connected, and his predictions are correct more often than not. I'm not suggesting we let him go. He can still be part of a winning team, just as he has been for the past three years. But he isn't anchor material."

"Why not?" Sal laced his fingers across his trim waist.

Renn wasn't sure whether the manager was asking these questions out of ignorance or merely giving Renn an opportunity to voice his opinion for the record.

"Taggart has none of the technical skills required for the job," he said. "Clark edited raw tapes, did voice-overs and created feature stories. All Taggart does is sit at the anchor desk and Monday-morning-quarterback why the local team won or lost. He never contributes to the production of a sportscast. He strolls into the station twenty minutes before airtime, reads scripts that someone else—most likely Marlee—wrote." A king on his throne handing down sports edicts. "If he gets the anchor position he'll need dedicated technical support. That means additional staff and more money in the budget."

Sal pursed his lips and stroked his chin. "What about that?" he asked Faye.

It was apparent from the set of her mouth and the way she tapped her fingers on the arm of the chair that she was fuming, but she was smart enough not to let her anger turn into temper.

"Renn's forgetting that the public doesn't care who does what behind the scenes. They want a face on the screen they recognize, one they can trust to give them the straight scoop. That's Taggart with a capital *T*. As for technical assistance, our existing staff can handle it."

"They're already busy full-time," Renn countered.

"We may have to do a little reorganizing," she admitted reluctantly, then added with conclusive certainty, "I really don't think it'll be a problem, Sal."

"I do," Renn shot back with equal fervor. He could feel her gray eyes drilling into him. "We don't have unlimited resources. If we tie someone up doing Taggart's work, he or she can't be doing their own."

"Supporting him will be their job." Faye heaved an impatient breath. "That's the point."

Renn shook his head. "We're playing a zero-sum game here, Faye. We have just so many people available to get our work done. Reorganizing isn't going to change that equation. Look, it comes down to this. There's nobody at this station whose job it is to support Taggart, and there's no money in the budget to hire someone."

She blew out a breath, frustrated by his adamancy. She wasn't used to being so openly challenged and clearly didn't like it, but Renn wasn't about to back down.

The irony was that he'd always been strenuously opposed to female sports reporters. Women had successfully assumed prominent roles in newsrooms. He had no problem with that, but sports coverage was different. While many female athletes had achieved international fame—and sometimes fortune—the realm of sweat and muscle was still dominated by men. There was a pact, a bond of camaraderie between males in those situations, that communicated itself to audiences and that a woman simply couldn't penetrate.

At least, that was what Renn had thought. He'd watched Marlee, intent on finding reasons to justify his prejudice, and found a bunch of little things to criticize. He hadn't hesitated to bring them up, either—often to Clark's amusement. At the end of the day, though, he had to admit she was at ease not only in front of the studio camera, but in the field, which was even more nerve-racking because live reports were usually on unfamiliar ground and sometimes in very tense situations.

"You're quite correct, Renn," Faye said now. "We can't afford to lose anyone. I can tell you this, however. Put Marlee Reid in the anchor seat and Taggart'll walk.''

''You've already discussed this with him?'' Sal asked, with raised brows.

Faye didn't miss the implied censure. Her composure stalled for a second. ''He asked me the other day about the job and said if he doesn't get it, he's out of here.''

For his part, Renn would have been happy to see the washed-up football player leave. Horace ''Tag'' Taggart wasn't greatly liked in the newsroom. His only other claims to fame, aside from his short-lived pro status, were his prodigious memory for sports history and stats and his notorious name-dropping. In spite of all that and his Hollywood-handsome looks, he really didn't connect with his audience. Renn was convinced the station would get over his absence with hardly a ripple of adverse reaction from viewers.

''Sounds like a threat,'' he commented, eyes narrowed.

''It's a candid statement of fact,'' she responded. ''The question is whether we'll be better off with Tag or without him.''

Sal raised his hand, palm out to forestall the remark he must have seen poised on Renn's lips. ''You really think he'll quit simply because we put Marlee in the anchor chair?''

''I can't see him working for a woman nearly fifteen years his junior, can you?''

The general manager shook his head. ''Clark's death has been unsettling enough. Taggart's a big name, a big draw. We don't dare throw that away.''

Renn tried to figure out if Sal was on his side or Faye's. He decided he probably wasn't on either. He just wanted to make money by keeping ratings up. Stations lived and died on numbers.

This discussion wasn't going anywhere, and Renn didn't want them painting themselves into corners they couldn't get out of without losing face. What would Clark do under these circumstances? *Temporize and compromise.*

"Maybe we shouldn't put anyone in the anchor seat for now," he said. "This soon after Clark's death, people might regard an abrupt change as disrespectful to his memory. I suggest we continue what we've been doing this past week—leave his place empty. Marlee can do the evening sportscast from the Live Center." This was the smaller set away from the anchor desk, normally used by reporters to introduce their stories before running them. "Taggart can give his weekly analysis by himself from the visitor's chair. That'll give everyone time to settle down."

Not an ideal solution, but it was better than being overruled outright. All Renn had to do now was explain to Marlee why she would be doing all the work of the anchor without getting the credit or the pay.

MARLEE RESISTED the temptation to pace. For one thing, her ankle hurt too much. She'd shunned the crutches during the funeral that morning and been fine until they'd gotten to the cemetery. The walk back to the car from the grave site had been pure agony. Renn had given her his arm to lean on, and she'd been grateful.

Actually, a little more than grateful. Disconcerted. She remembered crying on his shoulder the night Clark died, the gentle way he'd held her, soothingly stroking her back. He probably thought the words he'd mumbled had gone unheard or been unappreciated, but it wasn't the words that she'd valued. Never before had a man held her so innocently, so patiently, not demanding, only wanting to give comfort. At the cemetery, too, he'd been kind and generous. Perhaps it was her imagination, but she thought she'd also glimpsed loneliness.

As for pacing now, her cubicle was too small, anyway. The closets in her parents' lake house were bigger than this dinky cubbyhole. She'd just spin around in it and get dizzy.

She was probably naive to think she even had a chance at the sports-anchor job. In situations like this, stations often brought in new blood. A fresh face. Someone experienced. She'd been at KNCS-TV two years, two mostly wonderful years. Did she want to stay here now that Clark was gone? She'd never planned to remain in Coyote Springs indefinitely. In this business the only place an ambitious person stopped was at the top. But the prospect of job hunting depressed her. Clark had given her good evaluations; what about Renn? If Taggart became her boss and wrote her final performance review... Well, forget that. She wouldn't give him the satisfaction.

A fresh start was what she needed, but it wouldn't be easy. Despite all the policies and public statements about equal employment opportunity, women still had to fight an uphill battle in what was considered a man's domain. Renn Davis had made it perfectly clear from the outset that he didn't think much of women covering sports. Neither did Faye Warren, and Marlee had no reason to think they were about to change their minds.

The general manager was the wild card. Sal Bufano's interest was the bottom line. Profit, pure and simple. He was also a politician, the kind who didn't take chances. He'd bend whichever way the wind was blowing, and Faye could blow a pretty strong gust. Marlee mentally shook her head. She couldn't count on him, either.

She'd just about resigned herself to not getting the anchor job, when Renn strode to the door of her cubicle. "My office. Now, please," he said, and disappeared.

His abruptness chilled her. He didn't look happy, so obviously he didn't have good news. Surely they weren't firing her. They had no grounds. She hadn't done anything wrong, and her contract wasn't up for almost a year. Was Renn about to inform her they wouldn't be renewing it?

Marlee hit Close on the computer file she'd opened but not touched, lowered her foot from the desk drawer she'd pulled out and dragged herself down the thinly carpeted hall to the news director's office.

RENN HAD A DILEMMA. His chances of convincing Faye Warren to let him offer the anchor position to Marlee seemed slim to none, yet he didn't want to give up. For a couple of reasons.

First, he had scant respect for Taggart as a person, as an analyst or as a commentator. Oh, the guy was intelligent enough, but he was also shifty and devious—particularly unpleasant attributes when combined with vanity and laziness. He hid these true colors behind the good looks he so assiduously cultivated. Pretty boy spent more time working out at his health club and tanning salon than he did at the station.

Second, while he still wasn't sold on having a female sports anchor, Renn had to admit Marlee had earned his respect, however grudging, and most recently his unqualified admiration. She was hurting physically and emotionally, but she'd kept herself together, at least in the presence of other people.

Though Renn still wasn't thrilled with the prospect of a female sports anchor, he also realized he didn't want Marlee to bolt, which she undoubtedly would do if the sports analyst got the job. He didn't want to make too strong a point of it, but he liked having her around, liked the feisty way she responded to jibes and criticism. She was smart, no question about that, smart enough to know she'd never get a break working for Taggart. In fact, if he took over the sports department, Renn would be lucky if most of staff didn't quit within a few months.

All this ruminating didn't contribute one wit to how Renn was going to deal with her, of course. Tell her up-front she wouldn't be getting the anchor job and she'd be sending out résumé tapes to other stations in a heartbeat.

Yet he couldn't honestly assure her she had a decent shot at the job, either. There was only one solution. Tell her she had a chance. It wasn't a complete lie, and maybe it would buy him time to figure out how to get Taggart out of the picture. Which should be his real goal. Whether Marlee stayed or left, he definitely wanted Taggart gone.

"What's up, Renn?"

He whirled around. She was standing in the doorway, notebook in hand, her oval face framed by wavy honey-blond hair. Her blue eyes harbored sadness and grief. Renn felt suddenly hollow. When his time came, would there be anyone to mourn his passing as Marlee and Van Pelt's family mourned Clark's? Worry also darkened her features; he preferred to concentrate on that.

"Come in and sit down." His words sounded more harsh than he'd intended. As she limped forward, he circled the desk and closed the door behind her. "How's the ankle?"

"Better, thanks."

"Try to stay off it as much as possible."

"I do." She looked up at him, waiting for him to get to the reason she'd been summoned.

"I imagine you'd like to know what's going to happen around here," he said as he slid into his seat. He felt her nervousness and wished he could alleviate it, but he'd already expressed his sympathy. Nothing he added would make a difference. It was better to move on.

"No decision has been made about Clark's replacement," he announced. "His death is still so fresh in people's minds we felt that filling his position too quickly would be inappropriate. We want to give our viewers a chance to recover from the blow of this terrible tragedy before we make any abrupt changes. I'm sure you can appreciate that."

Suspicion lurked in her vague nod. Giving her Clark's job wouldn't exactly be an abrupt change. She'd filled in for him many times over the past two years—when he was on vacation, covering hand-picked sporting events or attending media functions.

"Are you planning to bring in someone from outside?" she asked.

"As I said, no decision has been made yet."

"Does that mean I'm being actively considered for the job?"

He could hear the hope in her voice. Destroying it would be cruel, especially under these circumstances.

"Absolutely," he replied too quickly, too positively. "Personally, I prefer to promote from within. Outsiders are disruptive." That much was true. "Taggart's being considered, too, of course."

She stared at him. He was the boss, yet he felt suddenly as if he were the one on trial here.

She compressed her lips and bowed her head. "I know you haven't been very happy with me, but—"

"That's not true," he countered, again sharply, maybe because he was annoyed by her honesty and sudden humility. The meek got nowhere in this business. Hadn't she learned that from her mentor? For all his integrity, Clark wasn't above blowing his own horn when circumstances dictated. If she weren't in mourning, she'd realize this was one of those times.

She raised her head and caught his eye, and something passed between them.

Straightening, she said, "I've always received favorable audience responses when I filled in for Clark. The focus group the station formed last fall gave me high marks, too."

He agreed, inordinately pleased with the return of that spark of determination, that fighting spirit. "You deserved them."

Her brows rose in disbelief.

"Clark and I discussed your performance," he said, to justify himself. "He was pleased with your work here, and so am I. I've been particularly impressed with your willingness to take criticism."

"But—" She looked more confused than ever.

"Marlee, just because I didn't compliment you every time you did something right and pointed out a few areas I felt could use improvement doesn't mean I've been unhappy with your overall performance."

She furrowed her brow skeptically.

"May I make a suggestion?"

"Of course." There was even more wariness in her reply.

"I don't think I have to tell you why Taggart is a serious contender for the anchor job."

"He's a man," she muttered.

"My advice is to do what you do best," he went on, ignoring her remark. "You're a good reporter. Audiences like reporters who pose the kinds of questions they'd ask if they were in your shoes. So capitalize on your strengths."

Her assent this time was more enthusiastic, though still uncertain.

"There's something else." He had her full attention now. "The job of sports director requires more than just anchoring a segment of the news or editing the highlights of a TUCS football game. You have to be able to supervise people, make bold decisions, be aggressive and dramatic. I don't have to tell you this business requires teamwork. You get along pretty well with the crews around here. Make sure you continue that relationship, not only with the people who support you—" he paused for emphasis "—but with your contemporaries."

In other words, get along with Taggart. Don't alienate him.

She pinched her lower lip as she considered his

words, spoken and unspoken. Finally she nodded and said, ''I understand.''

''For the time being, we'll be doing things a bit differently. Clark's chair will remain vacant. You'll announce scores and present your highlights from the Live Center.''

She gazed at him for a moment, her blue eyes appraising him, as if she were searching for some hidden meaning, some secret agenda. He was about to squirm under her scrutiny, when she said, ''I'll do my best.''

He exhaled a pent-up breath when she looked away. ''I know you will.'' He stood up. She did, as well. ''Thanks for stopping by.''

He crossed the room and opened the door for her. For a fleeting second, as she moved by him, he thought she was going to offer to shake his hand. He was unnerved by how much the notion of touching her appealed to him, but she just smiled self-consciously and hobbled out.

CHAPTER THREE

MARLEE WASN'T surprised that Renn showed no great enthusiasm for Taggart. The only one who seemed impressed by him was Faye Warren. The ex-jock certainly capitalized on his one year under contract to the Dallas Cowboys, as if he'd been a budding Joe Montana or Troy Aikman. In fact, he'd possessed just enough talent to be a low-round NFL pick in the early eighties. If he'd truly had some great untapped potential, no one ever got an opportunity to discover it. In his first, inconsequential, preseason exhibition game, he'd blown out his left knee. Despite surgery and a year of intensive rehab, he was released from his contract. Apparently, even as a long shot, the odds were against his ever actually making the team. He'd married his physical therapist along the way, but when his promising career was declared dead, he'd blamed his wife and divorced her.

A year or two of heavy drinking and debauchery had followed. Again, a woman came to the rescue. He sobered up, married her and used his short-lived NFL career to get hired on as a sports commentator by a national sports network. He covered professional football games, then partied with his old teammates— or more correctly with the cheerleaders. His second wife had failed to understand carousing was part of his job description. To hear him talk about it, she never really cared about him anyway, just his money, most of which she took when she divorced him. Poor guy. He was so distraught by her back-stabbing rejection that when a producer questioned some of the charges he'd made on his expense account, he lost his cool and slammed down a heavy microphone stand in a fit of temper. She claimed he threw it at her, and pointed to the hole in the wall to prove it. The network let him go. He settled the assault charge the producer had brought against him out of court. Bye-bye Ferrari.

He got a job as an assistant football coach at TUCS and married a graduate student. Shortly thereafter, he had a major clash with the head coach, was asked to leave—he claimed he resigned—and donned the sports-analyst hat at KNCS-TV. Four months ago his sweet young wife caught him playing stickball with her best friend and threw him out of the house, but not before burning all his pretty-boy suits. She then proceeded to have her attorney take him to the proverbial cleaners. He'd been crying poor mouth ever since.

Marlee figured he wanted the anchor position, not just for the prestige but because he needed the money. His ex was driving his Porsche and swimming in his pool, and he was still making payments on both.

If management brought someone else in from outside, Marlee felt confident she could work with him—that it might be another woman didn't even cross her mind—but if Taggart assumed the anchor role, she didn't see any future for herself at the station. The man was a blowhard of the first order. He put in a few minutes' face time on the air twice a week, while demanding other staff members write his material.

She'd end up doing all the work and he'd take all the credit. No career-advancement potential there.

Was that why Renn was buttering her up—because he would rather work with a woman than put up with Taggart? She laughed. Well, that was all right with her. Once she had the job, she'd prove her worth.

Or was he just stroking her so she wouldn't leave until he could find someone from outside?

Renn was right. She needed to go with her strengths. She was a damn good reporter, and she'd prove it.

Sunday, February 16

"I REALLY APPRECIATE you helping me with this," Audrey Van Pelt said.

"Hey, it's so nice having weekends off." Marlee touched her cheek to the older woman's. "I can't think of a better way to spend a Sunday than with you."

Audrey threw open the door to her husband's closet. Her sons had taken most of his tools, many of his books and a few mementos from his den, but Clark's clothes still hung where he'd left them. The boys had volunteered to cart off the things that could go to the Salvation Army, but she'd turned the offer down. Their time with her was too precious to waste packing boxes. At least, that was what she'd said. In truth, she hadn't been able to face the private space that harbored his smell, his presence, the sense of the man about to come home, but who never would.

"We'll get the place cleaned out today," Marlee said. "Next weekend we can paint it and you can spread your stuff out. A woman can always use more closet space.''

"If only for shoes," Audrey added, in a feeble attempt at humor.

Marlee smiled, assembled one of the cartons she'd picked up on her way over, sealed the bottom with strapping tape and set it on the king-size bed. They starting filling it with suits, while she explained what had been going on at the station.

"I can see why you're disappointed." Audrey grabbed a bunch of dress shirts, removed the plastic coverings and hangers and folded the shirts neatly before placing them in the box. "But I wouldn't be discouraged. A slam-dunk decision at this point would probably have gone against you."

"To Taggart." Marlee brought out casual and work clothes. "The recognized expert, the man," she groused.

"This delay gives you a chance to prove you're the better choice, and with Renn on your side, your prospects should be good. After all, the position comes under his direct supervision. He's in charge."

Marlee scoffed. "Seems to me if he was really in charge, he'd already have made a decision."

Audrey understood the younger woman's frustration. "He's new here. He can't very well go directly against his boss at this point and expect to keep his job. It's called politics, honey, and it's a fact of life."

She ran her hand along the top of Clark's bedside table. Dust. She hadn't had the energy to do much housework lately. Without him around there wasn't much point. With the boys having returned to their own lives, the place was so empty. Sean, their youngest, was in college back East. He'd be graduating in a few months—without Clark to watch him get his engineering degree. She brushed away an incipient tear. Their middle son, Jeff, had returned to his medical internship in New Mexico, and Steve, the model big brother, was an officer in the Marine Corps and stationed at Camp Pendleton. Having them home for the funeral had been a too-brief consolation but now they were all gone.

All except Marlee, whom they'd virtually adopted.

But Audrey's mind was wandering; it did that a lot lately. What were they talking about?

"The only reason Renn wants to give me the anchor job is that he can't stand Taggart. Not that I blame him."

"I bet there's more to it," she said. "You're much better qualified, and he knows it."

"You'd never guess it from all the grief he gives me."

Audrey had to smile. Clark recognized from the beginning that Renn was interested in Marlee but didn't want to admit it. Nitpicking, her husband claimed, was his way of establishing distance between them.

"He seemed pretty solicitous about you during the memorial service."

"Yeah, he was sort of sweet." Marlee paused a little dreamily, then snapped out of it. "But that was different. I mean—"

"Has he reverted since then?"

Marlee tossed a wire hanger on the pile with the others. "Well, no. He's been pretty nice, actually."

"And helpful?" Audrey prompted.

"Well, I suppose. He gave me some good advice on how I can compete with Taggart."

Audrey noted the subtle wistfulness in her statement and grinned. "Doesn't sound like a bad guy to me."

She paused over the expensive suit she'd bought Clark when he'd gotten the job at KNCS. Twenty years ago. She hadn't realized he'd held on to it all this time. Out of style now and probably too small for him. Her eyes welled up. She kept her back to Marlee and rubbed her nose with a tissue from her jeans pocket.

"I never said he was a bad guy," Marlee rambled on, "just that he doesn't like me."

Audrey wondered if she should clue the young woman in, that he probably liked her too much for his professional good. She neatly folded the suit and placed it in the box. "What do you think of him?"

Marlee shrugged. "He's my boss. What can I say?"

"He's quite good-looking."

Marlee sealed a box and assembled another, this one for shoes. "He's okay."

Oh, honey, Audrey wanted to say, *he's more than okay.* Tall, lean, square jawed, with blue eyes and dark hair. Maybe Clark had had it right after all. The two of them were attracted to each other but were terrified of admitting it.

"I like your hair longer, by the way. Letting it grow was Renn's idea, wasn't it?"

"It was easier to take care of when it was short," Marlee objected, but she kept her eyes averted.

Audrey smiled to herself. The attraction was definitely there.

They'd removed all the clothes from the closet. Marlee started on footwear, while Audrey began emptying the built-in drawers. She wasn't sure what to do with the rest of Clark's jewelry. Steve had taken his Rolex. Jeff and Sean had divvied up his gold cuff links, tie tacks and clasps. The rest was costume quality. She scooped it into a shoe box and deposited it in a corner of the carton on the bed.

In the bottom drawer of the wardrobe, she found Clark's military medals and awards. She removed them and set them aside to send to Steve in California. In the back of the drawer she discovered his grandfather's pocket watch.

"I don't think you've ever seen this." Audrey held it out.

Marlee examined the elaborately etched gold case. Audrey opened it so she could see the inscription inside the back cover and the date: 1889.

"It's beautiful," Marlee said reverently.

"Still works, too. A bit delicate by today's standards for a man, though." But not for a woman. "I'd like you to take it."

"I couldn't—"

"As a keepsake of Clark. You were the closest thing we had to a daughter."

"But—"

Audrey's eyes brimmed again. "He would want you to have it, honey."

They both had tears running down their cheeks as they embraced.

"I can't imagine what I would have done without you two all these years," Marlee said between sniffles. "Even when I wasn't living here in Coyote Springs, I knew I could count on you, that you'd always be here for me. I love you so much."

"And we loved you," Audrey whispered. "Still do."

They blew their noses, tried to dry their eyes and resumed cleaning out the closet.

"So what did Renn tell you to do to get a leg up on Taggart?" Audrey asked a little later.

"To be bold, aggressive and dramatic."

"Seems like good advice to me."

RENN SAT on the patio of his lake house, sipping coffee, munching a bagel and reading the Sunday newspaper. His thoughts kept wandering to Marlee and the hopeful determination he'd seen in her eyes when he'd told her she was being considered for Clark's job. It was a long shot; she must realize that—unless she did something to make a name for herself, not just at the station but with the public, something out of the ordinary.

Even if he didn't really want her to get the job as sports director, he did like the idea of her doing well as a reporter. Maybe he could help her out.

He flipped to the sports section. Rumor had it that Bill Parcells, the coach of the Dallas Cowboys, was in imminent danger of being fired. Parcells wasn't known to be particularly hospitable when dealing with the media, so he might flat-out refuse any overture for an interview, but if Marlee could get one with him, it would definitely put her on the radar screen for sports director at KNCS-TV, or anywhere else, for that matter.

Renn decided to check some of his contacts in Big D next week and see if Parcells might be receptive to talking with a young woman reporter from West Texas. Faye would scream bloody murder at the travel expenses, especially if Marlee and her photographer had to stay overnight in Dallas, since it would also mean separate rooms. But so what? That was the price for having a female reporter on the staff. The benefits to the station would far outweigh the costs.

Renn smiled as a sailboat glided by. Marlee needed to co-opt Taggart. Getting an interview with Parcells would definitely do the trick.

Friday, February 21

THE NEXT-TO-LAST GAME of the college basketball season was Friday night, exactly two weeks after the death of Clark Van Pelt. TUCS versus Angelo State, and it was a home game. Marlee had been covering the Coyotes for months, watching them practice, talking to the players and their coaches. She didn't need an expert analyst to tell her they were good. Their team captain, a six-foot-eight leaper by the name of Ty Jameson, moved with the grace and power of Michael Jordan. The Angelo State Rams had a couple of good players, as well, notably Stretch Higgins and Slim Brenner. Individually, neither of them could stop Ty. Combined, they promised an electrifying game.

"Bring plenty of tapes," Marlee told Wayne Prentice, her cameraman. "I'll need complete coverage." In two hours of taping, she might use a minute and a half, but without the raw footage, there was nothing to edit. "And save a blank for the after-game coverage. I want to do a couple of in-depth interviews."

"Got it," Wayne said.

She grabbed her press pass and notebook and charged out the door, while he lugged his fifty-thousand-dollar video camera with him.

TUCS's aging gymnasium, now called the athletic center, was located in a corner of the campus. Parking was at a premium. Fortunately, space was reserved behind the building for the press. Marlee pulled the white KNCS-TV van close to the back door that opened into a corridor between the men's and women's locker rooms. The voices of five thousand spectators echoed off the concrete-block walls. Excitement filled the heavy, humid air. The game wouldn't start for another thirty minutes, but cheerleaders were already warming up the masses. The Angelo State contingent, though small, was every bit as enthusiastic as the home crowd. The court was squeezed between bleachers stacked so intimately close to the players that fans were virtually on top of the action, becoming almost a part of the game.

While Wayne hauled his camera and tripod to the top of the stands behind the throng, above the madness, Marlee scanned the packed assembly from press row on the front line. Coyote maroon-and-gray banners were held aloft, while pom-poms darted and bounced. Home-team fanatics brandished painted faces, animal masks and outlandish hats.

A buzzer signaled the end of the twenty-minute warm-up period; the two teams lined up on their respective sides. A man's voice boomed over the PA system: "Please rise with us in singing the national anthem and remain standing afterward for a special tribute."

The cavernous room rumbled as people rose to their feet. When the last chords faded, the university athletic director stepped to the edge of the court, microphone in hand.

"Texas University at Coyote Springs and our community suffered a terrible loss two weeks ago when the bus bringing members of our high-school basketball team home from Del Rio was caught in a flash flood. Our own Voice of Coyote Springs, Clark Van Pelt, gave his life trying to save others. I ask you all to bow your heads in a minute of silence in honor to his heroism and in memory of those who perished with him.''

Marlee had had no warning this tribute was going to be offered, and the sudden, respectful silence of the assembled crowd sent a shiver down her spine. Staring blindly ahead, biting her lips and straining to hold back tears, she tried to picture Clark's face, his white hair, ruddy complexion, sparkling blue eyes. Panic swept through her when she realized she couldn't see him distinctly in her mind, as if his features had been rubbed out. Fear that his memory might fade terrified her. Her head shot up just as the athletic director said, ''Thank you,'' and invited everyone to enjoy the upcoming competition.

As she had expected, the ensuing game was up and down, each side running and gunning. By the end of the first half, the score stood at forty-eight all.

The second half was even more boisterous. The battle was clearly drawn between Ty Jameson and the two star players from ASU.

One minute to play. The score stood at ASU 107, Coyote Springs 106. Ty had the ball. He passed it to Tommy Remington, who dribbled to the left, spun, then whipped a behind-the-back pass to Ty. He pump-faked Stretch Higgins out of position, then slammed home a go-ahead bucket.

The crowd went berserk. The Coyotes were ahead by a single point. Everyone was breathing hard. The

Rams's Slim Brenner had the ball. He dodged to the side and passed it to Stretch. Ty knocked the ball away. One of the Rams grabbed it and dribbled down the court. Slim was waiting, caught the pass, took two dribbles, spun to his right, spotted Stretch and hit him with a perfect bounce pass. Ty tried to block him, but his smaller six-foot-six opponent was quicker. Slim's shot was launched with perfect rotation toward the rim. For an eternal minute the packed gymnasium was nearly silent. Then the ball ripped through the net, like a dagger through the hearts of the TUCS fans.

Fifteen seconds remained. TUCS called their last time-out. Half the crowd cheered; the other half prayed.

Ty inbounded the ball, then worked behind his teammates' defensive screen. Slim was guarding him, holding him, and the referee let him do it. With a sharp elbow to Slim's midsection, Ty broke away and took a pass from Tommy Remington. The clock was down to five seconds.

The crowd was on its feet now and screaming.

Ty decked Slim with a fake to the right, then darted left to the basket. He drew contact from Stretch and two other Ram players but got off a shot three feet from the basket. The ball bounced high, skipped off the backboard, then landed suspended on the front of the rim.

The clock showed :01.

The crowd lurched forward in hopes, in anticipation.

Finally, as this moment in time evaporated, the ball fell in. TUCS had just won a thriller.

The buzzer-beating basket caused an explosion. Fans jumped up and down in the stands. Voices shouted. Horns blared. Cowbells clanged. Men and women let out whistles that threatened to shatter eardrums. TUCS students flowed out of the stands onto the floor. Security was helpless to control them and after a few minutes stopped trying.

Marlee climbed on top of her chair and waved to Wayne in the upper reaches of the stands to join her. He was already threading his way down, his camera and tripod hoisted on his shoulder.

"Come on," Marlee yelled, as soon as he arrived.

She pushed her way through the mob and crossed the court toward the Coyote locker rooms. Everybody was shouting and screaming. Turning her head only enough to make sure Wayne was still behind her, she circumvented the compact mob that had gathered around the jubilant team.

The narrow passage between the locker rooms was only slightly cooler, as air was sucked through ventilation ducts.

"Position yourself at the end by the exit. No, wait." She ran into the unused ladies' locker room, searched around and grabbed a folding chair. After dragging it outside, she braced it in the corner near the back door at an angle, so it was unlikely to get knocked over. "Climb up on this. I want you to catch the team as they come toward the locker room."

Wayne stowed the tripod on the floor against the wall and quickly mounted the creaky wooden chair. "Gotcha."

"Do you have a fresh tape in?"

He heaved the minicamera onto his shoulder and fiddled with the Nikon lens to get the focus just right for the narrow area. "I put one in just before the final play.'' He looked through the viewer. ''Lighting's not very good. I'll have to use my halogen.''

''Whatever. This isn't the big shot, anyway—just a diversion. I wonder if the lights in the men's locker room are better than in the women's.''

Wayne's eyes went wide. ''You're not considering—Marlee, I don't think that's a real good idea.''

She wouldn't be the first woman to barge into a men's locker room. The Coyotes just weren't used to being treated like pros.

''Stay close to me when we go in and keep your camera rolling. We can edit out anything that—''

A change in the volume of the noise cut off her last words. A moment later, a long line of adrenaline-hyped males streamed into the congested passageway.

''Now,'' Marlee said, just loud enough for Wayne to hear.

She moved forward and had to practically shout into her wireless microphone. ''There's no denying the euphoria that possesses this team or the adulation they have for their star player. Ty Jameson saved the day in the last two seconds of this crucial game against the Angelo State Rams, their traditional conference rivals, and no matter what the future may bring, this day is his, and his alone.''

Coach Dreyfus brushed along the wall as the players hurried past him.

''Are you satisfied with the game your boys played this evening, Coach?'' she called out.

He hesitated. His place was with the team, but few public figures could resist the allure of a camera. He turned on his smile, genuine, not plastic, and beamed at her. ''You bet.''

"Do you think you have a shot, then, at the conference championship next week in Abilene?"

"No doubt in my mind. None whatsoever."

The brief exchange gave a newspaper writer and the sports reporter from the San Angelo TV station time to join them and follow up with a series of questions. Marlee didn't even hang around for the sound bites. She skirted the pack, dragged Wayne with her and slipped into the alcove leading to the locker-room door.

"You sure you want to do this?" Wayne didn't sound happy.

Sure? No, she wasn't sure, but she was determined. Renn told her to be bold, aggressive and dramatic.

"Roll 'em" was her only reply.

Prentice shook his head, took a deep breath and put his finger on the trigger. She placed the flat of her hand on the door and pushed.

The noise inside was every bit as loud as the cacophony outside—until someone saw her.

"Jeez, lady." The room went quiet as everyone turned to face her. There was a sudden flutter of white towels as naked males scrambled to cover themselves.

"What the hell are you doing in here?"

"Ever heard of the ten-minute cooling-off period?"

"Can't you read? This is the *men's* locker room! You've got no right to be in here. Get the hell out."

The guy she was after was only a few feet away, imposingly tall, his dark, broad-shouldered body glistening with sweat.

"Ty," she said with a coolness she certainly didn't feel. Actually, she didn't want to dwell on what she was feeling at that moment. She'd never gone in for beefcake pinups, but what she was looking at was definitely not two-dimensional. "You played a fantastic game this evening, the perfect end of the season. What do you—"

"Speaking of perfect—" another player moved in front of her, a towel immodestly dangling at his hip "—if you're writing a feature article, sweetheart, and want an exposé—" he grinned lecherously "—I'm your man."

She gazed up at his face and slowly scanned down his bare chest, his flat belly... Oh, yes, he had a very impressive physique. Her breathing caught and funny things were happening inside her. When her roaming eyes finally reached his knees, she reversed course. Everyone else, it seemed, had stopped breathing, too. She smiled sweetly at him. "Are you sure you want your shortcomings made public?"

"Oooh," chorused his teammates.

"So that's why they call you Tiny," one of his buddies wisecracked. "Tiny" was nearly seven feet tall.

He blushed all over, spread his towel strategically and attempted to withdraw to the back of the locker room, but his buddies refused to cooperate.

"Hey, Tiny—" the one next to him drawled out the nickname "—that's *my* towel." He snatched it away and held out a washcloth. "Here. This ought to be enough to cover up your *shortcomings.*"

Ribald guffaws and whistles sent the naked player scurrying red faced toward the showers.

"Ma'am," Ty muttered, as he looked down at her, "you really shouldn't be in here."

The sincerity of his concern and the note of protectiveness touched her, but she ignored his polite invitation to leave and the embarrassment of some of his team members. At least, she tried to. It wasn't easy.

"You scored forty-seven points in the game tonight, breaking the TUCS record set by Gibson Turner in 1989. How do you feel about that?" She held up the mike for his reply.

"I wasn't thinking about any records," he said modestly. "I just wanted to play my best."

"Still, you achieved a tremendous victory."

He smiled humbly, boyishly. "I didn't do it alone, ma'am. Everyone on the team won tonight."

Was he intentionally trying to make her feel old by calling her "ma'am"? "Your next game is with Abilene. They were the conference champions last year with a record of sixteen and one. How do you think you'll fare against them?"

"We'll win," someone behind him called out. They all had towels held or knotted at their slender waists now and were hovering around Marlee. She felt remarkably at ease, as if they were all protective brothers, a strange sensation she didn't fully comprehend, since she didn't have any brothers. But the warmth infused her with a kind of elation.

She looked up at Ty. "What about Conover?"

"He's tough," the muscular twenty-one-year-old acknowledged. His broad flat chest was smooth and hairless. "Which means we'll just have to play harder and smarter."

"Was the game plan to get you the ball tonight?" Marlee asked as a lead-in to her next question.

"What the devil's going on here?"

Everyone turned to see Coach Dreyfus standing in the doorway. Barely six feet, he, too, was dwarfed by the strapping young athletes. His outstretched arm held the door open. Wayne doused his floodlight and took his finger off the Record button.

"Lady," Dreyfus barked, "you have no damn business being in here. There's a mandatory ten-minute cooldown period for a reason. You've just violated a hard-and-fast conference rule by barging in here. Now, get the hell out before I call security."

"Just wanted to congratulate your team on their stunning victory tonight, Coach," Marlee said, pasting a friendly smile on her face.

He wasn't impressed. "Out." He stepped aside to let her pass.

She moved unhurriedly. "Thanks for the interview, guys. And good luck in Abilene next week. We'll be covering the game, of course."

"Or uncovering it, eh, Tiny?" someone quipped.

The scowl on the coach's face prompted her to maintain her forward momentum. "You can be real proud of them," she said as she glided by. He didn't soften.

She left the locker room and heard the door close swiftly behind her.

"Boy, is he ticked," Wayne muttered, as he lowered the camera from his shoulder.

"Is KNCS going in for skin flicks now?" Charlie Haskell, a sports reporter from San Angelo's TV station sniped. He was one of a snickering group of people in the hallway, all male. She was tempted to retort with a cute comment about the guys in there being real gentlemen, until she realized he had his camera trained on her. Taking advice she was glad most people didn't, she said nothing, didn't even crack a smile.

Realizing his taunt hadn't worked, Charlie signaled his cameraman to cut.

"Hey, Marlee, did you get any hot flashes... er...news flashes in there?" a print reporter asked in a loud voice.

Chortles surrounded her, but she refused to acknowledge the ribbing.

"I think I'll check out the women's locker room after the girls play Sunday afternoon," someone in the crowd said.

Marlee involuntarily stiffened. Surely her going in the men's locker room wasn't the same kind of threat....

"We'll take up a collection for your bail," another guy called out.

"The hell with bail," a third person objected. "I just want to know how much he'll charge for a copy of the tape."

"If the cops don't confiscate it."

They all laughed, then settled down to wait for the team to emerge so they could interview them. Having beaten them to the punch and gotten what she needed, Marlee led Wayne out the back door.

"Did you get everything?" she asked when she was sure they were out of earshot.

"Except for the coach's colorful language when he threw you out."

"He didn't throw me out," she countered, as they approached their van. "He invited me to leave."

Wayne was mirthful. "I have to hand it to you, Marlee. You got...well, the biggest pair of anyone in there. Pure shiny brass."

She had to laugh. ''Gee, Wayne. You say the nicest things.''

He smiled and grew serious. ''The big question is what's the boss going to say when he gets wind of this.''

CHAPTER FOUR

THAT SAME NIGHT, Faye took a satisfied breath and rested her head deeper into the fluffy down pillow. Beside her, Tag's heavy panting slowed. In a minute he would be asleep. He was an energetic lover, sometimes a bit rough, even frightening, but that was part of the thrill. There definitely wasn't anything soft about Tag Taggart. Yet it was at these moments, when he was spent and just a bit vulnerable, that she enjoyed most being with him. She leaned over and kissed him on the cheek.

He smiled, content with himself. "What was the matter tonight? You didn't come with me."

That he'd noticed surprised her. This wasn't the first time he'd taken the trip by himself.

She shrugged. "A little stressed-out, I guess. I've been under a lot of pressure lately." When he didn't respond, other than to fondle her left breast, she added, "Renn Davis wants to give Clark's job to Marlee."

Tag stopped his kneading but didn't remove his hand. "He's been here what...six months? You'd think by now he would have figured out the pecking order." He flicked his thumb over her tender nipple and opened his eyes. "It's a no-brainer, Faye. You're his boss. Tell him it's me or no one."

"I'll take care of it."

He propped himself up on one elbow and slid his hand between her legs. "We're good together, Faye." He smiled when she admitted his probing finger. "But I'm not going to play second fiddle around here anymore, certainly not to Marlee Reid. It's my popularity that's been carrying the sports segment. I'm the one who should have gotten the anchor job two years ago when Clark's contract was up. Instead, you renewed him for another five years."

She was having trouble concentrating on egos and business negotiations when all she could relate to was his touch and what it was doing to her. Tag could be so good with those big strong hands of his when he wanted to be.

"Clark was here a long time. An institution," she managed to gasp. "He had a following...beloved by viewers." She pressed herself harder against his palm. "He also had powerful friends. There was nothing... I couldn't just...usher him...out the door... even for you."

Tag leaned over and captured her left nipple between his teeth and used his tongue to toy with the sensitive tip, while his finger invaded deeper. Her respiration hitched. Her heart pounded.

He withdrew his hand. "There is now."

Air rushed out of her lungs, leaving her gasping.

"The show's worked well for both of you," she reminded him after she'd caught her breath. "You've been paid very handsomely for twenty-seven minutes of airtime a week."

He banded a leg over her, pressing his restored arousal against her thigh. "Baby," he murmured as he suspended himself above her, his lips curled, his eyes gleaming, "you know I've been worth every penny." He probed against her. She guided him in. "You've gotten your money's worth out of me."

Thinking was difficult with him filling her, moving almost languorously, building a spark into a fire, a fire into... She inhaled sharply when the first explosion burst inside her. He smiled, increased the tempo and pounded with renewed force that bordered on the painful. She cried out and tightened her grip on his back when the second wave nearly drowned her. He grunted a long guttural sound as he emptied himself, then collapsed on top of her. For a moment, his hard-toned body threatened to suffocate her, and she felt the weight of panic. He let out an exhausted sigh and rolled off her.

Again, they lay side by side. She wanted to curl up in the crook his arm, but this time he established distance, and she knew there would be no more physical intimacy between them—at least not for a while.

"I've brought a lot to KNCS," he said a minute later, and laced his fingers behind his head. "I've got firsthand, behind-the-scenes experience in the world of sports. I'm not just some spectator who talks the talk while second-guessing the guys who walk the walk. I've been there, done that. And I've taken awards—"

Faye threw her legs over the side of the bed. For a moment, she'd thought they had been making love. Now she acknowledged it had been merely sex. Damn good sex, but...

She shouldn't complain. She knew all too well that lovemaking was a fantasy, that for men it always came down to the physical. And Taggart was all man, physically and temperamentally.

"You don't have to remind me." She reached for the silk dressing gown on the chair by the window and flung her arms angrily into its sleeves. "I've heard it all before."

"Faye," he called out, as she made her way to the bathroom.

The edge in his voice had her involuntarily turning. He had his knees raised and spread enough to capture her attention. Oh, yes, definitely male and damn proud of it.

"If you want me to hang around—" he grinned "—you'll get me the anchor job."

"You agreed to stay on board for three years," she reminded him, matching the stridency in his tone.

His amber eyes squinted above the smile on his lips. "I don't have a written contract, Faye. You've been around long enough to know a handshake doesn't mean diddly in this business."

Was that a subtle hint about the six-year difference in their ages? Probably not—not consciously, at least. There wasn't anything about Tag Taggart that was subtle. Unfortunately, what he said was true. Their unwritten agreement constituted intentions, not promises. If he chose to leave, there wasn't a damn thing anyone could legally do about it.

"Get me the anchor job, Faye, or I'm out of here."

She didn't like being used, threatened, bribed. But, God help her, she didn't want to lose him. "This isn't the time or place to be discussing this," she said, and turned back toward the bathroom.

"That's because there's nothing to discuss," he said, as she closed the door.

Saturday, February 22

"SHE'S MADE US a laughingstock," Faye Warren stormed, as she slammed a newspaper down on Renn's desk the following morning.

He'd already read the article on the front page of Saturday's *Coyote Sentinel*. It noted that Marlee Reid, the only woman sports reporter at KNCS-TV—or in town, for that matter—had barged into the men's locker room after TUCS's upset victory over Angelo State the evening before to get an exclusive interview with Ty Jameson, the team's high scorer. It quoted Coach Dreyfus as saying he'd had to order the young woman out and that he would lodge a formal complaint with the television station for the unprofessional behavior of their reporter and photographer.

Renn had hung around the newsroom the evening before long enough to help Mickey Grimes put the final touches on a story about the upcoming fraud and embezzlement trial of the former school superintendent, then he'd gone home. There, he'd received the call from Dreyfus. Renn would have laughed at the situation if the man hadn't been so genuinely furious. Images of tall naked basketball players being confronted by a sexy, blond reporter who was undoubtedly trying not to stare at exposed body parts made it almost impossible to respond to the irate caller without a smile in his voice.

After about twenty minutes of sympathetic listening to the coach's harangue, Renn had gotten him to calm down. Dreyfus still wasn't happy about the situation, but he'd backed off on his demand that Marlee be fired. They hung up in time for Renn to catch the ten o'clock report and Marlee's sports segment. He was impressed. She'd done a good job, appeared unruffled in her close encounters with the male of the species, and the editing had been excellent.

His attempt to get her an interview with Bill Parcells, the Cowboys' coach, had failed, but so what? From what he'd just seen, she didn't need any help from him to make herself known. He'd considered calling her at the station to discuss the spot she'd put herself in but decided to let it wait until the morning.

All night he kept imagining himself in the naked players' position with Marlee gazing at him. *Be still my heart.*

Except in this case, the heart wasn't the organ most prominently affected.

He also asked himself how much responsibility he shared for what she'd done. He'd have to be more careful in his choice of words with her in the future. She seemed to follow his advice too literally and too far. Dangerous. But exciting, too. Life with Marlee Reid wouldn't be predictable.

"There's an adage," he said now to the seething vice president, "that even bad publicity is good."

Her gray eyes narrowed. "Are you condoning this?"

He ignored the question. "Did you see the story she put together last night?"

Faye's glaring silence verified his guess that she hadn't.

"The interview was excellent. She did a very professional job—"

"I don't call flaunting herself in front of a bunch of naked men professional—"

"Flaunting?" He snorted. "Marlee was the one with the clothes on."

''And neither does Sal Bufano,'' Faye charged on, overriding his observation.

Oh, great.

''She could have asked her questions outside the locker room like everyone else. She didn't have to invade their privacy, not to mention breach NCAA regulations by ignoring the ten-minute cooldown period.'' She took a pace in the cramped confines of his office, spun around and addressed him with an outstretched hand. ''What is she trying to do—get us banned from covering future games? This kind of conduct is inappropriate and unacceptable. I hope she had a good time, because she just kissed the anchor job goodbye.''

Renn shook his head. ''You're overreacting.''

She glowered at him.

''Marlee might have been a bit aggressive *for a woman.*'' He emphasized the last words and had the satisfaction of watching Faye's lips tighten. ''But I think you're forgetting an important factor.''

''And what might that be?''

''Our ratings during the sports segment soared last night. When word got out that Marlee had violated the men's locker room, people couldn't stay away.''

Any other feminist would have delighted in his choice of words, but Faye remained stone-faced.

''We want viewership, and we got it,'' he concluded.

She strode back and forth in front of his desk. ''Voyeurism in the locker room isn't the image we want to project.''

She didn't fool him. The notion of walking in on a bunch of naked guys titillated her as much as it had every other woman at the station. It was amazing how many of them just happened to stop by this morning to review the tape. Too bad there was no way to break out what percentage of their television audience the night before had been female.

"She and Wayne did a great job of editing," he pressed on. "Everybody knew they were in a men's locker room, but it was as chaste as a chapel."

She screwed up her mouth and rolled her eyes. "Hardly."

Actually, Wayne had been very discreet in his filming, to the chagrin of some of the staff, who talked him into letting them see the uncut version. Still, imagination was a potent faculty.

"It doesn't really matter. She won't have to do that again." He chuckled. "For the foreseeable future, people will be tuning in just to see what happens next."

They both knew he was right. He also understood Faye's dilemma and frustration. Marlee had broken the rules, breached conventional conduct—a perfect excuse to eliminate her from consideration for the anchor job. At the same time, however, she'd also increased viewership and placed herself in the spotlight in such a way that the station would probably take a beating from the public and come across as petty if they fired her. The overwhelming majority of the callers regarded the caper with humor, if not approval.

"Did you know she was going to pull this... stunt?"

So Faye suspected them of being in cahoots, conspiring against her. What would she have said if he'd snared the Parcells interview for Marlee? In this case, he almost wished he could claim credit. He'd told her to be boldly aggressive and dramatic. She'd done so in spades.

"I'm not even sure she knew herself before she actually did it," he said.

Faye didn't appear convinced. "It's still unacceptable behavior, Renn. She needs to be made aware of that. I want her formally reprimanded in writing. This is a family-oriented station. Another incident that brings our image into question, and she's history. Got that?"

He nodded but said nothing.

MARLEE WAS PSYCHED. The calls she'd received after the broadcast last night had ranged from highly complimentary to a few that condemned her to hellfire. She basked in the first and dismissed the latter. Her eternal salvation wasn't in the hands of her viewers, but her career was.

Most people treated her piece as a great lark. Except for Coach Dreyfus, of course. She'd stopped by his house this morning to see if she could soothe his ruffled feathers. He wasn't a bad guy, really. She'd just caught him off guard. Once she'd appealed to his good nature and sense of humor, pointed out all the positive publicity she'd generated for his team and promised not to break the rules again, he'd calmed down.

She'd tried, too, to imagine what Clark's reaction would have been. The thought made her smile. He probably would have wagged his finger at her and laughed.

Maxine Howard, Faye's secretary, caught up with Marlee as she was making her way across the newsroom to her work cubicle.

"I wish I had your nerve, girl." She giggled and gave Marlee a high five. "Just barging in like that. You must have really gotten an eyeful."

She and Wayne had had less than thirty minutes to edit the tapes. There'd been only a few shots that had to be censored, and a couple she left alone because they were provocative without being offensive.

Marlee chuckled. "They were pretty fast at hoisting the white flag...er...towel."

"But not fast enough, right?" When Marlee just pursed her lips and sucked in her cheeks without offering further comment, Maxine grinned lasciviously. "Tell me, is Ty...uh...as impressive up close and personal as he appears on the court?"

"Well," Marlee drawled, "let's just say he has big feet."

Maxine cocked her head, then let out a hoot, which she quickly suppressed with both hands.

Suddenly, Marlee sobered. "Maxine, what are you doing here on Saturday?" Faye's secretary worked Monday through Friday.

"Boss lady called this morning. Said she wanted me to come in and dig out some stats for her."

Lightheartedness fled, instantly replaced with panic. Was the VP going to fire her? Or was she satisfied now that Marlee was the person for the job, that she had the aggressiveness and cool to handle a hot situation? She snickered to herself. *Hot* was an understatement. She was a woman, after all, and she had been in a room crowded with virile young men. Oh, yeah, definitely hot.

"Has she ever asked you to do that before?"

Maxine shook her head and gazed at Marlee. "Nope. This is a first."

That didn't sound encouraging. Marlee had come in to see if Quint Randolph could use some help. The junior reporter was excited about taking over from her as weekend anchor, and he'd done pretty well so far, but she knew he was nervous about it. A little unobtrusive moral support never hurt.

"Where is she now?"

"They're talking."

Marlee didn't have to ask who her friend was referring to. Faye and Renn.

"What kind of mood is she in?"

Maxine frowned and leaned against the door frame. "She was practically wearing a trench in the carpet when I got here, pacing in front of her desk with the newspaper clutched in her fist."

Definitely not a good sign.

"She had me check last night's ratings twice," Maxine added, "and get her a detailed breakout of how they compared with the coverage we had before and after Clark's death, as well as Tag's last three analysis shows."

Now, that was interesting. "How did I stack up?"

Maxine grinned. "Except for the initial coverage of the bus wreck and drownings, you were higher than all of them, even Clark, and miles above Tag. Without Clark to pull his chain and feed him straight lines, pretty boy's numbers have tanked."

Being pleased by someone else's misfortune wasn't very nice, but in the TV news business there was no room for humility or charity. Besides, this was Taggart, the blowhard she had to beat. If Faye was being true to form, the higher ratings would weigh more in her judgment than any pique she might have over the unkind remarks about the station in the editorial section of this morning's paper.

"How long have they been at it?" Marlee asked.

"Just a few minutes."

She couldn't help but fidget. Was Renn up there agreeing that she'd stepped over the line, that she'd killed her chance to be seriously considered for a supervisory management position? He claimed he was pleased with her as a reporter, but his constant harping on her mistakes sure hadn't substantiated that. Maybe he'd been patronizing her because he saw how hard Clark's death had hit her. Maybe he'd never really wanted her to stay on at all and she'd played right into his hands with this episode.

"Has she said anything about the anchor job?"

Maxine lifted her chin. "Now, Marlee, you know I would never listen at doors."

"Of course not," Marlee responded with equally mocking seriousness. "But if you just happened to be passing by when the subject was being discussed, what do you think you might hear?"

Maxine snickered. "She usually keeps the door closed, but being as she spends a considerable amount of time in consultation with Taggart, it doesn't take much imagination to figure out they're not talking about the weather forecast."

As far as Marlee was concerned, their personal lives were their business—unless pillow talk became a conflict of interest. She could accept losing the job to someone more skilled and more experienced than she was, but Taggart didn't fit either of those categories.

Maxine stared across the wide expanse of desks to the main entrance.

"Well, look what the cat dragged in, on a Saturday, too."

Taggart sauntered into the reception area with the swagger of a teenager after his first sexual conquest. Head held high, he gazed around the nearly empty newsroom, an emperor surveying his domain.

"Looks like the Cock of the Walk is about to grace you with his presence," Maxine said in an undertone.

Both women watched him wend his way toward them through the maze of desks and filing cabinets.

"A fine figure of a man," Maxine added with a snort. "Too bad it's all on the outside. Inside he's full of—"

"Himself."

They both laughed.

Obviously, the subject of their jocularity hadn't heard the comments; otherwise he wouldn't still have had that cat-that-ate-the-canary grin on his perfectly tanned face.

"Quite a show you put on last night," he said to Marlee by way of greeting. He paid no attention to Maxine, who was standing beside her.

"Glad you liked it," she replied, not at all sure his remark was intended as a compliment.

"Very much," he acknowledged. The grin didn't fade; in fact, it seemed to intensify. "If there was ever any question that you're not suited for the sports director job, there isn't now. You proved that very effectively. Why, in one fell swoop, you managed to humiliate the players—"

"Gee, they didn't look humiliated to me," Maxine piped in. "From what I saw on the tape I'd say they looked real pleased to see her."

"Mind your own business," he snarled at her. "This is a private conversation."

"No, it isn't," she snapped back, unintimidated. "We're standing in the middle of the newsroom. No expectation of privacy here."

"Maxi…" Marlee cautioned, not wanting the woman to get called on the carpet or even fired for being a smart mouth, but her friend didn't back down. She just folded her arms and gazed defiantly at the man in front of her.

He glowered, seemed to weigh his options and apparently decided to simply ignore her. He returned his attention to Marlee.

"Let's see. You broke official NCAA rules, embarrassed yourself on camera and brought disgrace to the station. Nice going. Really impressive. I couldn't have set you up better myself if I'd tried. But of course I didn't have to. You're doing a very good job without any help from me." His eyes narrowed in amusement. "I must say, though, sweetheart, that I had no idea you were so hard up for the sight of a man's naked body. All you had to do was say something and I could have accommodated you with something worth looking at."

Maxine groaned. "Oh, brother."

Marlee was speechless. She couldn't believe he was being such an brazen ass, especially in front of a witness.

"But never mind," he went on, as if he hadn't heard his lover's secretary. "You probably wouldn't know what to do with it anyway."

"Do you know what sexual harassment is?" Marlee asked him.

"I believe it's what those *boys* can charge you

with.'' He smiled, totally confident he had the upper hand. ''I wonder if they will.''

Icy panic slithered down her spine. A slick lawyer could probably argue that as an older woman she was in a position of power—and she had gone in with bright lights and a cameraman. Oh, God. She'd never considered the possibility. Then another thought struck her. Wasn't that exactly the situation between him and Faye? An older woman in a position of authority. Marlee wondered if her lawyer could use that in her defense. Before she realized it, she was laughing.

Maxine tilted her head, unaware of the joke, her arched brows expressing eagerness to be let in on it. The smirk faded from Taggart's face. He'd just announced her career aspirations were toast, and she was laughing. Didn't make sense. He looked totally confused. Which only made Marlee laugh harder.

''Don't worry about me,'' she told him, after regaining control of herself. ''As with Mark Twain, the rumors of my death are greatly exaggerated.''

He shook his head in a attitude of pity. ''You can laugh if you like, but that doesn't change the situation. You're finished, sweetie. The station will never put you in the anchor seat now. When word of this spreads, if it hasn't already, you'll have a tough time getting a job anywhere in the industry.'' He touched his index finger to his forehead in a mock salute. ''Have a nice day, girls.''

They watched him amble down the hallway to his office. Everyone else rated a cubicle. Taggart had a room with a door.

''Uh-oh,'' Maxine intoned. ''There goes Renn. I better get back to the boss lady.''

Marlee glanced down the hallway but didn't see him. "Where'd he go?"

"Into his office. See ya." Maxine hurried over to the stairwell.

Barely fifteen seconds later, Marlee's phone rang. She knew who it was before picking it up.

"This is Marlee Reid. How may I help you?"

"Please come to my office," Renn said.

She tried to gauge his words. His tone was polite— he'd said *please,* which wasn't a word he used very often—but beyond that she detected nothing. Civility could mean he was in a good mood or he was furious, that he had good news to tell her or bad.

"Yes, sir."

Her fingers trembled as she grabbed a steno pad and pencil. Was he going to give her a pat on the back or a pink slip?

CHAPTER FIVE

THERE WAS NO SENSE putting it off. Renn moved from behind his desk, wishing for the hundredth time he didn't feel so boxed in. Someday, he promised himself, he'd have a job with a big picture window, preferably up high, and a panoramic view. A tap on the door tumbled his thoughts back to earth.

Marlee was wearing snug jeans and a long-sleeved red turtleneck that covered all but her hands and face, but it also clung to her body in a way that made the palms of his hands itch. Narrow waist. Nicely rounded hips. Breasts that were full and high…

"Sit down," he said. "We need to talk."

Her expression of concern told him he'd come across more sharply than he'd intended—again. He seemed to do a lot of that lately. He settled on the edge of the his desk, close enough to get a whiff of her delicate scent. The sight of her was as provocative as a red flag waved at a bull. Now she was transmitting pheromones. Could she really be oblivious to the effect she was having on him? Or was it all calculated?

It wasn't important, he decided. She was here because he needed to counsel her about her job performance.

How could he possibly reprimand her when she'd done precisely what he'd advised her to do? Well, not exactly. He hadn't told her to drag her cameraman into a roomful of naked men, to break conference rules, but... He liked her spunk. She brought the human touch to her work without being a powder puff, yet she still retained her femininity—a delicate balance few women in this hard-edged business achieved. The sweet ones didn't last; the tough ones often ended up like Faye Warren, corseted in stainless steel—and basically alone, the likes of Tag Taggart notwithstanding.

"You made quite an impact with your Ty Jameson interview last night. Our e-mails and voice mails have been about nothing else since you ran it."

The statement didn't require a response, and she gave him none, but the tips of her mouth curled slightly.

"Not all the calls have been complimentary," he added.

Her blue eyes were multishaded, with light and dark tones. "Most of them have."

So she'd been keeping tabs. Good for her. She wasn't apologizing, either. He liked that even more.

"Our vice president isn't pleased with the bad publicity we've gotten in the press."

"It'll pass," she said philosophically. "Our ratings spiked during my segment."

"No argument there," he agreed. "But there's also the station's reputation to consider. Your little escapade caused quite a stir. Coach Dreyfus complained to me last night and Sal Bufano. He demanded that you be fired."

Marlee paled. "The GM wants me terminated?"

Renn was quick to correct his syntactical error.

"Not Bufano. Dreyfus. He had some very unkind words to say about you."

If the general manager wanted her gone, she would be. Fortunately, Bufano didn't usually take an active role in the day-to-day operation of the station, certainly not in matters of personnel management.

Marlee took a deep breath, her color gradually returning. "I stopped by and apologized to Coach this morning. We're cool."

Smart move. "Faye's willing to be appeased with no less than a written reprimand for your unconscionable behavior."

Marlee looked up. She hadn't missed the jocular tone in his last statement. He could feel her trying to figure out whose side he was on.

"For unbecoming conduct that reflects poorly on the integrity and wholesome image of KNCS-TV."

She continued to stare at him. Petrified. Her guard up.

"How do you feel about that?"

She gazed at him warily. A written reprimand in her official jacket would make getting another job difficult, if not impossible, especially at an up-market station. "Does it matter?"

He stroked his chin. "In the end, probably not, but I'd still like to know."

She pursed her lips. He had the impression she was trying to decide whether to bolt or stand and defend herself. "It locks my jaws."

Renn had always been an admirer of understatement. It said so much so eloquently. His admiration for her grew. "Mine, too."

Then he smiled.

She studied him, her eyes clouded with uncertainty.

Gradually, almost by degrees, he saw awareness dawn, as if she'd just recognized a melody. Something communicated itself between them, and she understood for the first time that he was on her side. Relief softened her gaze and at last brought a smile to her lips. Suddenly, she was grinning. To him it was as though she'd opened a window in this sunless room and the clean, scented air of spring had just wafted in on a cool, refreshing breeze.

"When I told you to be bold, aggressive and dramatic, I didn't exactly have in mind for you to go barging into the men's locker room for a reveal-all interview," he said, trying to revert to a straight face—and failing.

"You didn't?" Her brows were raised in a way that suggested she was innocently surprised at the revelation, but the sparkle below them undermined any attempt at seriousness.

He slouched in his seat, his fingertips resting on the edge of the desk. "Wayne tells me one guy tried to proposition you."

"He was just being cute. I cut him down to size, so to speak."

Renn laughed. "So I heard. I'm not sure it's wise baiting seven-foot-tall athletes, Marlee."

"A pussycat," she assured him. "He'll probably think twice about *exposing* himself to criticism again."

Renn chuckled, as his mind conjured up the image of a strapping buck slinking off red faced with his hands between his legs. "I almost wish I'd been there."

"Wayne may still have it on tape."

In fact, he'd already viewed it and been impressed by the way she'd handled herself. The situation was decidedly entertaining, but it also alarmed him.

"Marlee, if those players had been veteran pros ten years older than you instead of college kids, you might not have been treated so generously. I hope you considered that before doing what you did."

Her eyes widened and warmed, as if the idea that he might be genuinely concerned about her welfare came as a shock. In fact, his unease ran deeper than a skittering anxiety. They weren't close friends, just business associates, but he worried about her.

The next moments of silence lingered into discomfort.

"You're in the doghouse at the moment," he finally said, attempting to reestablish a businesslike tone. "You brought our ratings up for a short time, but you also put yourself in the position of getting the wrong kind of reputation and giving Taggart ammunition to use against you."

"It won't happen again."

He rested his arms on the desk and leaned forward, inexplicably unsettled by her nearness, by the delicate floral scent that was uniquely her.

"My advice the other day still holds, Marlee. I don't think I have to remind you Taggart has certain advantages in his bid for the anchor slot. You need to demonstrate unequivocally that you're better qualified to be sports director than he is. Do you suppose you can do that—" he couldn't help but smile again "—without alienating half the community or putting your personal safety and reputation at risk?"

She rubbed her chin, her blue eyes twinkling above her slender fingers. "Watch me."

Saturday, March 15

"COACH HILLMAN, thank you for agreeing to this interview. I know this has been a very difficult time for you and for the members of the team, their friends and families. You have my deepest sympathy and condolences."

The fifty-year-old high school basketball coach had aged ten years in the five weeks since the bus carrying his team had been swept into the Devil's River. The teenagers had won a stunning victory against a formidable rival, which qualified them for the state playoffs and were undoubtedly euphoric on their way back from Del Rio when the tragedy struck. At the championship game the following weekend, they'd done respectably well, losing by less than ten points. Inevitably, people speculated whether they might have won if they hadn't lost two of their players. In a larger sense it was a no-win situation. Had they actually come out on top, their victory would have somehow felt disrespectful.

Marlee and the coach had agreed to meet this Saturday afternoon at his home. He'd greeted her and her photographer cordially and led them to his den, a large room that had been converted from a two-car garage. The dark wood-paneled walls were crowded with framed pictures of teams going back a quarter of a century. Awards and accolades lined shelves and bookcases. It was a pride-filled room, except that the man sitting behind the old wooden school desk had lines of defeat bracketing his thin mouth. The sadness radiating from him tore at Marlee, reminding her of the loss she, too, had suffered.

As Wayne Prentice set up his gear, she attempted to put their host at ease by asking questions and offering comments about some of the older memorabilia. When the room was artificially brightened by the halogen floodlight, she did a sound check and began her interview.

Over the next hour, she elicited information about his career. Coyote High had been only his second coaching position. In those twenty-five years, many of the young men he'd trained had gone on to play college basketball. Five had advanced into the pros, one playing for the L.A. Lakers, another for the Dallas Mavericks.

At last Marlee brought him to the fateful night. Hillman's proud mood sobered and the relaxed atmosphere she'd so carefully nurtured melted away.

"It'd been drizzling on and off for several hours," he said. "I'd checked with the highway patrol. They assured me all the roads were clear. No reports of flooding."

A few people in the community had accused him of negligence in attempting to return home in a winter rainstorm. His defenders, who included the parents of one of the dead players, far outnumbered them, however, but the damage had been done. Hillman had offered his resignation. It was declined.

"At the point where the highway parallels the Devil's River," he went on, "it started raining pretty hard, but we'd seen worse. This is West Texas, after all. When it rains, it pours, usually for only a few minutes, then it stops as quickly as it starts. We saw some standing water, and the normally dry fork was running, but the river was still within its banks."

"Did you consider turning back?"

He nodded. "Clark, Mel, the driver, and I discussed it, but the highway along that stretch was only two lanes, not wide enough for that big, long bus to do a simple U-turn. We would have had to go off the blacktop, and Mel was afraid we might get stuck. We would have been in real trouble then—and a danger to anyone else on the road. Plus, the storm was moving in behind us, which meant we were already cut off in that direction. Our only option was to keep going.''

''How were the boys handling it?'' Marlee asked.

''A few were antsy. Clark moved to the middle of the bus to keep them company.'' Hillman grinned sadly, as if recalling a fond memory. ''Those kids ate up his insider stories about all the famous people he'd met. He was a combination of big brother and wise grandfather, the kind of man they could look up to.'' Hillman's voice wobbled. He stalled. He and Clark had been good friends for many years.

''Mel started across the low-water crossing at the dry fork. Water was up to the edges of the pavement but not over it. He drove nice and easy, and—'' he inhaled deeply ''—that's when we stalled. Suddenly, everyone became quiet. Mel's hands shook as he turned the key, trying to get the engine started again. It almost caught a couple of times. Then someone noticed water coming in under the door.''

He bowed his head despondently. ''I couldn't believe the river had risen that fast. I looked through the windshield. The roadway had disappeared. Then a big tree limb slammed into the right side of the bus, and we began to slip sideways. Seconds later we were tossed on our side. That's when pandemonium broke out.''

Marlee tried to imagine the scene. The sheer terror.

The sense of complete helplessness in the face of such power and violence. Her heart beat faster. Hillman's breathing was audibly labored.

"Coach, would you like to take a break?"

He shook his head. "This isn't going to get any easier—for either of us," he added with a wan smile. "Might as well get it over with."

She liked this man, his honesty, his humility and compassion. Asking him to repeat the events that followed made her feel cruel. If at that moment he'd refused to proceed, she would have accepted it. But she sensed he needed to tell this story. He'd find a way to get on with his life, but the memories would never completely leave him.

"The lights in the bus had gone out. I'd banged my head against something and was stunned for a few seconds. The next thing I was aware of was Clark telling everyone to stay calm. He ordered the boys to open the windows on the topside and crawl out, to help their buddies and to hang on to the bus as long as it remained stable. From the lightning flashing around us, we were able to make out a high spot about twenty-five feet away. Clark had us hold hands and form a human chain to it. The rain was a torrent now. We were all soaked to the skin. The heat had been on in the bus, so we'd taken off our jackets. Most of us were wearing only T-shirts and were shivering from the cold. As soon as we reached solid ground, I took a head count. Three guys were missing. Brookshire, Stone and Tremont." He paused. "This had been Tremont's first game and he was jazzed. Stone was, too, because he'd been high scorer. I didn't think we'd ever get the grin off his face."

Hillman cringed at his poor choice of phrases. He

took a deep breath and went on, his voice husky. "Brookshire played nearly a perfect defensive game. No one could get over, under or around him. They were all fine young men."

"What happened after that?" Marlee prompted.

"Someone said they'd fallen asleep in the rear of the bus with the gear. Clark and I started back. The water was chest high by this time. He climbed through a window and got Dante Tremont out. The kid was dazed, his right arm broken. The other two guys were still inside. They must have been knocked unconscious when the bus rolled. The river was raging now, and the bus was beginning to shift. I threw Tremont over my shoulder and carried him to high ground."

His eyes glistening, he said nothing for a minute.

"I turned back to help Clark with the other two. The bus was practically filled with water by then. I expected to see him pulling someone out. What I saw was a huge wave rise out of the blackness, a wall of water and debris. All of a sudden, the big yellow bus capsized, trapping Clark and the two boys inside. I tried to go after them, but Mel and the others held me back." Hillman's whole body seemed to deflate. "It was hopeless. Between lightning flashes, the night was pitch-dark, and the rushing river… We stood there and watched the bus tumble steadily away. There was no way to get to it, nothing we could do, no way to save them. No way."

He fell silent. Marlee's eyes were moist. The camera rolled as they both fought to regain composure. After what seemed a very long interval, she found her voice.

"You saved twenty-seven lives that night, Coach."

Marlee ended the interview on a positive note. "Coach Hillman has established an athletic scholarship endowment fund in Clark Van Pelt's name," she said into the camera. "Anyone wishing to contribute should call the numbers on the screen or KNCS-TV."

Monday, March 17

RENN WAS BOTH pleased and moved as he watched the interview in the editing room. Marlee had handled an emotionally charged situation with sensitivity and compassion, revealing the coach's strength of character, yet offering the audience a glimpse of his vulnerability without in any way compromising his dignity. Not a small feat.

Discussing the last moments of Clark's life couldn't have been easy for her, either. That she was personally affected by the account of his heroism was unmistakable, but it didn't keep her from following through with gentle prompts and insightful questions.

"Outstanding, Marlee. I don't know of anyone who could have done it better. In fact, I'm going to nominate you for the Affiliated Press Award." In prestige it ranked close to a Pulitzer.

A self-conscious smile brightened her face. "Really?" she asked, almost breathlessly.

He grinned. "Really. A truly first-rate job. Clark would be very proud of you."

Her smile faltered and she bit her lip. When she looked at him again, tears glistened in the corners of her eyes. She tried to blink them away. "That means a lot to me, Renn. Thank you."

Their locked gazes lingered. The air between them grew charged. He had a sudden urge to wrap her in his arms, but touching wouldn't be appropriate, safe or wise. Probably not welcome, either. Besides, Wayne Prentice was sitting next to her, watching them.

"How would you present it?"

She'd shown it uncut, with only the long pauses removed. Even after final editing there'd be too much material for a single nightly seven-minute sports segment.

"We could do it in installments," Prentice suggested, although the question hadn't been directed at him. "Show a segment every night for a week."

Renn rubbed his jaw and concentrated on Marlee. He wanted to know her ideas.

"I think it would be better," she said, "to present it complete, as a special."

Renn nodded. "It'd lose its impact otherwise."

"Getting sponsors for it shouldn't be a problem," Prentice offered, as if he knew all about the subject. He'd been at the station for almost two years and was a good cameraman. His next goal was to get on the air as a reporter.

On this subject of sponsors, he happened to be correct. Clark had been popular enough that selling airtime for a special would not only be easy but would probably have companies competing for the privilege.

"Get it down to twenty-two minutes," he said. That was the actual amount of airtime for a half-hour program. "We'll put it on next Sunday evening—in place of Taggart's weekly analysis."

Even as he said it, Renn knew he was in for a fight.

CHAPTER SIX

Wednesday, March 13

"LIKE HELL you will," Taggart said, when Renn told him the following Wednesday he was preempting his sports analysis show Sunday evening for Marlee's special. "You're not taking my airtime so she can blow her own horn." Taggart stalked out of the room and headed directly for the stairs.

Renn understood Taggart's outrage, even if he didn't sympathize with it. Part of it was his losing his time slot, if only for one night, but the bigger issue was professional pride. A dozen reporters and journalists had tried for weeks after the bus tragedy to wrangle an interview with the grieving coach. Hillman had adamantly turned them all down. According to Renn's sources, the coach had been particularly caustic in rejecting Taggart's request. Something about when hell froze over. Which was understandable, since Taggart had made some scathing remarks in the past about Hillman's coaching style.

Three whole minutes elapsed before Renn's phone rang and he was summoned to the vice president's office. He was torqued as he climbed the stairs but was careful not to let his anger show when he stepped over the threshold.

"What's this about pulling *Going Overtime with Tag Taggart* this Sunday?"

Renn described the interview Marlee had conducted. "It's first-rate," he stated unequivocally. "There won't be a dry eye in the city when we show it."

"Let them cry on somebody else's time," Taggart snarled. "Not on mine."

Faye regarded him critically, probably willing him to calm down. The famous Taggart temper had lost him one job. Throwing a tantrum now wouldn't serve him well, even with her to defend him.

"Why can't she do it in installments next week during her regular sports segment?" she asked.

"This interview is much too special to be frittered away in sound bites," Renn said.

She eyed Taggart. Renn was convinced that if it were anyone else she wouldn't hesitate to give the go-ahead to use the Sunday-evening time slot, but she seemed to be blinded by this guy. Did she really believe Taggart was as important to the station as she claimed, or were there more personal reasons for wanting him to stay around?

Renn moved to her desk, picked up the phone and called downstairs to ask Wayne Prentice to deliver a copy of the edited tape.

"Once you see it," he told Faye, "you'll understand what I mean."

She frowned at his taking over but could hardly counter the order. A minute later Maxine opened the door and Prentice walked in. He went directly to the VCR in the television across from Faye's desk and installed the cassette. Renn thanked Wayne and dismissed him, then cued it himself.

Twenty-two minutes later there was no question that Marlee had done a magnificent job blending information, humor and poignancy in a well-balanced presentation.

"One thing she's certainly established," Taggart commented, "is that she's not a team player."

Were the man not so vain, Renn mused, he'd realize he had an opportunity to make points with his associates and the public if he'd graciously cede his time and offer to personally introduce Marlee's interview. Renn had planned to recommend just that but now changed his mind. Under the circumstances, he didn't want Taggart anywhere near Marlee's triumph.

"What are you talking about?" Renn asked, peeved at the man's grumpy jealousy.

"As soon as she got the old man to finally agree to an interview," Taggart replied, "she should have turned it over to me. I'm the senior member here."

Renn was so astounded by the man's gall that for a minute he was speechless.

"You've got to be kidding." He had to muster every ounce of self-discipline to maintain a civil tone. "That's ridiculous. Jim Hillman had already refused your request for an interview, as well as half a dozen others. The only reason he agreed to do this one is that he knew Marlee and Clark were good friends." He waved his hand toward the blank screen. "She got things out of that man even veteran reporters couldn't have dragged from him."

"I'm not talking about the interview itself."

"Oh. What are you talking about, then?"

Taggart sulked, unable to come right out and say she'd done an outstanding job. "I said she wasn't a team player. That goes a lot further than one session with a high school coach."

Renn couldn't let the statement stand. "Expecting

her to set up an exclusive interview, then pass it on to someone who doesn't even work for the station—'' Taggart liked to capitalize on the fact that he was a contractor, not an employee ''—is utterly preposterous. No reporter would ever do that, and I would never ask her to.''

He turned to Faye, who'd remained remarkably quiet. ''Instead of castigating Marlee for succeeding, you ought to be praising her. It's obvious the only reason Hillman agreed to talk to her is that he felt comfortable with her.''

''Because she's a woman,'' Taggart added bitterly.

The sexist remark drew a scowl from a tight-lipped Faye.

''You're probably right,'' Renn admitted. ''So what's your point?'' He again appealed to Faye. ''The subject was an intensely personal one. Men aren't comfortable showing that kind of emotion with other men. It's easier with a woman.''

Faye listened pensively, then slowly nodded.

Taggart started to object, but Renn cut him off. ''Your bold, brash style is fine in the rough-and-tumble world of contact sports. You've proven that repeatedly.'' He watched the other man's chest expand and nearly laughed. ''But it just isn't suited to the more…uh, sensitive, human-interest stories, not in this particular case, anyway.''

The chest deflated. ''I can be very sensitive.''

Renn struggled to control his facial muscles. Faye was observing him, not with amusement. She seemed afraid of what he might say next. Renn decided to take pity on her.

''I'm sure you can,'' he agreed without an ounce of sincerity in his tone. ''I suspect, though, that you would have been uneasy handling this interview. Some kinds of intimacy make a man uncomfortable. I imagine that's why you never do interviews with women athletes.''

Zing.

Everybody knew Taggart looked down his patrician nose at women in sports. As far as he was concerned, they were all amateurs who didn't deserve serious attention as athletes.

''Marlee should have let Tag know she'd set up this interview with Hillman,'' Faye finally said.

Renn was ready to explode, but one hothead in the room was enough. Besides, he didn't want to give either of them the satisfaction of getting to him.

''Why?'' he asked with a calm voice and a raised brow. ''She doesn't work for him.''

He didn't point out that Marlee hadn't informed him, either. Which bothered him, though it shouldn't. She didn't need his permission to develop stories or set up interviews. It wasn't as if she were his protégé, though she could have clued him in as a professional courtesy. She would have conferred with Clark about this beforehand and sought his guidance.

Renn mentally sighed. Had she asked his advice, he would have told her to do exactly what she'd done. Unlike the locker room incident. She was savvy enough to realize asking forgiveness was easier than asking permission. Besides, in spite of all Taggart's snide comments and Faye's umbrage, Marlee had pulled the interview off like a pro.

''Tell me,'' he asked Faye now, ''would you have expected Tag to inform her if he'd snagged the meeting?''

''That's different. He's the senior sports person.''

She didn't sound nearly as convincing as she'd probably intended.

"I could have given her some pointers and a few questions to ask the coach," Taggart persisted, a beat behind the discussion.

Disgusted, Renn shook his head. "Like what?"

When Taggart failed to reply, he turned to his boss, the businesswoman.

"You saw the tape. We'll get top ratings with this interview. I'm nominating her for an Affiliated Press Award. That'll reflect very well on KNCS-TV. In the meantime, I'm willing to bet this human-interest piece will be picked up by the Dallas market and maybe carried across Texas. You can't ask for better publicity than that."

Faye reclined into her seat, clearly unhappy with the dilemma she found herself in. She wanted to champion Taggart, but Marlee had pulled off a coup. There wasn't much she could do but applaud it.

"I'm not questioning the quality of the work, Renn," she said evenly. He noted that she didn't offer to endorse the nomination package. That was all right. The piece would stand on its own, and Sal Bufano would be happy to support it. "But I am concerned that she's a loose cannon. She handled this situation well, I'll grant you—"

"That publicity stunt she pulled at TUCS was a disaster," Taggart jeered.

"Like hell it was," Renn snapped too sharply. "It was very effective...."

Taggart tilted an eyebrow, pleased at Renn's slip in composure. "So you think it'll be all right if I barged into the girls' locker room after their next basketball game?"

Girls, Renn noted, not women.

He smiled. "I tell you what, Tag. You try it and we'll see."

Faye raised her hand. "It's one thing, Renn, for our viewers to wonder what surprises are coming. It's another when the people she works for don't know what to expect."

"She works for me, Faye, and I know exactly what to expect. Bold, aggressive, accurate reporting of high quality, delivered professionally and on time. As for another locker room incident, there won't be any." She'd already made her point and captured her audience, which Renn suspected was going to remain very faithful for quite a while.

"I hope not," she said with a dismissive downturn of her mouth.

Renn resented her grudging acceptance when she should be enthusiastically approving Marlee's achievements. Marlee Reid wasn't a good reporter *for a woman.* She was a good reporter. She wasn't undeserving of the sports director job *because she was a woman.* She merited it because she was the best qualified person for it, not just in competition with Taggart, but with any outsider they might bring in. He'd been a fool up until now not to see that, but he wouldn't be anymore.

"I'm putting the Hillman interview on Sunday in place of Taggart's analysis," he told Faye. He didn't say, *If you don't like it, you can fire me,* but his tone implied it.

"That's unacceptable." Taggart's perfectly tanned face turned an unpleasant shade of mauve.

"It's not your call, Taggart. It's mine." Renn glared at him. "Let's get something straight. You don't run the newsroom. I do. If you don't like the way things are being done around here, you can quit. You would also be well advised to remember that if you get the sports anchor job, you'll be working for me, so I suggest you learn to control your mouth and your temper. I'm an easy guy to get along with, but I don't tolerate insubordination. The next time you have a problem with one of my decisions, you discuss it with me, not run to my boss.''

He stabbed each of them with a penetrating glance. They seemed equally shocked by his outburst, though he hadn't raised his voice. In truth, it surprised him, too, but it also felt good. ''I hope I've made myself clear.''

Neither of them said a word as he strode out of the office.

His jaw was still clenched by the time he reached his office downstairs. He'd thrown down the gauntlet. He wondered how long it would be before his phone rang and he was summoned back upstairs to be reprimanded or even fired. After an hour, he decided the crisis had passed, but he had no illusions it was over.

Sunday, March 23

''HAND ME THAT bag of bonemeal, please.'' Audrey scooped out another trowelful of topsoil from the flower bed she'd been preparing in the far corner of the backyard.

Marlee brought it over and knelt beside her.

''Sounds like you had an eventful week and that you're getting good support from Renn.''

''He can't stand Taggart, which helps.''

''Yeah, it does.'' Audrey wondered if the younger

woman was missing the obvious. "I don't think that's the sole reason he fought so hard to get you airtime on Sunday, though. Do you?"

She didn't like gossip. It was so unreliable. "If what Maxine told you she heard at Faye Warren's door is true, the exchange between the two men was pretty heated."

"Taggart has a temper. It cost him one job and was probably the reason he left the coaching staff at TUCS."

"I'll take those lily bulbs now. Clark loved cannas. Especially the orange." She placed one in the hole and started covering it with soil. "What about Renn? Does he have a temper?"

Marlee shrugged. "Everybody does, I guess."

"But you haven't seen his?"

"He's pretty cool."

Audrey planted another bulb. "He likes you, you know."

"That's good to hear," Marlee replied with a chuckle, "since we have to work together."

"I don't mean just work."

Marlee paused before handing over the next tuber. "What do you mean?"

"The way he looks at you." Audrey had seen it. Clark had noticed it even earlier.

"Yeah, like an incompetent who can't figure out which end of a cassette goes in a VCR."

Audrey chuckled good-naturedly. "He really has been trying to help you."

"Humph."

Audrey threw back her head and laughed. "I bet you've noticed a few things about him, too."

"Like what?" Marlee was getting irritated and trying very hard not to show it, which only confirmed what Audrey already suspected: that she found the news director attractive and didn't want to admit it, even to herself.

"What color is his hair?"

"Dark brown. Why?"

"Wavy or straight?"

Marlee cocked her head to one side. "More wavy than straight, but definitely not curly."

"What color are his eyes?"

"Blue." No hesitation.

"Dark or light?"

"I'd probably say cobalt."

"Very striking." Audrey divided the next tuber. "How tall would you say he is?"

"Six-one."

"Weight?"

"Probably around 175."

"Skinny?"

"Lean, muscular."

"What's his favorite color?"

"Either blue or green—I haven't decided yet. He wears a lot of both."

Audrey grinned. "Still think you haven't noticed anything about him?"

Marlee jumped to her feet and went over for the new bag of bonemeal. "Doesn't mean a thing," she called back. "I could probably answer those questions about anyone at the station."

"Really?" When Audrey asked for the same information about Mickey Grimes, Marlee wasn't sure, and she actually got Taggart's eye color wrong. His were hazel-green, not brown.

"Close enough," Marlee insisted.

"Yeah," Audrey agreed. "Almost." She brushed off her hands and climbed slowly to her feet. "Anyway, it's nice to know you have someone you can trust in your corner."

Monday, March 24

ON MONDAY AFTERNOON Marlee was stunned when she arrived at work to find a huge plant sitting on the receptionist's desk with her name on it.

"Delivered around ten," Peggy said, with a big smile on her face. "Wonder who sent it."

The card wasn't sealed and looked a bit crumpled, making her suspect Peggy already knew. With her fingers shaking, she opened it. The signature under the "Thank you" surprised and disappointed her. She was happy that Jim Hillman was pleased with the interview and was thoughtful enough to send a gift, which definitely wasn't necessary, but she was also a little let down that it wasn't from Renn. After what Audrey had said over the weekend, she thought maybe he…

Silly notion. Even if Audrey was right and Renn was interested in her beyond the purely professional, he wouldn't send a potted plant. Cut flowers, maybe. But she had no right to expect anything from him, and having a gift delivered to the station would be embarrassing for both of them.

"Where are you going to put it?" Peggy asked.

The pink wax begonia was too big for her already crowded desk, and the light there wasn't very good. Besides, she had a decidedly brown thumb, which meant it would be dead within a month.

"It's so pretty," she said. "It'd be a shame to keep

it all to myself. Do you think I could leave it out here for everyone to enjoy?''

"You bet," Peggy said, her face lighting up. "It'll fit perfectly on the end table by the couch. I can pick up a grow light to put in the lamp.''

"Good idea, but let me pay for it,'' Marlee told her.

"I'll water the plant for you, too, if you like,'' Peggy volunteered. "I know how busy you are.''

Over the next few days the station received an unprecedented number of cards, letters and phone calls praising Marlee for the interview with the high school coach. She continued to present the sports segment of the evening news from the Live Center, while Clark's regular place on the news set remained vacant, and Taggart gave his analysis from the visitor's chair next to it.

The following Thursday afternoon she was in one of the editing booths, reviewing a tape she and Wayne Prentice had shot of the TUCS track team doing wind sprints for the upcoming state finals, when Renn stopped by—the fourth time this week.

Prior to Clark's death, she'd seen little of the news director except on the set; lately, he never seemed to be far away. She'd taken umbrage at his close presence initially, as if she were some rookie who needed close supervision—before she understood he wasn't checking on her work, just lending moral support.

She wanted to tell him it wasn't necessary, until she realized she kinda liked him hanging around.

Maybe Audrey was right. Maybe he really was interested in getting her the anchor job. These past six weeks had brought out a different side of him. Was it possible she'd misjudged him, that she'd read into his remarks a negativism that wasn't there? She'd regarded him as nitpicking and petty. She realized now that he'd actually helped her improve her presentations. Just because he didn't sandwich his criticism between positive strokes didn't mean he didn't mean well. Touchy-feely just wasn't his style; he went for the direct approach.

Touchy-feely. There had been a few occasions when his hand had brushed hers, when he'd looked over her shoulder to read an article, to examine a tape or mutter words of advice in her ear. Each time his closeness had set her pulse skittering. If his opinions and suggestions had been pesky before, they were unnerving now. She was much too aware of the heat of his body close to hers, of the low-voltage hum between them.

"Thanks for giving Quint a hand with the weekend stuff," he said. "He's enthusiastic, but green."

Clark had hired Quint Randolph, a broadcast-journalism graduate from TUCS in December, as a second reporter. The rookie had filed only a couple of stories from the field before Clark was killed. When Marlee had taken over the weekday role, Quint had been thrust into her weekend anchor spotlight. He was a hard worker, but his inexperience showed. Fortunately, he was still humble enough to ask for assistance.

She shrugged. "People helped me when I was coming up. There's no substitute for on-the-job training. Actually, he's not doing too badly under the circumstances."

Renn grinned. "Think he'll ever get over his stage fright?"

She shouldn't laugh, but she couldn't keep from

chuckling. The lanky six-footer stumbled over his words, his voice was flat and he came across as an only slightly animated robot. His performance was painful to watch. A few viewers had registered complaints about his amateurish presentations, but most were patient and encouraging. Their forbearance wouldn't last indefinitely, of course. If he didn't start showing marked improvement soon, people would turn him off.

"Clark felt the guy had potential," she said, "and he had good instincts about people."

"Like you." Renn grinned, making her nearly blush. "What was your debut like?"

She shivered dramatically. "I don't even want to think about it." Studying Renn's face, she decided this wasn't idle chatter. He was sincerely interested. "No better than Quint's. Probably worse. My voice came out too high and whiny." She snorted. "I sounded like a strangling chipmunk."

The gleam in his eye lasted only a second, but in that instant the two of them ceased to be business associates. He was looking at her the way a man gazed at a woman, with the kind of teasing assessment that conjured up images of assignations, candlelight suppers and shadowy bedrooms.

He laughed. "I doubt that. We're our own worst judges."

"And you?"

He covered his eyes with his hand and peeked between the fingers. "I don't want to talk about it," he intoned with mock seriousness. He dropped his hand and shook his head. "It's too embarrassing."

She'd never seen this bantering, self-negating side

of him before and found it both amusing and endearing. "It couldn't have been that bad."

He arched his brows, while his eyes sparkled playfully. "You wanna bet? I had two stories back to back, one about the president giving a speech at an international economic summit. The other was a local-interest piece about a circus that had just rolled into town."

"Uh-oh." She wrinkled her nose, suspecting what was coming.

He wagged his head. "It's not as simple as you think. I didn't just reverse the tapes—I got the pages of my script mixed up and was so intent on reading the words correctly that their meaning didn't register. By the time I finished, the president of the United States had performed a double reverse somersault on the high trapeze, and the Great Wallendas had joined with the British prime minister in calling for international tariff reforms."

Marlee threw back her head and laughed.

"And then there was the fly?"

She forced the words out between chortles. "The fly?"

"On my nose. Naturally, I didn't want to swat it away. Instead, I kept staring down at it between sentences. I was cross-eyed during most of the telecast."

She rocked with laughter, not totally convinced what he was telling her was true, but it didn't matter.

"What did your boss say?"

"Nothing. She was laughing too hard. In fact, for the next month, she started giggling every time she saw me. Definitely embarrassing. Not only that, she kept threatening to turn a bee loose in the studio for my next broadcast, just to see what would happen."

"Apparently, you survived."

He smiled and grew more serious. "Yeah. A lot of people helped me, too. So I guess we owe Quint the benefit of the doubt. You don't mind mentoring him?"

She shook her head and ejected a tape from one of the editing decks and changed the annotation on the label. "I enjoy sharing what I know with people."

She stacked the cassettes in the order she wanted them presented and started down the hall to the video bay where the tape operator would cue them up to show on the air. Renn followed closely behind her.

"I'm even willing to show Taggart the ropes," she added, "if he's interested."

He stopped, touched her arm with his hand, compelling her to face him. "You'd do that?"

She was as surprised she'd made the offer as he was. With a shrug, she said, "He's going to have to learn it sometime."

"That's awfully generous, Marlee, considering he's gunning for the job you want."

"You said be a team member," she reminded him, and resumed walking down the corridor.

She could feel him observing her. At the door to the control booth she nervously pressed down the corner of the top label. The grin on his lips when she finally looked up matched the gleam in his eyes. More seemed to lurk in their depths than the acknowledgment that she was competing against a pompous ingrate. The complexity of Renn Davis never failed to intrigue and confuse her. He could be harsh and lighthearted, stern and tender.

"If I don't teach him," she commented, "someone else will."

At that moment Taggart approached from the other end of the passage on his way to his office. Renn called out a greeting and invited him to join them.

"What's up?"

"I want to try something new tonight," Renn said. "Your numbers have been slipping lately, probably because viewers are used to seeing you with Clark. I'd like to put you and Marlee on together tonight."

Taggart stroked his chin. "I'll be sitting in the anchor chair, of course. That's fine with me."

"No," Renn corrected him matter-of-factly. "You'll still be in the visitor's seat and Marlee in the Live Center, but we'll bounce camera coverage between the two of you. Marlee will give her usual reports. Then, after each one, I'd like you to reply with an analysis."

Taggart eyes roamed as he tried to decide if this was some kind of trap. "She'll have to give me what she's going to be reporting on, so I can be prepared," he said, as if she weren't standing there.

"Fair enough."

"And if you can tell me what your comments will be, I can give you an appropriate lead-in," Marlee said.

"I need to know what you're going to report, but it isn't necessary for you to know what I'll say."

Renn slanted her an inquiring glance that said she could back out of this if she wanted.

"That's fine," she agreed. "I'll get you a list of my reports."

"By the way," Renn added to Taggart, "Marlee's willing to teach you the technical side of the business. Come in for an hour or two every day, and she'll show you what she does and how she does it."

Taggart stared at him, then shifted his gaze to Marlee.

"No, thanks, sweetheart," he said with a feral grin. He turned back to Renn. "She's not going to get any free labor out of me like some college intern. I'll do what needs to be done when I get paid to do it. Not before."

He looked again at Marlee. "Nice try, though. I'll be in my office waiting for your list," he said, and walked away.

Renn stiffened, his hands tightening into white-knuckled fists. Marlee touched his wrist and called out after her antagonist. "Just trying to be a team player."

Taggart didn't acknowledge it.

"If you want to bring sexual harassment charges against him," Renn grumbled between clenched teeth, "I'll gladly testify on your behalf."

"It's tempting," she acknowledged, "but under the circumstances I'm afraid I'd just be labeled a troublemaker. Thanks anyway, though."

"Document this meeting," he said, "and so will I."

His righteous indignation encouraged her. "Is he as confident of getting the position as he pretends?" she wondered aloud. "Am I wasting my time even trying?"

"More like he's afraid to show the depths of his ignorance," he countered. "And you're not wasting your time. Don't give up, Marlee. I haven't and I won't."

His unconditional confidence bolstered her more than she imagined it would. Something had changed between them. She couldn't say what exactly. There was still a tension, but it was different—and strangely appealing.

One thing she did know was that if Taggart was hired, she wouldn't be hanging around to tutor him. A pity, really. She'd miss watching him fall flat on his pretty face.

Leaving KNCS-TV would also mean saying good-bye to Renn Davis, and she realized with a jolt, she didn't want to do that.

MARLEE SMILED into the camera. "And what will no doubt prove to be a watershed event in the world of sports, Annika Sorenstam received a sponsor's invitation for the Colonial Golf Tournament in Dallas, the first woman to compete with her male counterparts on an even playing field, so to speak. No special treatment for this brave lady. Annika will be driving from the same tees as the men. All I can say is, may the best person win. Tag, what's your take on this revolutionary event?"

The control room switched coverage to the news set, where Taggart sat in his accustomed place.

"This is a joke, right?"

"Well," Marlee drawled innocently, "Billie Jean King did beat Bobby Riggs in the battle of the sexes back in '73."

"Only because he was twenty-five years older," Taggart retorted. "In an even match men are always better at sports than women. It's a scientific fact. This poor woman is going to be humiliated." He shook his head, not looking regretful at all. "Of course it'll be her own fault. I mean, come on, does she really think she can compete with the guys? I do feel sorry for any man who finishes behind her, though. Yeah, the view may be spectacular, but the term everybody will use to describe him afterward will definitely end with the word *whipped*. She's not even going to make the cut. What's your next item, Marlee?''

Not sure whether to laugh or scream, she went on to her next story, confident they hadn't heard the last of Taggart's most recent analysis.

Friday, March 28

THEY SAT NAKED in her Jacuzzi side by side, while the warm water surged around them.

''You better give me that anchor job pretty soon, Faye.'' Tag sipped from a glass of chilled white wine. ''My creditors are murdering me.''

Faye let herself be buoyed by the roiling currents. ''You're not doing much to help me.''

''Help you?'' He peered at her.

She shifted so that one of the jets massaged the tension in her right shoulder.

''You're the boss, sweetheart. Just order Davis to do it.'' He took another mouthful of wine, reached over and refilled his glass from the bottle in the ice bucket. ''This isn't bad.'' He examined the label. ''Where'd you get it?''

''The Cellar on Travis.'' It was one of their most expensive domestic vintages.

He smacked his lips. ''You ought to buy more of this stuff. It's good.''

She needed to get the discussion back on target. ''Every time I think I'm in a position to tell Renn to hire you, Marlee does something positive.'' *Something adventurous and brazen, like I used to do when*

I was her age, before I settled into the hollow safety of success. "Or you do something stupid."

He settled beside her, wrapped his fingers around her upper arm and squeezed. "I don't appreciate being called stupid, sweetheart." She winced and he released her. "Remember that."

"I didn't say you. I was referring to what you do."

"Marlee's the one who's been screwing up."

To distract him from her transgression and soothe his wounded pride, she reached over and began fondling him.

He smiled appreciatively. "She's the one who busted into the men's locker room. Speaking of busts…" He reached over and gently stroked her erect nipple.

Faye hitched a short breath. "Renn's nominating her interview with Hillman for an Affiliated Press Award. Hard—" which is what he'd become "—to fire her under those circumstances."

He moved his hand down her body. "I should have gotten that interview."

"Expecting her to turn it over to you was just plain—" His scowl discouraged her from finishing the sentence. "Then Renn does you a favor by integrating your show with Marlee's—"

"I was doing her the favor."

"Either way, you blew it." She continued undaunted, "You alienated every woman in the audience, and probably a sizable percentage of the men." She removed his hand and hers and turned to face him. "What the hell were you thinking when you made those sexist remarks about Sorenstam? God, Tag."

He reached for his glass and took a swig. "Doesn't anyone have a sense of humor anymore?"

Faye climbed out of the tub, reached for one of the towels she'd draped over the small table a few feet away.

"Nobody's laughing." She began drying herself. "Sal isn't. His wife isn't. Our sponsors aren't. You managed to get more mail than Marlee did with the Hillman interview, Tag. The difference is that yours was all negative."

"I'll be vindicated, Faye. You'll see. Sorenstam isn't going to qualify. When that happens, people will forget their little hurt feelings." He climbed out and took her towel from her. "I like you wet and slippery." He pressed himself to her. "I need that anchor job, Faye."

CHAPTER SEVEN

Friday, April 4

GLENDA SOAMES breezed into the reception area of KNCS-TV the following Friday morning with the force of a tropical storm and an equal amount of color. No dull grays or tans for Glenda. Parrot greens and reds, sunshine yellows and cerulean blues draped her statuesque figure. She might have been a movie star—an early avocation she nixed when she found out casting meant sleeping with the director. Not that she was averse to an occasional tumble in the straw, she admitted, but she reserved the right to choose with whom she tumbled. Besides, she had no thespian talent and couldn't sing worth a toot.

KNCS's advertising executive looked around. The usual daytime air of busyness pervaded the newsroom, but today there was an added atmosphere of anticipation, like when a big story was about to break.

"What's going on?" she asked Peggy Faykus.

"The bigwigs are meeting in the GM's office," the receptionist informed her. "They're still trying to decide what to do about replacing Clark."

"When will they be out?"

Peggy shrugged. "Should have broken up half an hour ago."

"Marlee with them?"

Peggy shook her head. "In an editing bay, putting together her highlights for tonight's roundup."

"Still getting accolades about her interview with Coach Hillman?"

"Yep, and Taggart is still miffed at being preempted," she added with a snort, "and the hate mail he's getting over his male-chauvinist remarks."

The guy was a class-A jerk, but that didn't mean he wouldn't come out ahead. He was in Faye's knickers, and there was a good chance his head was overruling hers. Anatomy counted, and she knew from personal experience Taggart's body parts could be very persuasive—if you ignored the ego attached to them.

He'd hit on her the first time they met, when he was still coaching at TUCS. She'd put him off, of course. Never accept the first invitation. They'd gone out twice after that. She didn't believe in jumping a guy's bones on the first date, either. She'd had no illusions that their liaison would be anything more than a diversion for either of them, but when the second date ended with them engaging in the old bouncy-bouncy, she'd found him too selfish to be truly satisfying. He was one of those guys who thought size was everything—and in his case, it was.

Her curiosity satisfied, she discouraged any further relationship. It would have been nice if he'd shown the least regret, but he hadn't. A month later, he married the graduate student she discovered he'd been engaged to all along.

"Sounds like Marlee can use a breather. If anyone comes looking for her, she's out for lunch and can't be reached."

Peggy smiled. "Just what she needs."

Glenda strolled down the dimly lit corridor behind the receptionist's desk and turned right into a warren of cubbyholes and booths. Marlee was standing in the third stall on the left, staring at a screen and pressing buttons on a remote control. Since the red sign over the doorway wasn't illuminated to indicate recording was in progress, Glenda strolled in.

Marlee's initial annoyance at the intrusion quickly morphed to delight when she saw her friend.

"Hey—" she froze the image on the screen "—figured you'd be around one of these days."

"I could say the same about you. How's it going?"

"Busy."

"No excuse. It's time you took a break, girl."

Marlee didn't argue, but she did hit the Play button.

Glenda took a step back and pointed both index fingers at her. "Now, put down that control device," she ordered the way a cop would command a felon to drop his gun. "You're coming with me."

Marlee laughed. "Oh, yeah?"

"To lunch at the Mesquite Grill," Glenda declared.

Marlee pressed Stop, laid down the remote and pulled away, her hands up. "No, no. Not that. They have so much food there, scrumptious beef and pork ribs…and chocolate desserts." Her eyes gleamed and her lips curled in a mischievous grin.

"Just what the doctor ordered."

"Hmm." Marlee slouched. "You must give me the name of your M.D. I think I like him already."

"Her," Glenda corrected.

"Better still."

Glenda wasn't a small woman, nor was she a featherweight. She harked back to the full-figure days of Marilyn Monroe and Jane Russell and was very much at home in her skin. She'd been married once to an investment banker, who turned out to be deeply involved in some very shady deals. After he was convicted of fraud and embezzlement and sent to the slammer for ten years, she'd divorced him and reverted to her maiden name.

They took Glenda's Lexus. Marlee always found riding with her friend an adventure. Glenda drove with the same zest and apparent recklessness with which she approached every challenge. Yet Marlee felt remarkably safe with Glenda behind the wheel. As far as she knew, her friend had never been in an accident or even received a traffic ticket. Of course, with her extrovert personality, she could probably talk her way out of anything.

They were seated at a table near the front window of the restored nineteenth-century mercantile building, where they could observe passing cars and pedestrians. Their waiter offered menus, but Glenda waved them away. "We'll have the buffet."

Marlee just smiled at him. Glenda was in charge.

"So those boneheads haven't made a decision yet, huh?" she remarked when they returned from the long buffet, their plates piled high with barbecued brisket, pinto beans, cottage-fried potatoes and green salad.

"They don't want to replace Clark too quickly. Afraid they'll come off as callous. Everybody loved him."

Glenda tried as a matter of habit not to dwell on unpleasant subjects. She'd attended the memorial service for the dead hero, whom she'd regarded as one of the last true gentlemen on earth, then gone back to her ad agency and fought like hell to get a contract with the biggest soap company in the nation. Succeeded, too.

Glenda screwed up her mouth as she slathered butter on a piece of corn bread. "They're messing with your head, sweetie."

Marlee chuckled. "They're weighing their options."

Glenda didn't smile. "For two months? I don't think so."

"What…what do you mean?" Marlee could always count on her friend to tell it like it is. A valuable trait, but one she suspected this time she wouldn't welcome.

After cutting into a thick slice of slow-roasted beef, Glenda raised a piece to her mouth, then lowered it again to her plate. "There's no reason you shouldn't be sitting in the anchor chair right now. You're the senior reporter, the weekend anchor, and you've filled in for Clark a dozen times. It's not as if you don't have the experience."

"They don't want to move too fast," Marlee observed but without as much conviction as she'd felt only a few minutes earlier. "They're afraid the public will see them as—"

"Callous. Yeah, I heard you the first time." Glenda shook her head. "Honey, they could easily have named you his replacement the day after he died, saying it was what Clark would have wanted, which is the absolute truth. The public would have been very supportive. You were like a daughter to him. That's why Audrey asked you to speak at the funeral."

Recollection of that day flashed before Marlee's eyes, and the words she'd used to honor the man she'd grown to love—honor, loyalty, integrity—echoed in her ears. She thought of the gold pocket watch Audrey had given her as a memento and stopped eating, not sure she could get anything past the lump in her throat. She missed him, but she'd developed this technique of not thinking about him as dead exactly, more like not available. Being reminded of the permanence of his absence and the way he died opened a painful wound.

Glenda was brash, but she wasn't insensitive. "I'm sorry, honey." She reached across the table and placed her hand on Marlee's. "I ought to learn to keep my big mouth shut." Her face softened. "Especially when I'm picking up the tab for this glorious spread."

Marlee forced a grin, then put her heart into it. Having someone who understood was nice. They resumed eating, though not with quite as much gusto.

"If they wanted to do something really touching," Glenda went on a minute later, "they could have left Clark's chair empty for a week or so and have you host the program from the other seat. Instead, those nincompoops stick you in the Live Center, as if you're not good enough to replace him—"

"Maybe I'm not—"

Glenda peered across the table. "Don't ever say that." Her tone hardened. "Don't even think it."

Marlee worked her jaw, not sure how to respond.

"Listen to me, kiddo. You are a damn good sportscaster. Anyone with half a brain can see that. Clark certainly did. That's why he hired you."

Glenda put down her knife and fork, folded her arms on the edge of the table and leaned forward. "Let me tell you something else. The sponsors know it, too, and they're the ones who pay the bills. Don't ever sell yourself short.''

Marlee wondered if her friend ever doubted herself, if the pushiness was a kind of compensation for lingering insecurities. She'd grown up in poverty, failed as an actress, failed in her marriage. Or maybe she'd just found herself. She was definitely successful as an advertising agent, selling products and services—and herself.

''If you weren't such a hotshot reporter, if you weren't anchor material, they wouldn't even be considering you for the job. It's because you are that they have a dilemma on their hands.''

''Tag Taggart,'' Marlee mumbled.

''Faye Warren,'' Glenda countered. ''He wants the job, but so what? The station isn't going to miss him when he leaves—''

''You mean *if*.''

''Trust me on this, honey. It's *when*. I know all about phonies. They don't last. They have to keep moving. I went to seven schools before I finally left home because my daddy was always checking out some great new opportunity. In fact, he was running from the ones he failed at because he was too lazy to work at them. Then there was Don. Dear sweet Don, my wonderful ex-husband, emphasis on the *ex*. He wasn't lazy. Actually, he was damn energetic.'' She winked and grinned. ''And he was ambitious, which were two reasons I loved the rat. I thought he was smart, too, till I found out he was only slick.'' She shook her head. ''Listen to me, playing sob sister.'' She waved to the waiter for more iced tea.

''Your problem is Faye,'' she continued after it was poured, ''and her problem is she's got a stud in her bed, and she's afraid to let him go, afraid of the prospect of sleeping alone for the rest of her life.''

Glenda's judgment was harsh, but Marlee suspected it was also accurate. Behind Faye's tough facade, Marlee thought she detected desperate loneliness.

''She wants to give him the job to hold on to him.'' Glenda skewered a piece of potato. ''She knows he's not qualified, but the need to keep her boy toy between her…sheets has clouded her mind.''

She looked Marlee directly in the eye. ''What she's really trying to do with this ploy of not dishonoring Clark is rob you of legitimacy with the public.''

The statement shocked Marlee. What hurt even more was the realization that it was true. At least, she thought, Renn had been helping her. He'd stood up for her over the locker room debacle, and he'd preempted Taggart's airtime for her special.

Glenda picked up a crispy French fry with her fingers, displaying her long, perfectly manicured nails, and dragged it through a dollop of ketchup. ''Have you been keeping track of ratings?''

The question was rhetorical. Everyone in the business, especially the on-air talent, watched ratings religiously.

''Everybody expected them to fall,'' Glenda went on, ''after the first shock of Van Pelt's death wore off, but the stats are still good. Damn good. I haven't had any trouble selling airtime.'' She looked across the table directly at her companion. ''Management may not be willing to credit you with this, Marlee, but I hear things they don't—or won't listen to. Taggart isn't the reason numbers are up. You are.''

The compliment pleased her on a personal level. It

also meant she had an advantage in her bid for the anchor slot.

"What you've got to do, though, is make it clear to Faye and Sal Bufano that you're the reason for the high scores."

"How do you propose I do that?" she asked after a spoonful of pinto beans, slow-cooked southern-style with slab pork and onions. "Barge in with a news flash?"

"That would be one way," Glenda agreed, then grinned. "Not as much fun as crashing a men's locker room, though."

Marlee didn't return the smile. She was weary of having the incident brought up, successful as it may have been.

"Make yourself the personification of KNCS-TV wherever you go," Glenda continued more seriously. "Ratings are high, but they're not enough. Taggart can and will exploit them to his advantage since they can't be tied to either of you directly."

She was right. Being on the air more than her competitor wouldn't keep him—or Faye—from using the program's popularity to blow *his* horn, because the station really didn't care who earned the marks, as long as the stats allowed them to sell air time at increased rates.

"Are you going to the *Alegre* fund-raiser next week?" Glenda asked.

Alegre, which meant *joyful* in Spanish, was the local therapeutic riding center in Coyote Springs. Clark had cofounded it nearly fifteen years earlier with Talia Preiser, a widow whose adult daughter had been severely injured in a car accident. Herself an accomplished equestrian, Talia had read about the therapeutic value of horseback riding for people with handicaps. Enlisting the aid of a friend, she'd taken her daughter on short trail rides three times a week. Clark had done a story on the success of her program and been so impressed, he'd convinced her to establish a permanent organization to help the handicapped recover from injuries or live better with permanent disabilities.

"Audrey's invited me," Marlee replied.

Audrey was a certified therapeutic riding instructor who contributed a day and a half a week to the center. Marlee planned to take an active part, as well, as soon as her schedule slowed enough to give her time. For the moment, however, she was too busy doing her job—and Clark's.

"Good." Glenda thanked the waiter for the bowls of warm peach cobbler á la mode he'd set before them. "Clark was the Voice of Coyote Springs. Now it's time for you to assume that mantle."

The very idea was intimidating. Would people think she was being presumptuous if she dared cast herself in that role?

"How about you?" she asked.

"Wouldn't miss it for the world. You going with anyone?"

Marlee shook her head. "Haven't had much time for a social life lately."

Glenda regarded her with a critical eye. "Girl, you have to make time. All work and no play isn't good for the hormones."

EVERY MARCH the TV station contributed a thousand dollars to sponsor a table at the annual *Alegre* fund-raiser. This year the dinner had been postponed because of the sudden death of Clark Van Pelt, who had been one of its charter members.

Renn received two of the tickets and now had to decide whom to take with him. He wasn't keeping regular company with anybody at the moment, but there was someone he would definitely like to escort to the affair.

He observed Marlee and Glenda when they came back from lunch. The two women were different in so many ways. Glenda was outgoing and gregarious. Her glib tongue and no-nonsense approach served her well in sales.

She'd been one of the first people he'd met outside the immediate television crew when he'd arrived at the station almost eight months ago. True to form, it was she who'd invited him out. They'd spent a pleasant evening at a nice restaurant, laughing like old pals about any number of things. She was easy to be with, smart, witty, confident. They'd gone dancing for a couple of hours afterward. Neither of them tried to hide the fact that they were exploring possibilities. The night could have ended in his bed or hers, but it hadn't. They liked each other, enjoyed each other's company and became good friends, but the spark of sexual attraction hadn't quite caught. They ended the night with a chaste kiss and never dated again.

Marlee was much more low-key, but no one could accuse her of being timid. How many women had the daring to march into a room full of naked men and conduct an interview? The image still made him smile. But she was also reserved and private. In all the months they'd worked together, she'd spoken very little about herself—at least to him. That element of privacy was probably as much his doing as hers. His vow to steer clear of women in the media had driven him to keep his distance.

"I'd like to talk to you," he told Marlee, as she picked up her messages at the reception desk. "When you get a chance. No hurry."

"I need to speak with you, too," she said. "Be there in a minute."

She turned back to Glenda, virtually dismissing him. Something in her eyes, in the way she spoke to him, made him uneasy. He stood there a moment, then returned to his office.

His secretary, Trish, had placed the latest ratings figures on his desk. Newscast viewership was steady. The swell they had experienced immediately after the death of Van Pelt had gradually leveled off to previous levels, except for the sports segment. Normally, there was a slight decline in the number of viewers immediately after the news and weather, since sports didn't have the same universal appeal, but the drop wasn't nearly as sharp as it had previously been. Because of Marlee? She seemed the only explanation. Taggart's ratings for his solo analysis show were actually falling.

He tried to anticipate how Faye might interpret these statistics in Taggart's favor and couldn't come up with a single rationalization. He had a sinking feeling, however, that she'd invent something.

A tap on his open door caused him to raise his head.

Marlee stood before him in sensible chinos and a plaid cotton blouse. He'd gotten to touch her—a hand under her elbow, an arm around her back. Not exactly intimate gestures, but they were enough to raise his awareness of her, of his reactions to the feel of her flesh, her scent.

"Come in," he said.

Her hair had been short and sassy when he'd arrived at the station months earlier. He'd mentioned at one of their early meetings that she might consider letting it grow. He'd been afraid from the quirky expression she'd given him that he'd offended her, but then she'd followed his advice. The shiny, golden-blond hair was shoulder length now and wavy—the kind of casual style that made a man want to comb his fingers through.

"What's the status of the anchor job?" She settled into the chair by the side of his desk. The question was curt.

"We haven't come to a decision yet."

"So I'm still giving my reports from the Live Center?" She sounded annoyed, and he had to admit she had a right to be.

He nodded.

"Why?" The word was spiked with impatience and a sharp-edged emotional barb he hadn't observed in her before.

"I explained—"

"That was two months ago, Renn. What's your excuse now?"

He fell silent, taken aback by her caustic tone. In the past she'd always been coolly businesslike. Now she was fiery, confrontational.

"You don't really want me to get the anchor position, do you? You just want to make sure Taggart doesn't."

Sweat broke out on his forehead. He wasn't prepared for this attack, and wasn't quite sure how to handle it. The easiest, safest and least complicated course, he'd long ago discovered, was telling the truth.

"Initially, that was true." He saw her blanch. "I didn't think then Taggart was the right choice. I still don't."

"And the only way to keep him from getting it was to use me."

He exhaled, wishing he didn't have to admit any of this. "You were a compromise." *Temporize and compromise.*

Her face darkened. She was upset and insulted. He couldn't blame her. She sprang from the chair and turned her back on him. He wondered if she was crying, then decided she wasn't. Tears, if there were going to be any, would come later.

"Please sit down, Marlee, and let me explain."

She spun around to face him. "What's there to explain?"

He sucked in an unsteady breath. "We...I've come a long way since Clark's death. At the time I thought you could make a good anchor. That's why I recommended you." Her blank stare made him feel like a fraud. "I'm a selfish man, Marlee. I have to consider about my own career. Nominating you for a job I wasn't confident you could handle would jeopardize my reputation. I can't afford to do that."

She plopped down into the chair again. Because she wanted to hear what he had to say? Or because she was too upset to stay on her feet?

"How glib," she drawled, answering his question.

"Obviously, Sal Bufano thinks you're suitable for the job, too," he reminded her. "Otherwise he would have rejected my recommendation out of hand. He didn't.''

"What about the Live Center?'' she demanded. "By placing me there you've robbed me of legitimacy in the eyes of the public.''

She was right—to a point.

"Faye wanted to put Taggart in Clark's seat because he has seniority. I was the one who proposed leaving it vacant and having you report from the Live Center.''

The admission made her raise her eyebrows.

"I had no idea making this decision would take so long,'' he said.

She rolled her eyes. "I'm not stupid, Renn. By delaying the decision, the station saves money. I'm doing Clark's job without getting paid for it, and half of Quint's job, too.''

"That was never my intent.''

She half closed her eyes and clicked her tongue.

"The problem is Faye still wants to give the job to Taggart, and I'm still saying no. That's what our meeting was about today.''

So Glenda had been right. The obstacle was Faye, not Taggart. Not Renn, either, if he was to be believed. She wanted to very much.

"Marlee, I'm more convinced than ever that you're the best choice for the job, regardless of who the other candidates might be.''

Other candidates? "Is there someone else besides Taggart?''

"No, it's still just between the two of you. Look, don't worry about the Live Center,'' he went on. "Audiences block out background after a while. That's why we change sets periodically. People don't really care where you stand or sit, as long as you appear to be comfortable with your surroundings. They're interested in what you have to say. When you do move to the anchor desk—'' he offered her an encouraging smile ''—they'll applaud and say it's high time. Until then, just stay focused on content.''

She nodded, then started to get up. ''Oh, is that why you wanted to see me?''

''Uh...no.'' He waved her back into her seat. ''I was wondering if you were planning to attend the *Alegre* dinner. The station's bought a table—I guess they do every year. You'd know that better than I would.'' He was rambling. ''I've been given two tickets, and I thought...if you haven't already bought one...we might go together.''

Her eyes widened. He was unable to determine if it was in pleasure or disapproval.

''Of course, if you have other plans or already have a date—'' he started.

''No,'' she said quickly, then stopped, as if her haste were giving something away.

The important message was that she didn't have a date, which meant she would be free to go with him and that she probably wasn't seeing anyone steady. Unless, of course, she had a boyfriend who was out of town.

''I mean I am planning to go to it. Audrey asked me to be her guest.''

''Oh.'' He should have realized Clark's widow would want Marlee by her side.

''Actually, Mrs. Preiser asked me if I would put together a tribute to Clark, since he was the person who inspired her to establish *Alegre* in the first place and was such a help in getting it organized.''

The mood had suddenly changed, and he began to hope. "I knew it was Clark's favorite charity."

"Would you be willing to help me with the tribute?" Marlee asked. "I'd like it to be multimedia. I figured we could use some film clips and still photos. I'd appreciate your advice writing the script. I'm probably too close to be objective."

Renn felt a kind of glow inside. He hadn't heard about the tribute. Apparently, the station hadn't been informed. Marlee, of course, was the perfect one to give it, but her wanting him to lend a hand set his pulse tripping.

"I'll be glad to help in any way I can." He smiled happily at her. "This is really a great opportunity, not just to honor Clark, but to put you in front of people as his successor. It's perfect."

The careworn lines on her face faded, replaced by the vivid animation Renn had come to treasure.

"I'll get together with Audrey and Mrs. Preiser this weekend," she said, "and see what they have to contribute."

"Good, good."

He felt like a teenager who couldn't believe the homecoming queen had agreed to go to the prom with him.

She checked her watch. "I've got to run. It's almost show time."

For a moment he considered apologizing again for her having to use the Live Center, but decided it would be a downer on what had turned out to be a very positive encounter.

CHAPTER EIGHT

MARLEE LEFT Renn's office with a smile on her face. She wasn't quite sure what was happening, but whatever it was, it made her feel good. This was the first year she was able to attend the dinner. In the past it was during March Madness, when all the college basketball teams were ending their seasons with championship competitions, and she'd spent most of her time traveling from game to game to cover them.

This was also the first time Renn had asked her out socially, and he was going to help her with Clark's tribute. They'd be working closely together on something personal. The prospect stirred ripples of panic, yet warmed her blood in a way that was...stimulating.

She was probably reading too much into this. The *Alegre* dinner wasn't exactly a date. Not like he'd asked her out to a restaurant or dancing, although it was a dinner, and there would be a band.

This was a business function, a PR event, she reminded herself. He hadn't even bought the tickets; they'd been given to him by the station.

No, this wouldn't be a real date.

She returned to her cubicle and sat down, the bubbly sensation still showing on her face.

"Are you going to let me in on the secret?"

Marlee's head shot up. Trish Beasley, Renn's secretary, was standing in the opening between the partitions.

"Looks awfully pleasant whatever you're daydreaming about," she said.

"Oh, nothing."

"Uh-huh." Trish grinned. "What did he want?"

Marlee shuffled papers on her desk. "To know if I was going to the *Alegre* fund-raiser."

She pictured them in a slow number, their bodies close, touching, his legs brushing up against hers.

"I just put the tickets on his desk. He sure didn't waste any time asking you."

"We're going to be working together on a tribute to Clark."

"Ah, so that's what has you smiling like a satisfied cat. What else are you going to be doing together?"

"Nothing," Marlee snapped. "And don't start spreading rumors. That's the last thing I need. Faye—"

"Will be taking her boyfriend. Hey, Renn's hot. No reason you can't—"

Marlee felt a moment of panic. She wasn't getting involved with him, and she couldn't let people think she was. "Please, Trish, don't make this any more complicated than it already is."

Her friend's face melted into a conspiratorial smile. "My lips are sealed. But remember, you're the one who brought up complications."

Thursday, April 10

"OH, NO! Oh, crap!"

Marlee raced into the editing booth. Wayne was fumbling frantically with the buttons on the front of a cassette deck while the machine screeched, followed by a crackling pop as the tape snapped.

"Turn it off! Turn it off!" Marlee ran over and hit the Power button. The recorder ground to a halt.

Wayne's hands shook, his eyes wide, as he stared at the malfunctioning equipment.

"What happened?" she asked.

"I don't know. I was rewinding Mr. Taggart's interview with Bill Parcells and all of a sudden it started making these weird noises. I hit the Stop button and then the Eject button, but nothing happened. Oh, God, he's going to kill me."

Judging from the sounds she'd heard, she suspected it wouldn't be salvageable. "Is there a dupe?"

The photographer shook his head. "This was the only copy. I was rewinding it, getting ready to make a backup…. He's going to kill me. I'm going to be fired. I know I am. What am I going to do? I can't afford to lose this job, not now. Not with the new baby. Oh, God, how could this happen?"

"Let's see if we can recover any of it," she suggested.

"First, we have to get it out of the machine," he said, without much hope.

He turned the machine on again. The same high-pitched whine ensued. Marlee instantly hit the Power button. After trying unsuccessfully to pry the cassette drawer open, she picked up the phone and called Charlie Walhof in Maintenance and asked him to bring his tools.

Ten minutes later, the repairman had removed the plastic cassette and broken open the case. What was left inside was curled, stretched and broken beyond redemption.

"When was he supposed to run this?" Marlee asked.

"On his show this coming Sunday."

"Not now, he isn't," Charlie muttered as he ran his fingers through the skein of magnetic filament. There was hardly a foot-long length that wasn't mutilated in some way.

"What the hell is this?"

They all turned to see Taggart standing in the doorway, legs spread, hands on his hips.

He stared at the pile of ruined tape. "That better not be what I think it is."

"I'm sorry, Mr. Taggart," Wayne said. "I don't know what happened. I was just rewinding it when something snapped and—"

"Are you telling me that's my interview with Bill Parcells?"

Wayne recoiled at the savageness of the other man's tone. "Yes, sir."

"There damn well better be a backup."

"I'm sorry, sir. I didn't get a chance to make one."

Taggart took an aggressive step into the room, his hands curled into hard fists. The younger man instinctively retreated.

"Bill doesn't do interviews. He did this one as a special favor to me, and now you've destroyed it."

"I'm real sorry, sir," Wayne repeated, unable to hide his fear. Marlee sensed the young man was right to be afraid. Taggart was known to have a violent temper; he certainly had the physical power to inflict pain on the much smaller man.

His face beet-red under the perfect tan, Taggart suddenly growled at Marlee, "You're responsible for this."

"Me?" she cried in shock. "I had nothing to do with it."

"You instigated this." Taggart was breathing hard. "I know you did." He glared at the photographer again. "I hope she paid you well, because whatever it was it's going to have to last you a long time."

"Please, Mr. Taggart," Wayne begged. "It was an accident. I swear."

But Taggart wasn't listening. He stormed out of the room and turned right toward Renn's office.

RENN SLOUCHED in his chair and scrubbed his face. Taggart had just left, after demanding that Wayne Prentice be fired. He'd also intimated that Marlee was behind the plot, as he called it, to discredit him.

"You're in on it, too, aren't you?" Taggart had sniped. "I should have known."

"Known what?"

"You're not fooling me or anyone else."

"Be very careful about making accusations you can't substantiate, Taggart," Renn had warned, "unless you want to find your ass hauled into court on charges of slander and defamation of character."

"I want Prentice fired."

"What I do about Prentice is my business. Now, get the hell out of here."

Taggart had left, but his venomous attitude still poisoned the air. At the sound of a tap a few minutes later, Renn looked up, to see Marlee standing in the doorway.

"What are you going to do to Wayne?"

Renn took a deep breath, pleased with the sight of her. For a moment, at least, things didn't seem so bad.

"Taggart's out for blood," he said, "and I can't

blame him. That was an important interview, one he's bragged about on his Sunday-night show for a couple of weeks. Not delivering the goods will make him look bad to his public.''

''I don't suppose he could redo it.'' Marlee took the seat across from him.

He shook his head. ''Not a chance. Taggart was able to corner Parcells into this one only because he was in town visiting his ailing aunt who lives in a retirement center here and supposedly knew Tag from back when. Not that there was much to it. Wayne said it didn't last very long, about five minutes, and wasn't all that informative. I seriously doubt the coach said anything new, anyway. The whole point of it was for Taggart to upstage your interview with Hillman.''

''Would it be possible for him to do a telephone interview in its place?''

Renn's brows rose. He scratched his chin. ''Not quite as effective, but it might work. Tag could show some archive clips while they're talking. Good idea. I'll suggest it to him. Parcells probably won't go for it, but it's worth a try.''

''Don't fire Wayne.'' Marlee implored as much with her eyes as her words. ''It was an accident. This isn't the first time a tape's gotten mangled in a machine. Wayne has a wife and baby at home—and probably a mountain of bills.''

She was really worried about the kid, and Renn couldn't blame her. With a young family to support, the guy probably didn't have any resources beyond his weekly paycheck. Renn had no doubt, though, that Taggart would be running to Faye about this, undoubtedly with his outlandish accusation that everybody was out to get him. Taggart couldn't demand to know what action was taken against the photographer, but she could.

"I'll give him a written reprimand," Renn said after a brief pause. "If nothing else happens, I can pull it from his records in ninety days, and no one will be the wiser."

"Thanks," Marlee said. "You're doing the right thing."

He smiled, and refrained from quipping that no good deed went unpunished.

Saturday, April 12

THE CRYSTAL BALLROOM on the mezzanine floor of the Coyote Hotel had been refurbished several years earlier, its crown molding, friezes and fresco medallions restored and revived. The dominant feature was the huge crystal chandelier in the middle of the ornate ceiling, flanked by two smaller ones at both ends of the two-story, oblong room. Tall, multipaned, arched windows constituted the outside wall, their heavy damask drapes pulled back into pleated folds.

A small orchestra, made up of students from the university music department, was set up on a platform in front of a floor-to-ceiling antiqued mirror at the far end of the ballroom. The sweet strains of Mozart and Haydn were interspersed with classical renditions of The Beatles and The Grateful Dead. Beverage bars occupied the two opposite corners of the vast room.

The town's movers and shakers were all present. Ranchers who donned faded jeans and dirty boots during the week were dressed tonight in tuxedos and patent-leather shoes.

Marlee was wearing a slinky satin, full-length burgundy gown that hid her legs but didn't disguise her breathtaking curves. Her blond hair was held aloft by a band of pearls. Matching streams of smaller pearls dangled from her ears. Renn hadn't missed her attractiveness when she was dressed in street clothes and jeans, but, dear Lord, how could he have missed this overwhelming beauty? She radiated charm, sophistication and more sex appeal than he'd ever imagined. He was unnerved when he realized, as they stood in the doorway surveying the other guests, that his palms were sweating.

At the bar he ordered white wine for her, red for himself. She smiled her thanks when he handed her the glass. The curve of her lips, the soft glow in her eyes brought a physical response. He wasn't a teenager anymore, hadn't been for a long time, but his body seemed to have forgotten that obvious fact. He definitely didn't feel his thirty-six years.

"You look beautiful tonight," he said impulsively, like a fool. He'd already told her that when he'd picked her up. She'd think he didn't usually regard her as pretty, which wasn't true. It was just that tonight—

"You're very handsome in your tux, too."

He resisted the temptation to pull at his collar, which suddenly felt uncomfortably snug. Actually, all his clothes seemed tight, restricting.

A man came up from behind her and put his hand on the small of her back. She turned to him, took his hand and leaned up to kiss him sweetly on the cheek. "Danny, how are you? Haven't seen you in ages…I didn't know you were in town. Oh, excuse me." She turned to Renn. "This is Danniker Milburn. Renn Davis, my boss at the station."

Renn studied the guy. Late twenties with wavy blond hair, a smooth tan complexion, pale blue eyes, white teeth and dimples in his cheeks.

He held out his hand. "Call me Danny. Pleased to meet you."

Renn muttered appropriate words.

"We were so sorry about Clark. Terry and I were in Mexico at the time and didn't hear about his death till we got back, or we would have come to the funeral. What a terrible tragedy."

Marlee's chin quivered. "He was a good man. I miss him."

Danny squeezed her hand before releasing it. The three of them migrated away from the bar.

"Have you been sailing lately?" Danny asked.

She chuckled. "Haven't had time. Renn here is a slave driver. Besides, I don't own a boat anymore."

"Sailing?" Renn's interest was instantly piqued. "You never mentioned that you sailed."

"She's one of the best," Danny told him.

Renn pictured her in a bikini on the deck of his catamaran, her silky skin bathed in sunshine, wind blowing through her golden-blond hair.

"Is Terry here with you?" she asked her friend.

Danny's grin softened into affection. "Yep, and we couldn't be happier." He nodded toward a couple across the room—a tall buxom redhead in a low-cut dress, who was talking to a shorter dark-complected man.

Marlee touched his hand. "I'm glad. So are you living here now?"

"Still in Dallas. Just came into town to meet with a few clients and attend this function."

"What kind of business are you in?" Renn asked.

"Commercial software development, heavy on video graphics. We tailor packages for specific needs and provide technical services."

"Is it going well?" Marlee asked.

"Very. One reason we're here is to look into expanding our business to West Texas. We've been doing a lot in this area via online support, but we think it might be time to establish a local presence."

Marlee laughed. "You're traveling in circles. You started out here, went to Dallas and now you're talking about coming back."

Danny chuckled. "That about sums it up."

"What are you sailing these days?" she asked.

"We have a twenty-five-foot ketch on Eagle Mountain Lake, west of Fort Worth. Don't get out nearly as often as we'd like, but it's great when we do."

Renn glanced over at the redhead who was now engaged in a conversation with one of the local bank presidents. She didn't strike him as the sailing type, though he couldn't say why. Appearances could be deceiving. Consider the surprises Marlee had already produced.

"Your parents aren't here?" Danny surveyed the crowd.

"They'll arrive soon," Marlee replied. "Stylishly late. They can't pass up an opportunity to make a grand entrance."

Renn couldn't decide if he detected sarcasm or humor in her tone. What shocked him, though, was learning that her parents would be here. On the three evenings when they worked together designing the tribute to Clark—disappointingly brief, purely technical conferences with several other people in attendance—she'd never mentioned them. Since she always referred to Clark and Audrey as being like parents, he'd assumed her real ones were deceased.

Danny snorted, his smile one of sympathy. "I guess some things never change." He glanced toward the door. "Speak of the... Here they are now."

The expression on Marlee's face tightened for a fraction of a second as she shifted her attention to the entranceway.

"It's been great seeing you again, Marlee. I haven't had a chance to catch you on the air, but from all the reports I've heard, you're the best." He held out his hand and took hers. "Let's keep in touch. If Terry ever gets tired of me—" he kissed her affectionately on the cheek "—I'll be looking you up."

The familiarity between them bordered on intimacy and made Renn suddenly jealous.

She laughed. "You know where to find me. Give my best to Terry if I don't get a chance to later."

Danny offered Renn his hand. "It was nice meeting you. Take good care of her—she's very special." His handshake was firm.

Renn's awareness was instantly drawn to Marlee. The tension he'd observed a few moments earlier still skulked behind her carefully composed features. She'd been at ease with Danny, so it must be the approach of her parents that had her on edge. Renn knew she was originally from here, but he'd assumed Reid was her married name. That she might be one of The Reids of Coyote Springs hadn't occurred to him.

"Marlee, darling." A whiskey voice insinuated its way between them. "I told your father we'd find you here."

The slender woman was nearly as tall as Marlee, her lush brown hair perfectly coiffed. She wore a black satin dress with a diamond-and-sapphire necklace that was large, elegant and probably worth a fortune.

The man beside her was equally imposing. Over six feet tall, he was massive in frame and stocky rather than portly. His curly, light-brown hair was thick, cut short and salted with gray. Renn easily pictured him in whites on the tennis court at the country club.

"Hello, Mother, Dad." Marlee's greeting was proper but not particularly warm.

"You haven't come by since the holidays," her father said.

"I've been busy at the station." Marlee's reply sounded defensive, which took Renn by surprise. He'd known her to be contrite when the circumstances warranted, but not defensive.

"Mother, Dad, this is Renn Davis, the news director at KNCS-TV. My parents, Anthony and Myra Reid."

The two men shook.

"You must be very proud of your daughter. She's doing a fantastic job at the station."

"She's certainly made herself newsworthy," Myra said with a smile, an unvoiced sigh in her tone. "I suppose that's what she wants. I must say it's not what we expected of her."

Renn cocked his head toward Marlee, who was clearly uncomfortable. "And what might that have been?"

Mrs. Reid glanced at her daughter, her expression

one of disappointment. "Let's just say something more ladylike than barging into boys' locker rooms."

"They were men, Mother, not boys," Marlee said with a vicious grin. "Definitely men."

Mrs. Reid pursed her lips, but refrained from responding to the barb.

Renn suppressed the urge to chuckle. "Rest assured, Mrs. Reid, your daughter never lost her dignity. In fact, she's earned the respect of everyone for her composure and decorum."

The older woman didn't appear to be mollified, but a quick wink from Marlee indicated she appreciated his attempt to salvage her tarnished reputation.

"I see that man is still here. I thought he'd left town."

Marlee gazed in the direction of her mother's glance. "Danny? He's here for a visit. He lives in Dallas now."

Her mother snorted with disapproval.

"I thought that with the weather warming, you might come out to the lake," her father said, changing the subject, though Renn got the impression he wasn't any more happy with his daughter's choice of profession or friends than her mother was.

A very unsettling thought struck Renn. Clark had given Renn thumbnail sketches of the people in the sports department: how long they'd worked at the station, whether they were married, how many children. He'd mentioned that Marlee was divorced, no kids. Renn had gotten the impression the marriage had been brief. He'd never thought to ask what her husband's first name had been. Hadn't Trish said something about him also being in the media? Graphics software. They used a good deal of it in the television industry, and it was always being upgraded and modified.

He looked over to where Danniker Milburn was talking to the redhead. The smaller, swarthy man was limping toward the bar with two empty glasses in his hands.

Ex-husband would explain Danny's easy familiarity with Marlee and her parents' hostility to him.

Renn wasn't sure what he felt. Marlee and Danny were still friends, still cared for each other, so their divorce must have been amicable. Why had they broken up? Renn had detected no jealousy on Marlee's part for the other woman. If anything, she seemed genuinely pleased that they were happy together. He gazed at her with new interest. A complex woman and infinitely fascinating. Mystery added to intrigue.

"I just haven't had time, Dad," Marlee said. It took Renn a moment to remember what they were talking about—going to the lake. "Ever since Clark's death, I've been completely tied up."

"That was months ago," her mother observed. "Surely you could have found a few hours to go sailing with your father."

"I would have liked to, but—"

"We've bought a cabin cruiser, you know."

Marlee gazed at her mother. "No, I didn't." She smiled at her father. "Not for the lake, I presume."

He chuckled. "Down on the coast. A forty-foot sloop. I've had it out twice. A real beauty. Sleeps six, complete galley. Handles like a dream. Has all the latest electronic equipment. You really ought to come down to Corpus Christi and go out on it with us."

"I'd like that. In another month things should have settled down at the station and Renn can give me some time off." She quirked a grin at him, one that rippled clear down to his toes.

"Do you sail, Mr. Davis?" Anthony Reid asked.

Renn acknowledged that he did but on a much smaller scale than oceangoing cabin cruisers. They talked about boats, from regattas to schooners. The conversation turned relaxed and pleasant—people discussing things they mutually enjoyed. After a few minutes, however, Renn sensed Marlee was eager to break away.

"Oh, there are the Carters," Myra said. "Tony, I need to talk to Leona about the art exhibit at the museum. If you will excuse us." She extended her hand, palm down. "Very nice meeting you, Mr. Davis."

Seconds later the older couple had moved away.

Marlee seemed relieved at their departure, making Renn wonder what issues separated parents and daughter. Even disappointment over her career choice didn't explain the chill that existed between them. Not that he could offer much in the way of consolation. His own family background was nothing to brag about, nor did it give him any clues on how happy families successfully coped with problems. Maybe it was something he and Marlee had in common, this dysfunctional relationship between generations.

He noticed Audrey Van Pelt walk into the ballroom with Talia Preiser, which meant the formalities would soon begin.

"Shall we stop by the KNCS table and say hello?" Renn suggested. "I think they're getting ready to start serving."

She nodded and turned. He placed his hand on the small of her back, aware of the tension that still gripped her. They wended their way among the attractively set round tables, each with a floral arrangement in the middle.

Renn had seen Faye and Taggart arrive several minutes before Marlee's parents. Sal Bufano and his wife were already there, as were Fred Sanders, the station owner, and his wife. Glenda Soames and Andy Crawford, a radiologist she'd been seeing for several months, were also at the television station's table. Crawford was a compact man, an inch or two shorter than Glenda, with thinning hair and a quick wit. He had everyone laughing at a joke he'd just told when Renn and Marlee joined them.

"What a lovely dress," Faye told Marlee. "I adore that color. Did you buy it locally?"

It was probably the most personal question Faye had ever asked her. Marlee nodded. "At The Smart Shop."

"Dora has some lovely things," Sal's wife commented, referring to the shop's owner.

"You look quite dapper this evening," Glenda said to Renn. "Men are so lucky," she added, to the group at large. "All they have to do is put on a tuxedo or a uniform and they sparkle. Women spend hours dolling themselves up with creams, powders, scents and jewelry, and half the time only other women even notice."

"Not tonight," Renn assured her. "You look good enough to eat."

"Careful," Andy Crawford chimed in with a nonthreatening smile, "she's all mine."

"I hear you two aren't going to be joining us," Taggart said. "Going to be at the head table."

Renn wondered if he'd intended the remark to come out sounding snide, or if he just couldn't help it. He'd been predictably furious when he'd learned they were making the presentation and he wasn't invited to participate.

"Marlee, dear," Mrs. Bufano said, "I just wanted to tell you how much I enjoyed your interview with Coach Hillman. What a wonderful piece, very touching and poignant."

"Thank you," Marlee said.

"I completely agree," Mrs. Sanders echoed. "That poor man, seeing his friend and those boys die like that and unable to do anything about it. You handled the subject very well, pointing out that he was a hero, too, helping to save so many others."

"I know Hillman personally," Sanders piped in. "He told me he had serious reservations about agreeing to the interview, said you were very considerate and sensitive. He really appreciated that."

Renn shot a glance at Taggart and Faye. His jaw was tight. Her eyes were averted.

"He's a good man," Marlee confirmed. "I just wanted to let people see that."

Talia Preiser and Audrey Van Pelt came up to the group.

"Thank you all so much for coming tonight," Talia said, after the usual greetings were made. Seventyish, with silver-gray hair and sparkling hazel eyes, she carried her trim figure with straight-backed dignity that was almost regal, yet she had a personality that put people instantly at ease.

She turned to Fred Sanders. "I want especially to thank KNCS for their wonderful support over the years. *Alegre* wouldn't have been possible without Clark's inspiration or the sponsorship of your station."

"We're honored that you asked Marlee to put together this evening's presentation."

"I'm sure your new sports anchor has done an outstanding job," she responded.

Renn tried to gauge the people around him. Taggart seemed about to bluster, when Faye nudged him.

It was Glenda who broke the moment of tension. "I'm sure she'll do us all proud," she said happily.

Everyone who understood the significance of Talia's remark breathed a sigh of relief.

The music paused and chimes sounded, calling everyone to take their assigned seats.

The two ladies excused themselves and moved off. Renn had been observing Audrey. The sly grin on her face as she turned to leave told him she'd put the older woman up to the remark. He would have winked at her if he could have done so surreptitiously.

"Enjoy your dinner," he said to the group, and escorted Marlee to the head table, just as waiters began serving the shrimp cocktail.

"Relax," he whispered in Marlee's ear as he held her seat. "This is supposed to be fun, remember."

But she didn't.

CHAPTER NINE

MARLEE GAZED OUT over the assembled crowd. She knew many of the people here and liked most of them. Her parents were sitting with a couple of bank presidents, a prominent attorney and their wives. Danny and Terry were at a table of businessmen and women. Glenda and Andy Crawford were chatting and laughing with the station's executives. Everybody was having a good time. Except her, and she wasn't sure why.

Running into her parents didn't matter. They'd reached a kind of truce, which was about the best she could expect, even if her mother did like to snipe from time to time. Part of her discomfort was seeing Audrey without Clark. The love they'd shared had been so perfect, so inspiring. How many of the couples in this room had achieved what Audrey and Clark had? Certainly not her parents. She considered the man beside her. She liked being in his company. Did he yearn for a family? He'd never said anything to suggest it, and that inexplicably added to her sadness.

Mrs. Preiser referring to her as the new sports anchor was disturbing. Marlee had no doubt the comment had been sincere or who was behind it. Audrey meant well, but pulling the tiger's tail was a mistake.

Faye would accuse her of spreading rumors, misrepresenting herself.

She was halfway through her prime rib when Renn commented, ''You and Danny are certainly on good terms.''

''Why shouldn't we be?'' she wondered out loud. ''We've been friends since elementary school.''

''Your parents don't appear to be nearly as forgiving.''

She slanted him at quizzical glance. ''Forgiving? For what?''

''The divorce,'' he mumbled between bites of meat.

What was he talking about? Then it dawned on her and a slow grin crept across her face. She understood now the reticence he'd shown in talking with Danny. She'd been disappointed by his attitude, which she realized now she'd misinterpreted.

He was jealous. Oh, this was too sweet not to savor. She took another forkful of baked potato, crunched on the bacon bits and sipped her wine.

''The divorce, huh?'' She pouted at him. ''Do you see where Danny is sitting? Over there, to the left, second table from the bar. Do you see who's sitting on his right?''

His brow furrowed. ''The guy with the limp. So?''

She grinned broadly. ''That's Terry.''

He gaped, then turned very slowly to her. ''Terry is a man?''

She sucked in her cheeks and barely suppressed a chuckle. ''They've known each other since high school, went on to college together and majored in computer science. In their senior year Terry was badly injured in a car accident. After months of recovery he continued his rehab with *Alegre.* That's how they became associated with the center.'' She couldn't help snickering at the embarrassed expression on Renn's face. ''Danny's a good friend—'' she placed her hand on his ''—but our affection is strictly platonic.''

Glancing over to where the two men sat, Renn felt a sense of relief. Marlee had caught him being jealous of a guy he thought was her ex-husband, which was embarrassing, but it also stripped away any pretense that his interest in her was strictly professional. This was dangerous—for both of them. Sexual attraction was a quagmire. He needed to back off, pull away. His brain was still functioning well enough to register that resistance was the sensible course.

The mayor tapped a spoon on his wineglass and made his way to the podium. After welcoming everyone to this fifteenth annual *Alegre* banquet, he formally introduced the people at the head table. Renn could feel the hostility radiating from Faye and Taggart when Marlee was referred to as a close friend of the Van Pelt family and Clark's protégée—and the new Voice of Coyote Springs.

He placed a reassuring hand atop hers, felt the warm skin and the pulse beneath it. ''Ready?''

He rose from his seat and held hers. Together they walked to the rostrum. He thanked Audrey Van Pelt and Talia Preiser for giving Marlee and him the privilege of making this presentation. He punched a button on the podium, and two screens descended over the mirrored wall on the north end of the room. Another button dimmed the room's lights. Finally, he activated the computerized projector that had been set up in the middle of the dance floor during dinner. The

KNCS-TV logo appeared on one screen, the *Alegre* logo on the other.

"Clark Van Pelt," Renn said in a smoothly professional baritone voice, "had a distinguished career as a television sports reporter, writer, anchor and teacher that spanned three decades. He came to KNCS-TV as a reporter in 1983 from KDAL-TV in Dallas."

The screens were filled with still and motion-picture clips of a much younger man, his hair dark, his face unlined, as he stood behind a microphone in a crowded football stadium, in front of a baseball field, beside a shimmering swimming pool. Background sounds included the muffled roar of a crowd, the crack of a bat, the splash of water.

"Since then," Marlee said into her mike, "he earned national and regional awards, twice serving as president of the Sportswriters Guild. Two years ago he was awarded the Lifetime Achievement Award by the National League of Sportscasters for his work in fostering athletics and sportsmanship among poor and disadvantaged youth."

There were shots of him holding a large glass plaque before an applauding audience as flashbulbs strobed in quick succession.

Renn again took over. "He was a distinguished member of the faculty of the School of Broadcast Journalism at Texas University at Coyote Springs for the past fifteen years. His courses on sports journalism and ethics in the media have received national and international acclaim. Clark Van Pelt was awarded an honorary Doctor of Humane Letters by the state university last year."

Footage of the ceremony rolled across both screens,

his wife standing on one side, the governor of the state on the other.

"Clark was an active member of the Coyote Springs community," Marlee said, "who generously contributed his time and energy to many charitable causes, but he is best remembered for his role in helping establish *Alegre,* the Therapeutic Riding Center for handicapped adults and children."

A clip showed him with a helmeted young woman with braces on her legs, her face wide with an endearing, beaming grin, as she sat atop a horse. The film was nearly fifteen years old. Talia's daughter had died two years later of complications resulting from the injuries she'd sustained in the car accident that had crippled her. Marlee had hesitated showing it, but Talia had given her enthusiastic permission. Marlee wondered what effect it was having on the woman sitting a few seats away.

A montage followed: boys and girls with a variety of disabilities, adult men and women, some quite aged. All of them smiling broadly as volunteers walked beside their horses and ponies.

Renn summed up. "Clark Van Pelt is survived by his wife of twenty-eight years, Audrey Dempsey Van Pelt, and their three sons. He died the way he lived, an unselfish hero."

Mrs. Talia Preiser, dry eyed and smiling, joined them at the podium, as the audience applauded. She gave Marlee a heartfelt hug, warmly shook Renn's hand and kissed him on the cheek.

"Clark gave hope and inspiration to the hundreds of clients we've served in the past fifteen years," she said into the mike a minute later. "He touched the lives of countless children, of old people, of people who have had to fight to maintain their dignity in the face of traumatic, life-altering injuries and diseases. We miss him, but he hasn't really left us. His good works live on.''

Renn glanced over at Marlee. The tears of a couple months earlier were under control now, but the sadness in her glazed eyes was no less intense.

Clark's portrait filled both screens, and the dinner guests gave a standing ovation as Audrey joined the three at the podium and embraced them all.

Awards were then distributed to various members of the *Alegre* staff, including Audrey Van Pelt herself. Thanks were given to various individual and corporate sponsors, Anthony and Myra Reid among them.

Throughout it all, Renn was most aware of Marlee, but he also kept an eye on Faye and Taggart. She smiled and clapped at the appropriate times and seemed genuinely touched by the ceremonies. Taggart, sitting beside her, had a perpetual scowl on his face.

The formalities concluded, the ballroom staff removed the big round tables from the middle of the room and the orchestra returned. Instead of classical music, they played the big-band sound of the thirties and forties.

''Would you like to dance?'' Renn asked, when the musicians broke into Hoagie Carmichael's ''Stardust.''

''I'm not sure we should,'' she said.

''I am. We're here to socialize, so let's be sociable. Other people are dancing, including Faye and Taggart.''

She searched the room and saw them. Not exactly hanging on to each other, but they were dancing.

"I'd be delighted," she said.

They moved to the middle of the floor, directly under the massive chandelier, which had been dimmed to make the room more intimate. He took her hand in his and circled her waist. They left a modest inch between them, but propriety didn't last. By the second verse they were touching. By the third they were in still closer contact.

Her hair brushed his cheek. Her scent seeped into him. Renn closed his eyes and luxuriated in the sensation of her body, her feminine curves ranged against him. His pulse tripped. He felt himself hardening and wanted to bury his head against the soft column of her neck. Cruelly, mercifully, the music ended and they established space between them.

The next number was "In the Mood," a fast one. Marlee started toward a small table that had been set up on the perimeter. Renn grabbed her wrist, spun her around and lowered her into a dip. Her startled expression—one of surprised delight—shot adrenaline through his system.

"Up to it?" he whispered, as he looked down at her.

Her lips curled. Her eyes narrowed. "Try me."

Woman, his libido screamed, *don't tempt me.*

With a sure, strong tug, he pulled her up, and they began a lively jitterbug. Within a minute the floor had cleared and people were standing around it, their toes tapping as they watched Marlee spin and kick to the magical beat.

Applause and cheers greeted them when the music stopped. Still holding hands, they grinned at each other and bowed to their appreciative audience. At the bar in the corner, they both asked for soft drinks to quench their thirst while they received the congratulations of those around them.

Taggart came up and ordered a couple of Manhattans from the bartender. "You two have been practicing," he said with a grin that would have been perceived as friendly on anyone else.

"As a matter of fact," Renn replied, "this is the first time we've ever danced together. How about you and Faye? Your maiden voyage, too?"

The question caught him momentarily off guard. He was about to say something, when the man behind the bar handed him his cocktails. "You were both very good out there. I was impressed," he said, quickly turned away and started wending his way back to where Faye sat with several other guests.

"Gee," Renn said, "I think he paid us a compliment. I wonder why."

Marlee chuckled. "Probably to throw you off track. You notice he got away without answering your question."

Renn laughed. "How about some air?"

"Definitely."

He opened the French doors behind the portable bar, and they slipped outside. The balcony was big enough for only two people, so they were assured of privacy. The night was cool and dry, the slight breeze refreshing after the heavy air of the ballroom.

"Where'd you learn to dance like that?" she asked.

He grinned. "I was about to ask you the same thing."

"Mother insisted I take ballroom dancing lessons when I was a teenager. I hated them at the time, but I can do the waltz, the polka and the tango, as well as several other numbers no one has performed in a century or two.''

''Great for costume parties. I noticed she wasn't one of the people rushing to congratulate us on our twinkle toes.''

Marlee chuckled. ''In case you haven't noticed, my mother is a snob.''

He lifted an eyebrow at the bitterness behind the sarcasm. ''I gather you're not close.''

''I've failed her,'' she said, half-mockingly. ''She wanted a debutante and got a tomboy.''

He smiled. ''Is that why you went into sports reporting instead of news?''

''It was a natural choice for me. When other girls were playing with dolls, I was kicking around a soccer ball or shooting hoops. They took ballet lessons. I enrolled in gymnastics. They learned nursery rhymes. I memorized batting averages and handicaps.''

''Athletics gave you poise and grace,'' he noted.

She liked being complimented, but her shy grin intimated that it also made her uncomfortable.

''Please don't tell my mother that,'' she quipped. ''She thinks I learned it from walking around with a book on my head at Madame Carmine's Academy for Young Ladies.''

He chortled. Marlee Reid was beautiful, intelligent and successful in a highly competitive profession, yet she couldn't win the approval of her parents.

She was also close enough on the narrow balcony that Renn had only to raise his hand to brush his knuckles across the fine line of her jaw. ''Not a tomboy,'' he said softly. ''A very charming, sophisticated woman of the world.''

She lowered her eyes, took hold of his hand and placed a delicate kiss on it. "Thank you."

He wanted to wrap his arms around her, experience once more the caress of her body against his. "You'll have to teach me to tango sometime."

"I suspect you'll be a quick study." She took a sip of her ginger ale.

They stood beside each other. Below them the Coyote River meandered its way through town, dark swaths of pecan and live oak trees lining its banks. A nearly full moon hung in a cloudless sky, illuminating the stiff gothic forms of commercial buildings and the graceful gables of residences.

"Tell me about your marriage." He kept his eyes straight ahead, but he was fully aware of the woman standing beside him. She didn't stiffen at the invitation to discuss what must have been an unhappy episode in her life, but she did pause before responding.

"His name is Barry Taylor," she said quietly. "We went to TUCS together and majored in broadcast journalism, got married right after graduation and considered ourselves blessed when we were both hired by the same TV station in the Southeast, he as a news reporter, me as a sports producer. He was good. Within fifteen months he received a dream offer from one of the top-twenty stations in the country. I still had nine months remaining on my two-year contract, so Barry went on ahead. Three months later I decided to surprise him with a visit. Well, the joke was on me. I found him exploring cloud nine with the weekend weather bunny."

She fell silent. Renn sensed old pain and that resignation had supplanted anger. She'd loved the guy and he'd hurt her badly. That kind of wound took a long time to heal. It also left scars.

"I divorced him and went my own separate way."

Fighting an uphill battle because of gender bias in this high-profile industry, Renn reminded himself, a bias he'd bought into and propagated. He covered her fingers clutching the ornate, wrought-iron railing, felt the gentle throb beneath the soft, smooth skin, lifted the hand and coaxed her around to face him. Leaning closer, he kissed her on the lips. A gentle touching. No more. But it was enough to confirm what he'd hoped: that she wasn't averse to his proximity.

Her eyes were still closed when he pulled away. He was tempted to reestablish contact, when she opened them. Her gaze lingered before she caressed his cheek, then she turned and stared out across the drowsy city.

"He was a fool," Renn murmured.

She seemed to weigh his words, not sure if they were true. "We better go back inside."

He wished she weren't right. The company of others wasn't on his mind at the moment. Only hers.

Over the next hour, between conversations with people they knew and accepting compliments on the program they'd presented, they were able to squeeze in a waltz and a polka. No more slow, intimate fox-trots, though. Marlee wondered if it was because of Taggart's remarks and his insinuation that their relationship went beyond the purely professional. No tango, either. That would have to wait for another time.

Not that her mind had really been on her footwork or his. She kept recollecting the sensation of his kiss.

A chaste kiss, she reminded herself, though chastity wasn't exactly what his lips had stirred.

He never did tell her where he'd learned to dance, Marlee ruminated later as they were driving back to her place.

"It's not very late," he said.

She checked the digital clock on his dashboard. Nearly midnight.

"How about a cup of coffee?"

Caffeine didn't really interest her, especially at this hour. She was stirred up enough just being with him, but the thought of going home to her empty apartment held no appeal. Not tonight.

"If I can get decaf."

"I think that can be arranged."

"Where do you want to go?" The only place she knew of that would be open was a twenty-four-hour truck stop on the outskirts of town.

"My place."

What was he proposing? One little, innocent kiss… Surely, he wasn't suggesting…

"I have something I'd like to show you." He didn't look over at her, just concentrated on the dark road ahead.

"Your etchings?" she jested.

"Would you like to see my etchings?" He slanted her a crooked smile. "I was referring to my boat."

"Boat?"

He chuckled. "It's nothing fancy. Just a catamaran. But when I heard you talking so fondly about sailing this evening…well, I thought maybe you'd like to see it."

"At night?" Humor flavored her voice. She had a sudden image of them groping in the dark. The notion brought heat to her face and a strange stirring in her belly.

"I have dockside lights." He glanced over at her this time. "If you'd rather not... I mean, we can do it another time, if you're even interested."

His sudden shyness emboldened her. If she hadn't worked with him for more than half a year and gotten a glimpse of his more gentle, caring side, she would have said no. Maybe she was being foolish, too credulous, but she felt safe with him.

"Do we need to stop off for decaf?"

He looked over and grinned broadly. "Yes."

She laughed. "There's a supermarket two blocks over that stays open late on Saturday night."

They went inside together, he in his tuxedo, she in her evening gown. He bought a pound of premium beans and a tin of Danish cookies. The clerk at the checkout smiled at them.

"Been to a prom?" she asked.

"Not in about twenty years," he told her. "But thanks for asking."

"The *Alegre* dinner," Marlee explained.

"The therapeutic riding group? Oh, aren't they great?" the woman exclaimed. "My neighbor's eight-year-old son has cerebral palsy and goes there every week. He absolutely loves it, and so does his mom. Say, you're Marlee Reid, aren't you? I've seen you on TV."

Marlee smiled. Being recognized was always a boost to the ego.

"Your interview with those basketball players was a hoot. I don't usually watch the sports—unless my son or one of his friends are going to be on. He plays midget soccer, so that doesn't happen often. Austin isn't very good yet, but his father swears next year he'll be the star kicker. Anyway, when I found out where you did that interview I had to watch. Wow! You were way cool, a lot more than I would have been. I mean being right there, surrounded by all those—'' She looked up at Renn and actually blushed. ''Well, you know.''

Marlee chuckled. Complete strangers often discussed the most intimate details with people they recognized from TV, as if they were old friends.

''I bet you miss Clark,'' the woman continued more seriously, as if glad to change the subject. ''I never met him, but he seemed like a nice man. Are you going to take over for him now that he's…er…gone.''

Marlee could feel Renn studying her. ''Nothing's been decided yet. It's still too early.''

''Well, I hope you do get it. I don't like that other guy, Maggot, or whatever his name is. Reminds me of my sister's husband. A real jerk.''

Renn handed her a twenty-dollar bill, winked at Marlee and accepted his change.

''Y'all come back now, hear,'' the woman said, as they left.

''You got a vote in there,'' Renn commented, starting his car.

''Too bad it's not a popularity contest.''

Marlee's attention was soon diverted when they pulled into Renn's driveway. His lake house wasn't especially big or luxurious. Quite ordinary, really. But the moment she stepped inside the front door, she felt comfortable in it.

The large living room constituted almost half the floor plan and had a picture window that offered a sweeping view of the lake. Tonight the moon-struck water sparkled like diamonds on black velvet. To her right she glimpsed a small kitchen and breakfast nook. On her left were two rooms, one of which appeared to be an office. The furnishings throughout were simple and masculine, but what captivated Marlee was the air of serenity about the place. This was the home of a man who was content with himself.

The kitchen, she discovered when she followed him there, was utilitarian, though there was a healthy pothos plant on the windowsill. The room was also neat and clean. Whatever happened to the bachelor image of dirty dishes piled up in the sink and greasy frying pans left on the stove? *He probably doesn't cook that much,* she thought. Yet when he went to a drawer to get out a coffee filter and to an overhead cabinet for cups and saucers, the impression was of a place used, not just occupied.

He ground the beans and set the coffee machine to gurgling. ''Let's go outside.''

They stepped through the breakfast nook's sliding-glass door, onto a flagstone patio. It was cooler here than in the heart of town. The air was more humid and scented with lilac.

''Are you chilly?'' he asked. ''I can get a sweater for you to throw over your shoulders.''

''I'm fine,'' she said, not sure she was. Would he put his arm around her if she shivered?

''Come take a look.'' He clasped her hand and led her down a narrow redbrick path to a wooden dock. Tied to it was a twenty-foot catamaran, its single mast folded down. She read the name emblazoned on the side.

''Why *Calico*?'' she asked.

"After a cat I used to have. She liked to go sailing with me on my old boat."

He'd had a cat. She hadn't seen one inside. "Used to have?"

"She died about a year ago at the ripe old age of seventeen. I've thought of getting another one, but I'm home so little these days that I don't think it would be wise to leave it alone for hours on end, especially a kitten. Did you have pets when you were growing up?"

She shook her head. "They're messy and leave hair all over the place." At least, that was what her mother had said.

"I'm sorry." He was still holding her hand. He tugged her around to face him. "Kids need pets," he murmured. They were only inches apart. Another inch and—

When he kissed her this time, she was prepared. At least she thought she was. His mouth covered hers. His tongue slipped forward and nudged her lips. He explored slowly, tentatively. A soft, sweet moan escaped her when their tongues collided, parted, touched again. Tasted. His arms encircled her. If she had been cold before, she wasn't now. Heat cascaded through her as she settled into the comfort of his embrace.

Her mind, what little of it was functioning, told her this was crazy. He was her boss. Sex and business didn't blend.

She pulled away, breathless, hardly able to get words out. "We shouldn't."

She could feel his reluctance when he released his hold, and wished he hadn't. She shivered, not from the cool night breeze coming in off the lake, but from the absence of his warmth pressing against her, surrounding her.

His lips curved. His eyes danced. "Ready for coffee?"

Her head was swimming, her body tingling. Again, she was aware of the aroma of lilac on the air, but it was the scent of Renn that lingered in her mind. The allure of a man. It had been a long time since she'd experienced the excitement of intimacy, the kind that started with a kiss.

"One cup," she said, and hugged her arms around her waist. "And then I need to go home."

"One cup," he echoed.

Sunday, April 13

WHAT HAD HE DONE? He'd kissed Marlee Reid, not once but twice. Forget that she was his subordinate. Forget that he'd committed himself to getting her Van Pelt's job as the sports director and anchor for KNCS-TV. He'd done something far more serious than compromise his professionalism. He'd opened a door and let in a tempest. The peaceful, secure, serene world he'd created was being shattered, and he wasn't sure he'd be able to put all the pieces put back together again.

He couldn't afford to have a woman complicating his world. He didn't need hormones distorting his judgment. Maybe if she wasn't in the industry, he could entertain the notion of letting her into a compartmented corner of his life, the way he had from time to time with other women. But he'd vowed never again to get involved with anyone in the media. There wasn't room for two of them, not in his house or his heart, because it was his heart that would suffer. Call him greedy. Call him selfish, but he didn't want to expose himself, lay himself open once more to the pain of disappointment and loss.

He'd watched his parents' marriage writhe and finally break because they were so rarely together, because when they were his mother had questioned his father's fidelity and because in truth his old man had been unfaithful. When Renn had met Pamela, he'd convinced himself they could do better. He'd been a news reporter at a local television station; she'd been freelancing for one of the networks. Their love affair had been an exciting series of stolen moments from both their jobs. Eventually, they'd accumulated enough time together to decide they were deeply in love.

They'd set a wedding date, then postponed it because she latched on to a feature story halfway across the country that she just couldn't pass up. Since they'd opted not to have a big church wedding, delaying the small private civil ceremony was no great inconvenience. They set a new date, and again, a plum assignment—this one overseas—popped up. He was beginning to have serious second thoughts about the wisdom of their union, when he received word that she wouldn't be coming back. The peaceful demonstration she'd set out to cover had turned violent, and she'd been killed.

At work on Monday, Renn decided, he'd ignore Marlee. He'd forget about the kisses, go about his job and let her go about hers. They were dedicated, ambitious professionals, after all. A kiss or two couldn't change that.

Could it?

MARLEE TOSSED and turned, dozed off once or twice, but reawakened each time with the phantom sensation of Renn kissing her. As if she'd never kissed or been kissed by a man before. She had. Plenty of times. What was it about Renn Davis that made his kisses linger on her lips, in her mind, in her dreams?

She slept late the next morning, crawled out of bed, showered, dressed and fixed herself a cup of instant coffee. She rarely used her coffeemaker. What was the point for just one person? Renn had used his machine last evening for two cups, but that was different. He was entertaining a guest. Did he normally brew a pot, or did he use instant as she did? Did he have company very often?

It was Sunday. Audrey had invited her over for dinner, but that wasn't until late this afternoon. She went for her morning run. The ankle had healed long ago, but she was still being extra careful. Afterward, she combed the sports page in the newspaper, checked scores and flipped through the TV channel that carried national and international athletic events. Channel surfing used to drive her parents crazy when she lived at home, but it was a way of life for people in the media.

Forget about Renn, she told herself, as she drove to the studio. She'd missed Quint Randolph's sportscast the previous night and wanted to review the tape to see how he had done. Forget Renn's kisses and the way he made her feel when he held her in his arms. What they had in common was the same thing that would drive them apart, just as it had with Barry.

CHAPTER TEN

Wednesday, April 16

RENN WAS WALKING through the newsroom Wednesday afternoon when he overheard an exchange between Taggart and the producer for his analysis show.

"Where are the highlights from the Yankees game?"

Lacy Ewell lifted her chin. "You said the Giant game because it was going to be so close." Her tone was a mixture of defensiveness and apprehension.

Taggart screwed up his mouth scornfully. "If you'd taken the time to notice the score, you'd have seen it wasn't anywhere near close, and I didn't say it was going to be. I said it might be if they lost their starting pitcher, which they didn't."

"I did exactly what you told me to do," she insisted.

"You did what was easy," he countered. "The Yankees were on a roll. Too bad you didn't bother to check."

"You weren't here," she enunciated between clenched teeth.

"What's the problem?" Renn asked, as he stepped into the editing bay.

Taggart scowled. "I'm all set to comment on the

Yankees, and what she gives me is boring shots of the Giants getting trounced.''

Lacy was a widow in her midthirties, trying to support her two kids and ailing mother. The woman appeared tired and upset.

''He told me to get clips of the Giants. I did exactly that, and now he's complaining because he doesn't have footage on the Yankees. He never said anything about wanting coverage of them. I'm not a mind reader.''

Renn regarded Taggart, who seemed oblivious to the woman's frustration. ''Is that what you asked for?''

''She's supposed to get me *interesting* material, not snoozers.'' He took a deep put-upon breath.

''Did you tell her to edit the Giants?'' Renn asked him pointedly.

Taggart rolled his eyes. ''I said to check them out, and if the game looked close, to get me a few clips.''

''He didn't say *if* it looked close,'' Lacy retorted, her normally pale face bright with color. ''He said to tape the Giants, and that's what I did.''

''The Yankees game was an upset. That's the one everyone's going to be interested in.''

Renn had to agree about the Giants game—it was a drag—but that wasn't the issue. He'd never known Lacy to screw up an assignment—or to lie. She was conscientious about her work and asked for clarification if something wasn't clear. She had good instincts, too, and wasn't afraid to go with her gut. Working with anyone else, she probably would have taken the initiative and switched coverage. Taggart, Renn suspected, was a victim of malicious obedience.

"Is there still time to edit the Yankees feed?" Renn asked her.

The woman glanced up at the clock on the wall. "I'll find something."

"That's right. You will," Taggart said disdainfully.

They watched him stride away. Down the hall, Renn caught a glimpse of Marlee coming through the main entrance, balancing a shallow white box.

"He's driving me crazy," Lacy told Renn. "I tried to call him yesterday, to see if he wanted me to switch coverage, but he wasn't home."

Renn placed his hand on her shoulder and squeezed gently. "Hang in there. We'll get through this."

"I sure hope so," she said despairingly. "And it better be soon. I've enjoyed my job till recently, but without Clark to run interference, it's been hell around here."

"Wow. Pineapple upside-down cake." They both turned at Peggy Faykus's exclamation.

Marlee was standing at the coffee bar with a glass platter in her hands. The tangy aroma of pineapple and brown sugar wafting through the air was enough to bring a sudden surge of people toward the reception area. Taggart came out and leaned cross-armed against the wall.

"Playing homemaker?" he asked sarcastically. "Smells like you've finally found your real talent."

Renn had an urge to connect his fist with the guy's face, but he'd never been a violent man. Instead, he watched Marlee for her reaction and was inordinately pleased when her shoulders didn't stiffen or her composure falter. She simply ignored him.

Peggy removed paper plates from the compartment under the coffeemaker. "What's the occasion?"

"I couldn't sleep last night, so I thought I'd do something productive."

"Your insomnia is definitely to our advantage," Renn commented, as he stepped forward.

She jerked around and stared at him. He smiled. She blushed, then quickly redirected her attention to cutting the moist cake into neat squares. She held out a generous piece, complete with a cherry and half a pineapple ring.

"Brave enough to try a piece?" she asked.

"Haven't I told you? I can resist anything but temptation." He accepted the paper plate and plastic fork with both hands. Their fingers briefly touched. "Looks and smells sinful."

"Buttering up the boss?" Taggart sneered, as he moved forward.

"Nope, telling him to stuff it." She handed another piece to Lacy and resumed cutting. Trish, Quint and Wayne joined them. "I'd offer some to you, too, Tag, but I'm afraid the caloric overload might put you in cardiac arrest or diabetic shock, or you'd get a big belly."

"To go with his big head," Trish muttered.

"Still, if you're willing to take a chance—" Marlee said, holding out an equally large portion to him.

"I don't eat sweets." He scrunched up his mouth, turned on his heel and retreated.

The women all had the good grace to wait until he'd returned to his office before they cackled.

Peggy snickered. "I could see him drooling. The guy's a real jerk."

"I was just teasing," Marlee said innocently. "I really didn't mean to offend him."

"Honey," Peggy said, "to do that, he'd have to have feelings."

"He's still bent out of shape because the guy in the control room Sunday night was slow with his clips," Wayne explained. "Every time he introduced a play, it took like three seconds for the footage to appear on screen."

Three seconds didn't seem like much, but in a business in which every second counted, the delay felt like an eternity. The audience would forgive one such occurrence, but a pattern of miscues had the effect of making the person on the screen appear disorganized.

Renn understood what was happening. People at the station were voting for their candidate for sports anchor in the only way they knew how. While Marlee brought in homemade cake, Taggart was complaining about things not going smoothly enough for him. Some of his charges were probably legitimate, such as producers cuing him in late or too early, but many of them were of his own doing, such as this problem with coverage of the Giants versus the Yankees.

What Taggart obviously didn't understand was that when the people he depended on had no reason to like or respect him, they could figure out all sorts of subtle ways to undermine him. From now on, Renn would make it a point to be very visible during live broadcasts, but he couldn't be everywhere at the same time. He just hoped the staff's attempts to promote Marlee didn't backfire.

"SHE OWES ME," Taggart snarled a little while later. "Big-time."

Barely half an hour remained before going on the air, and the esteemed sports analyst insisted he needed two minutes of Marlee's broadcast to properly analyze the footage Lacy had culled of the Yankees game and their prospects for a pennant later in the year.

"She doesn't owe you anything," Renn shot back. They were standing in the middle of the newsroom. Nobody was overtly watching them, but everyone was tuned in.

Marlee stepped out of the tape library, several cassettes in her hands. Renn waved to her to join them.

"What do you have lined up for today's show?" he asked her.

She rattled off a list of national and local events she was featuring.

"Are you covering the Yankees game?"

She shook her head. "Only the scores. Then I have a spot on Hayley Wickenhauser, the Canadian woman who's playing on the Finnish men's hockey team."

Taggart snorted derisively.

"Followed by a promo for the local golf tourney this weekend at the country club for the rehabilitation center."

"Can't cut that." Renn was about to tell Taggart to go climb a rope, when Mickey Grimes returned to his desk. "Mickey, how tight is your coverage this evening?"

He eyed Taggart warily. "What do you need?"

"Two minutes."

"That's pushing it." He pursed his lips in thought. "I can cut a little from the Middle East story and maybe a few seconds from the South American summit, since it's been in session for three days and is expected to go on for a couple more."

"How much time?" Renn asked.

"A minute and half."

"Good." Renn turned to Taggart. "There you go."

"I need two minutes."

"That's the best I can do. Take it or leave it. I really don't care. Which will it be?"

Taggart clicked his tongue. "I'll take it." He walked away.

"You're welcome," Renn called after him, but got no response. "Thanks," he said to Grimes.

"To help Marlee, it's a pleasure."

Friday, April 18

MARLEE SPENT most of the next two days putting together her Friday night wrap-up and highlights of local high school sports. It was the most popular segment of the week, watched by virtually every parent of a teenager in town. Having your name mentioned on the air set off a glow in people that could last almost indefinitely. Those ten or fifteen seconds of glory might be recounted at reunions for years to come. Marlee understood that and treated it with respect. Following Clark's example, she did her best to be as inclusive as possible. She also knew the Friday-night sportscast was the one that would gain her the most community support. Mention kids in a positive way and she'd have their parents and friends in her pocket.

Because of the popularity of this particular segment, she had a full eleven minutes, instead of the usual seven. The top two of the stack of tapes she handed Wayne to deliver to the control room were of national coverage. The last five were local.

With a microphone clipped to her blouse and notes clutched in her hand, she stood in the Live Center, greeted the television audience and gave them the teaser for the stories to follow. During the two-minute commercial break, she quickly reviewed her notes, though the text was on the teleprompter. The two national stories were short but mandatory. Texans loved to hear about home teams, even if the games themselves were uneventful. When she was cued in again, she covered them quickly, checking the monitor facing her as the tapes she'd selected were run.

"Turning now to local sports…"

She talked about the high-school baseball game, naming the two players who'd hit homeruns back-to-back. One was a new outfielder with an impressive batting average and potential to go pro someday.

On the screen, she saw girls' volleyball, which was supposed to be her second story. Trying to remain unfazed, she simply apologized for the mix-up, explained what the audience had just seen and went on to the next story—about the college men's swimming team. Except the tape that ran was of a varsity soccer match.

She smiled into the camera and again apologized for the mistake, once more explaining what had just been presented and being very careful to credit names.

She went into her third story, this time commenting wryly before the tape was run, "Let's see what comes up this time."

It was the first clip on the baseball team.

She laughed good-naturedly into the camera. "Does anyone know what the term *FUBAR* means? For the uninitiated, it stands for Fouled Up Beyond All Recognition." She grinned mischievously. "I think we're seeing it in action. Okay, I have an idea.

Let's show the tape first, then I'll give you the story that matches. Who knows, we might start a new trend.'' Viewers saw her nod to someone off screen. ''Run the next video, please.''

She waited until it appeared on her monitor, then went into her spiel. The downside was that she had to speed up her delivery to make up for lost time.

''How much was I over?'' she asked the producer.

''Fifteen seconds,'' Shelley Chester told her. ''No problem. Mickey can adjust. After all, he recouped Tag's half-minute overrun the other day. What I really want to know is what the hell happened?''

Marlee's stomach jittered now more than when she'd been on camera. ''I'd like an answer to that question myself. Who's working the control booth?''

''Dexter Lamont.''

Renn joined them. ''Somebody want to explain to me what's going on?'' He eyed Marlee with concern.

''No idea. I went over my script three times and verified the sequence before sending the tapes to the control booth. Let's go talk to Dex.''

The three of them marched down the hall toward the control booth and were almost there, when Faye appeared at the other end of the hallway.

''Uh-oh,'' Shelley murmured. ''I smell trouble.''

The vice president strode toward them. ''Renn, Marlee, in my office. Now.''

''Let me check—'' Renn began.

''Now,'' she repeated imperiously.

With a barely perceptible shrug, he nodded and followed. Marlee trailed behind him.

''By the way,'' he said, as they marched up the steps side by side, ''I think you did a great job recovering. Clark would have been proud of you.''

The compliment, coming from Renn, especially in association with Clark, sent a warm glow through her, followed immediately by the sadness of his absence.

Renn put his hand on the door handle at the top of the stairs. "Let's see what the dragon lady has to say."

They stepped into the carpeted hallway and walked down to the VP's suite. The outer reception area was empty; Maxine had already left for the day.

"Let me handle this," Renn whispered, as they approached Faye's open door.

Marlee hated the idea of standing mutely by while someone else defended her, but Renn wasn't just anyone. He was her boss. She trusted him, and he could probably get away with things she couldn't.

"Depends on her and what she says," she murmured in reply.

"Please," he implored.

She nodded to acknowledge his plea, but she still reserved the right to speak in her own defense.

Faye was pacing behind her desk. There were two guest chairs. She didn't invite either of her employees to take them.

"Do I have to remind you, Marlee, that this is ratings month?" she asked in a scathing tone. "When things are supposed to go smoothly around here, when people aren't supposed to screw up." She paused to catch her breath. "Your sportscast tonight was a disgrace. You embarrassed yourself and made this station look ridiculous. You also did a shameful disservice to the memory of Clark Van Pelt, the guy you claim to respect so much."

Marlee was stunned by the vitriol of Faye's attack. She could understand her outrage at the screwup, but invoking Clark's name against her was more than Marlee could bear, especially after Renn had just complimented her on the way she'd handled the situation. She started to open her mouth to speak.

"Just a minute," Renn cut her off. "That last remark was totally uncalled for, Faye. You owe Marlee an apology."

His boss glared at him.

"Yes, the tapes got mixed up," he continued. "It's unfortunate, but those things happen. I don't know exactly why, because you didn't give me a chance to find out. I'll investigate and make sure it doesn't happen again, but putting the blame solely on Marlee is unreasonable and unfair."

Faye was clearly flustered by the force of his reaction.

"It was her broadcast," she argued back, her voice raised. "She's responsible for what goes on during it."

"So if a tape breaks or the power fails, it's her fault? Come on, Faye. You know better than that. This station and everything that happens here is a team effort. Each of us has to depend on and have confidence in the people we work with. Let me check into this and find out where the weak link is."

"You better." She peered at Marlee. "I'm putting you on notice, as of now. If our ratings fall, it'll be because of your sportscast today, and I promise you, it will have consequences. The same goes if any more of your segments are messed up—for whatever reason. Is that clear?"

Marlee worked her jaw, not in shame, but in building anger at the woman's immoderate attitude.

"Now, get out of here. And Renn," she added, as

he turned to leave, "I'm holding you personally responsible for this, too."

At the bottom of the stairs, Renn gazed at Marlee, his expression sympathetic. "Don't let her diatribe bother you. She's just blowing off steam. Ratings week isn't a good time for the system to go FUBAR." He smiled.

Marlee didn't. "She blames me."

"Because you're the easiest target." He put his arm around her shoulders. The warmth and gentle strength of his touch smothered for a moment her anger and hurt.

"Relax," he murmured in her ear. "We'll straighten this out."

She wanted to believe him, and with his body so close to hers, not falling under the spell of his confidence was hard. But someone had sabotaged her.

They returned to the newsroom. Most of the day staff had gone home, replaced with the much smaller evening crew. Mickey Grimes was sitting at his desk, sorting through messages and notes.

He glanced up and tilted his head toward the stairwell door. "I guess she's on the warpath, huh?"

Marlee snorted. "In full paint."

"Mix-ups happen," he said. "The timing on this one was really rotten. You handled it like a pro. I'll give you that. Keeping your cool...ya done good, girl."

"Thanks," Marlee said with a wry twist of her mouth. "Now, if only Faye and our viewers see it that way."

He rose to his feet. "I'm getting ready to take my dinner break. You guys care to join me? All-you-can-eat spaghetti and meatballs tonight at Luigi's."

"You're not going home to eat?" Marlee asked. "Where's Lilly?"

"Visiting her sister in Abilene. Cassie had a baby girl a couple of days ago, and Lilly couldn't stay away."

"Congratulations, Unc." Renn held out his hand.

He laughed. "I didn't have anything to do with it, but thanks anyway. You coming?"

Renn shook his head. "Maybe another time."

"You're missing great garlic bread. See you later."

He snaked out from behind his desk and with a wave headed for the front door.

"Let's talk to Dex," Renn suggested to Marlee.

As soon as they entered the control booth, Dexter Lamont held up his hands and backed away. "I swear I put those tapes in exactly the way they were given to me. Marlee," he implored, "you know I wouldn't mess up your broadcast."

"Do you still have them stacked in the order you showed them?" Renn asked him.

"Right here." He motioned to the work counter of the equipment console a couple of feet away. "Just like they were handed to me."

Renn nodded to Marlee. "Could the sequence have gotten reversed?"

She shook her head. "I considered that when we were talking to Faye, but my first two clips appeared in the right sequence. It was only when I got to the local stuff that everything went haywire."

"I swear," Dexter repeated, "I played them exactly the way Quint delivered them to me."

"Quint?" Marlee's head shot up. "I gave them to Wayne."

Renn's eyes darkened. "Did he say anything to you when he handed them over?"

The technician's dark brows narrowed. "Not as I recall. Just said they were for Marlee's segment and left. Usually, he hangs around to gab. Sometimes, he helps me load them. But today, he seemed to be in a hurry."

Renn thanked him.

"Maybe Quint put them down somewhere," she speculated when they were in the hall, "and somebody checked to see what they were and got them out of sequence. Or he dropped them and didn't realize he'd picked them up in the wrong order."

She was groping and they both knew it.

"Possibly." Renn said without conviction. "Let's go find him."

Quint ran into them in the hall. "I've been looking for you," he said. "I don't know what could have happened." It was becoming a much repeated refrain.

"How did you get the tapes?" Marlee questioned him. "I gave them to Wayne."

"He brought them to me in the editing bay and asked me if I would drop them off for him. Said his wife called and he had to run home. Something about the baby being sick."

"What did you do with them?" Renn questioned.

"Took them directly to Dexter."

"You didn't put them down anywhere, maybe leave them for a minute to go to the rest room?"

He shook his head emphatically. "No. Even if I had, I would have taken them with me."

"You're certain you didn't rearrange them?" Renn asked.

"Absolutely." He looked worried. "Why would I?"

The guy had come a long way in the past two and a half months, thanks largely to Marlee, who'd assumed the role of coach and mentor, very much as Clark had for her.

"I don't know. That's why I'm asking. Did you drop them on the way?"

"No." He was angry now. "I took the stack exactly the way Wayne handed it to me and immediately walked down the hall and gave it to Dexter." He fingered back his sandy-brown hair. "If I'd dropped the tapes I would have checked with you to make sure they were back in the right order. There was plenty of time."

She touched his hand. "I believe you."

Quint gazed at her a moment, nodded and returned to the editing bay.

"Come to my office and let's discuss this," Renn said to Marlee.

She followed. Her later sportscast would be essentially a repeat of the one she just did, except this time she would make certain the tapes were in their proper sequence.

"I don't understand." She took the seat across from her boss. "I can't imagine Wayne doing this, not intentionally."

"Especially after the way you went to bat for him," Renn agreed.

"I suppose it's possible he did it inadvertently."

"More likely Quint fumbled and doesn't want to admit it," Renn posited.

"I don't know. It seems out of character for him. If he was at fault, I think he'd own up—"

Renn saw the note on his desk to phone Glenda Soames. It was important. The time marked in the top-right corner indicated she'd called when they were upstairs with Faye.

"I wonder what she wants," Marlee commented.

"You can never tell with Glenda." He picked up the phone and dialed the number on the paper.

"Hi, Glenda, what's up?"

"Is Marlee there with you?"

Smart woman. "She's sitting across from me."

"Have you figured out what happened to her telecast?"

"We're looking into it now."

"What I have to say is for both of you, so close the door and put me on speaker."

He couldn't help but smile. Always in charge. He was also intrigued. "Yes, ma'am."

He obeyed orders.

"I caught the sportscast this afternoon," Glenda said, "and saw what happened. Honey, you handled it perfectly. Clark would have been damn proud of you."

Marlee bit her lip. "Thanks."

"But that's not the reason I called. I overheard something this morning I didn't think much about at the time. I suspect now it might be significant."

Renn exchanged glances with Marlee, both of them equally baffled.

"This was before you came in, and Renn, I don't think you'd returned from lunch yet. Anyway, I stopped by to oversee a commercial that was being shot. When I pulled up in the parking lot, I was surprised to find Tag's car there, since he doesn't usually deign to show his pretty face on days that he isn't due to go on the air.''

''Did you know he was here today?'' Marlee asked Renn.

He shook his head.

''He was in the lounge,'' Glenda continued, ''with Wayne Prentice.''

Renn and Marlee stared at each other.

''They didn't see me,'' Glenda went on, but I managed to overhear part of their conversation. Taggart was playing the big-daddy role, if you can believe that, telling the kid he had great talent with a camera, but that the real money was on the other end of the lens.''

''I don't imagine that took much convincing,'' Marlee commented. ''Wayne's never made any secret of his ambition to be a reporter.''

''Well, here's the important part. Taggart said you'd blown any chance of becoming sports director with all your screwups, and that Faye was only waiting for the dust to settle to give the job to him. He said if Prentice wanted to stay on at KNCS when Tag took over, he'd have to make up for ruining the Parcells interview and show he wanted to be on the winning team, not Marlee's. If he did, Tag promised to make him a reporter, with plenty of airtime.''

Marlee lowered her head.

''What did Wayne say?'' Renn asked, after a pause.

''Mumbled something I didn't catch. Whatever it was, Taggart didn't sound pleased. I figured Prentice had enough loyalty and integrity to tell him to take a flying leap, so I didn't give it any more thought.'' Glenda huffed. ''After what happened this afternoon,

I'm beginning to wonder. Whoever sabotaged your telecast, you can be sure Taggart was behind it. Maybe Faye, too.''

Renn didn't agree. ''She wouldn't undermine her own position as VP by doing something like this during ratings week.''

''Taggart, on the other hand, has nothing to lose,'' Glenda observed.

The room and the telephone line remained silent for a long minute while Renn watched Marlee. She was hurt and had every right to be. He looked for anger, but it hadn't surfaced yet. He knew it would in time.

''Thanks, Glenda,'' he finally said. ''I appreciate your calling.''

He hit the button that ended the connection.

Marlee worked her lips in and out, her eyes pink, her expression blank. Renn waited.

CHAPTER ELEVEN

MARLEE REACHED for the phone and dialed a number.

"Hi, Kim," she said into the receiver. "Haven't talked to you in a while. How's that sweet little three-month-old? I heard you called because Johnny was sick. You didn't? Oh, I guess I misunderstood. Must have been somebody else. I'm glad to hear the little guy's okay. Uh, Kim, is Wayne there? I need to talk to him. He's not home yet?" Marlee looked over at Renn. "Well, when he does come in, would you let him know I figured out what went wrong this afternoon. He'll understand. Yes. Tell him I'll see him Monday. Yeah, you have a good weekend, too. I'm glad the baby's doing so well."

"She didn't call about a sick kid," Renn stated, when Marlee hung up.

"Johnny's fine and Wayne isn't home yet," Marlee reiterated.

Renn shook his head sadly. "I'm sorry, Marlee. You went to bat for the guy, and this is how he repays you." His tone hardened. "Well, you won't have to worry about him sabotaging you anymore."

"Don't fire him," she pleaded.

"What?" He gaped at her. "Why the hell not?"

"For one thing, we're already shorthanded."

"Darius Smith can take up the slack until we hire someone else."

"The guy's already pulling down nearly twenty hours of overtime a week. If you fire Wayne, the wrong people will get hurt."

"You mean his wife and son."

She nodded. "Besides, we really don't know for sure. It's a matter of finger-pointing. We can't prove who rearranged the tapes or that it was intentional."

"The circumstantial evidence is pretty convincing, Marlee. After what Glenda overheard... Stop and think about it. Why would Wayne even give the tapes to Quint when all he had to do was walk a few more yards down the hall and give them to Dexter himself?"

"I don't think firing him is necessary," she persisted.

He cocked his head to one side. "Mind telling me why?"

"People will figure out he was the one who mixed up the tapes, and everybody'll be looking over his shoulder to make sure he doesn't do it again. Under that kind of scrutiny, he may decide to quit on his own, but that'll be his choice. I don't want the reputation of getting him fired."

Strange, Renn thought, some people would relish the power trip of being known as a hard-ass. Her approach, however, while it bore some merit and was filled with compassion, smacked to him more of weakness than strength. She was letting Prentice get away with stabbing her in the back.

"Are you sure?" he asked. "The guy did a number on you. You don't owe him a damn thing."

"I'm sure."

He mulled her recommendation over for several minutes.

"I disagree with you on this, but I'll respect your wishes. If you change your mind, let me know. Prentice can stew this weekend, but Monday morning, I'm putting him on probation. This is two strikes against him. If there's one more incident in which he's even remotely involved—whether he's directly at fault or not, he's out of here." It suddenly occurred to him that he sounded just like Faye. Had Marlee noticed? Did she think less of him for it?

"I'll also inform Wayne he has you to thank for his job—again," he said a moment later.

She nodded without saying a word.

Saturday, April 19

AUDREY'S WEEKEND had been delightful. Marlee had come over Saturday afternoon, and they'd gone shopping at the mall. Not that she bought much. The companionship was what mattered. Afterward, they'd rented a movie—a comedy—picked up some Thai takeout and returned home to relax with a bottle of premixed margaritas. For a few hours the numbing loneliness of widowhood had been banished.

She watched the sports news every evening to see how Marlee was doing, so she was aware of Friday's debacle and was pretty sure it was at least partly responsible for Marlee's surprise visit. That she used it as an excuse to drop by didn't bother Audrey. Being needed and sought after for advice was what counted. Patiently, she waited for her adopted daughter to bring the subject up, which happened with the second salt-encrusted tequila drink.

"Renn was great," she said happily. Audrey

sensed more than pleasure at a compliment from her boss. "He said Clark would have been proud of me."

"He's right. You handled the situation like the pro you are." Audrey managed a chuckle. "He'd probably have his chest puffed out like a proud papa, telling anyone who'd listen he taught you everything you know."

"He did."

When Marlee teetered on the edge of becoming maudlin, Audrey asked, "So what happened? How did your tapes get out of sequence?"

The explanation shocked her. "That ungrateful little twerp. I assume Renn fired him on the spot."

"He wanted to, but I talked him out of it."

"Why?"

Marlee's rationale made a certain amount of sense. Audrey liked her compassion for Wayne's family, the innocent victims of his dishonor, and she said so.

"But I really wonder if it was a good idea, honey," she commented. "Renn's right. You'll spend all your time looking over your shoulder when he's around. What about Taggart? Is Renn going to confront him?"

"I don't know. I can't imagine it doing any good. Taggart will just deny it. Even if Renn gets Wayne to admit Taggart put him up to it, it'll just be a disgraced photographer's word against the great analyst."

All day Sunday Audrey debated with herself about what she could do to help Marlee.

Monday, April 21

THE QUIET LIFE Renn had so carefully honed for himself was falling apart. At work people were on edge, waiting for a decision about who would get the nod for sports director. They were beginning to vote in the only way they knew how. Renn sat in on all Taggart's shows now to make sure things ran smoothly. There hadn't been any more mangled tapes or late cues, but the spirit of cooperation and teamwork that had been the hallmark of Clark's stewardship was decidedly missing. People did their jobs, but that was all. At least as far as Taggart was concerned.

Marlee, on the other hand, could do no wrong. They all knew she'd saved Wayne's butt—again. The first time, they figured, he'd deserved it. This last time, he definitely hadn't, but they respected Marlee's willingness to give him another chance for the sake of his wife and baby.

There was another aspect of his job that was driving Renn crazy—being around Marlee. Until he'd kissed her he was able to convince himself his attraction was simply the normal, uninvolved appreciation of a healthy man for a beautiful woman. The kiss, or rather kisses, had changed that. *Appreciation* was much too mild a word, and *uninvolved* definitely didn't apply. Not anymore.

They'd managed to avoid being alone together since the night of the ball, the night he'd held her in his arms, taken her home, stood hand in hand with her as they gazed out across the moon-glittered lake. It didn't do any good. He was still stirred by the thought of her, and judging from the way she avoided eye contact with him, she was aware of him, too. If circumstances were different, he'd ask her out, but aside from the little detail that she was on his do-not-touch list, Coyote Springs was too small and she too well-known for them to go anywhere in public. Which was unfortunate, because he would very much like to find out if she was as good at the Texas Two-step as she was at jitterbugging.

Monday, April 28

"YOU WANTED to see me?" Marlee asked, as she approached the door to the vice president's office.

"Come in." Faye motioned to the chair on the right side of her desk.

The room was chilly, or seemed so to Marlee, who was wearing a short-sleeved blue cotton shirt and brown slacks. Faye had on a medium-gray gabardine suit with pointy lapels, over a sage-green silk blouse.

"Because of budget cuts, we've been reviewing and revising all our contracts, yours among them."

She opened a folder on her desk and removed a sheaf of papers, which she shoved across the desk. "Please read this contract carefully. If you have any questions, I'll answer them for you."

Marlee was stunned.

At the lowest levels, assistant producer and some technical people, contracts were standardized and basically nonnegotiable. As you moved up the ladder to producer and on-air personality, they became individually tailored. At the highest echelons, no two were alike and their specific provisions were highly confidential. Revisions were common when contracts were renewed and often involved lengthy bargaining. Marlee's would be coming up for consideration soon, but she hadn't expected to see an actual offer this quickly.

Her heart started pounding. Did this mean she

wasn't getting the anchor job? Or was this a contract for it? And where was Renn?

"I'll give you a few minutes to read it over," Faye said blandly, rose from her chair and left the room.

Marlee's fingers trembled as she picked up the file, which was several pages long and stapled in the upper left-hand corner.

Her eyes skimmed past the boilerplate information, her name, social security number, address, and raced down to the text. The words didn't register. She had to take a deep breath, slow down and concentrate on their meaning.

Reporter, not sports director.

The contract ran for three years. Nothing new. Only veterans like Clark were offered longer contracts. The first significant change that jumped out was compensation. Her pay was being cut ten percent. Overtime would be recompensed in time off rather than cash. In other words, she wouldn't be paid for her long hours on the job. Comp time was essentially a joke, because it had to be used within a specified period or lost, and there was rarely an opportunity to take it. Contributions to her retirement were likewise reduced.

Marlee's heart sagged and a wave of depression washed over her. She kept reading. The clause on termination was also significantly altered. Her current contract provided for six months' notice. Under those circumstances, she received severance pay equal to that amount of time. The provisions of this new contract were for only thirty days' notice.

Marlee hadn't hired an agent when she'd applied for this job because Clark had personally recruited her and had made sure she was given favorable terms.

Since she'd had no on-air experience, she had very little bargaining power anyway. What she needed now was an agent who could fight on her behalf or, more likely, a headhunter to find her another job somewhere else.

Did Renn know about this? He hadn't been at the station when she'd arrived. His secretary said he was at a special meeting with advertisers, which was definitely out of the ordinary.

Her depression deepened. He'd already admitted to using her as a foil to prevent Taggart from getting the job. Where was he now? Why wasn't he here?

She'd been naive to think she had a chance at Clark's position. Had Renn been sincere when he led her to believe she did, or had he just continued to string her along? And his kisses. Were they part of the game?

Faye reentered the room. "Have you read it?"

"Why is my pay being cut?"

"I told you—because of budget constraints."

The temptation to call her a liar was nearly overwhelming. "I find that very hard to believe," she said firmly. "You've saved big bucks by not paying a sports director salary for nearly three months. What are you doing? Banking money because you'll have to hire someone to do Taggart's work when you give him the job?"

Faye inhaled sharply. "You're out of line. The details of our budget are none of your business."

"Having my pay cut is my business."

Faye resumed her seat. "Do you want me to recite the litany of things you've messed up around here?"

"Shall I show you the numbers that clearly demonstrate our ratings haven't been hurt?" Marlee countered. "In fact, they've gone up over the past few months."

"In spite of your screwups." Faye eyes locked with Marlee's in a hard stare.

This wasn't getting them anywhere. Glenda had warned her that Faye would give Taggart credit for any good news.

"I need to have my agent and lawyer review this before I make a decision."

"Of course. I'm not asking you to make a decision this minute. Take a few days to think things over. I will tell you this, Marlee. This contract is not negotiable. Have your people examine the fine print so you understand what it means, but this offer is a matter of take it or leave it."

"And if I choose not to sign?"

"Then," Faye said, "you'll be given notice of immediate termination." She folded her hands primly in front of her and looked Marlee in the eye. "You will, of course, be compensated under the provisions of your existing contract, which means you will receive six months' severance pay. Under the noncompete clause you will also not be allowed to work at any other station within fifty miles of Coyote Springs for one year. The choice is yours, but as I said, the offer's nonnegotiable."

An ultimatum. One Marlee didn't like; one she wasn't expected to like. One, Faye no doubt hoped, she would reject.

"If I do sign this new contract, will I still be considered for the sports anchor job?"

Faye's smile was brittle. "Of course."

Except Faye would be able to use the argument that Marlee didn't have much confidence in her own abilities, since she'd just signed a contract that cut her pay.

Marlee picked up the papers and rose from her seat. "When do you need my answer?"

"By Friday before your broadcast. If you decline this offer, someone else will give the sports segment of the news."

Marlee moved to the door. She didn't have to ask who.

CHAPTER TWELVE

RENN WAS GETTING ready to go for a sail when the doorbell rang. He rarely had visitors, so he assumed it was a salesman. There'd been a number of them making their rounds along the lakefront the past month. His immediate inclination was to ignore the bell, but whoever it was would see him when he went down to the dock and would probably pursue him.

He yanked the door open. "Whatever it is—" His heart stopped. "Marlee. What are you doing here?"

His bark flustered her and he immediately regretted the harsh tone. He seemed to use it a lot with this woman, always unintentionally, but that didn't change its impact.

"If I'm interrupting…"

Her meekness and the sad look in her eyes stabbed him.

"Sorry for snapping." He chuckled, hoping to put her at ease. Something was definitely wrong. He'd never seen her so downcast. A death in the family? Another accident? "I thought you were a salesman. They always seem to attack at dinnertime."

"You're eating your supper. I'm sorry. I should have called. I'll…another time." She started to turn.

He reached out, clasped her upper arm and coaxed her around to face him. "Marlee, what's the matter?"

"I…"

"Come on in," he said, "and tell me what's bothering you."

He gave her arm a gentle tug. She entered demurely, shyly.

Not a death in the family, he decided. She could cope with that, and she would say it outright. Whatever was troubling her had her confused and perhaps angry. He couldn't quite read her expression.

"I was getting ready to go out for a quick sail before it got dark. Join me," he said.

"I really…"

"Sure you can."

She was about to refuse his invitation. The pale-green blouse and buckskin-colored slacks she had on weren't exactly suited to manning a catamaran.

"If you're worried about your clothes, I have a sweat suit you can wear. It'll be a little big, but I bet it'll work. How about it?" He could see she was tempted. "Please, join me."

"I really ought to get back to the station."

"Sorry I missed your five o'clock broadcast."

Faye had asked him to meet with a group of their advertisers while she was tied up with the station's lawyers. A waste of time. One of those interminable sessions that had no focus and accomplished nothing. By the time he was able to break loose it had been after five, so he'd come straight home. He planned to watch a tape of the program at the station in the morning.

"Is that why you're here?" He'd felt safe leaving because Taggart wasn't around, and Mickey promised to call if he showed up. "Did something go wrong during your show?"

She shook her head. "Everything was fine."

"Let's get you those clothes." He headed for his bedroom, but paused when he realized she wasn't following. "Unless you really don't want to."

Hesitation vanished. "Actually, a sail sounds like fun." She made an effort to smile as she moved toward him. "I haven't been out on the lake in over a year."

"While I'm digging out the sweat suit, phone Mickey and tell him to have Quint come in and do the ten o'clock broadcast. You deserve a night off after all the hours you've been putting in. Tell him to call me if he has any questions."

"Take comp time?" She burst out laughing, and for a moment he thought he detected a note of hysteria. He certainly didn't hear merriment.

She used his bedside telephone while he rummaged in his closet. He'd inadvertently washed a new pair of cotton sweats in hot water right after he'd bought them. They'd shrunk, but he hadn't gotten around to dropping them off at the Salvation Army.

"Here you go." He snatched them off the hanger and brought them out. She was just cradling the receiver. "I'll wait for you outside."

In the kitchen, he removed two steaks from the freezer and zapped them in the microwave long enough to partially defrost them. He stuck them in the refrigerator, set the oven, retrieved two large potatoes from the pantry, jabbed them with a fork and put them in to bake. All the time, his mind was conjuring up images of Marlee removing her outer garments and slipping into his. The fantasy was having a predictable effort on him.

She appeared in the doorway, her hair not as neat as it had been, but she didn't seem self-conscious about it. The outfit, though oversize, wasn't as baggy as he'd expected. Even though it gathered loosely around her waist and bunched at her ankles, the cloth clung to her breasts, outlining them to pure distraction.

"Not a bad fit," she allowed, "considering." She plucked at the side of her waist. He saw, or imagined he saw, the peaks of her nipples beneath the stretched material. "I don't suppose you have a pair of deck shoes, too."

On a deep breath, he looked down at her bare feet. He didn't have a foot fetish—at least, he never had before—but he found her feet very sexy, or maybe it was simply the bare skin that was causing his nervous system to short-circuit.

He located a pair of white canvas sneakers for her. The fit wasn't nearly as accommodating. They flapped as she walked down the path beside him to the dock.

"I feel like a platypus," she said.

He shot her a sly grin. "May I touch?" He took her hand in his. "I've always wondered what a platypus felt like."

She grinned over at him, and in that instant her eyes seemed to look into his soul. The sensation made him uncomfortable, but he didn't want her to stop. They both laughed.

He liked hearing her high spirits and seeing the lightness return to her features. He hadn't yet asked what was upsetting her, and she hadn't offered. Eventually, when the mood was right, they'd discuss it. Until then, he tried not to speculate, which wasn't all that difficult, since his attention was locked on the sight of her wearing his clothes. He kept visualizing her naked body inside the downy cotton.

He'd already raised the mast on the catamaran. It didn't take more than a few minutes to hoist the sail and cast off. Marlee sat forward, he at the tiller. The gentle breeze moved them into the middle of the lake. Soon they were alone in the world, the only sound the delicate lapping of the water as it curled away from the twin hulls. The low-angled sun glinted off its surface in multiprismed colors.

They floated in silence for the better part of an hour. Renn kept his eye on the contemplative woman in front of him, enjoying the sight of the wind ruffling her blond hair.

She slung around, her knees still pulled up in front of her chest, her arms wrapped around them. The earlier depression had dissipated, but the melancholy that remained tore at his heart.

"Thank you for bringing me out here," she said in a voice just loud enough to carry over the rushing air. "I'd forgotten how peaceful sailing is. Helps put things in perspective."

"What things might they be?" he prodded gently.

"I'll tell you later. Now I just want to enjoy the moment."

"Is there a particular place on the lake you'd like to go?"

She shook her head. "Around in circles is fine. I love the quiet, don't you? The serenity. A person is small out here. I've often wondered why that's a comfort."

"I've never thought of it as making me feel small," he confessed, "so much as being in harmony."

"In harmony. Yes. That's a better way of describing it. Anyway, thank you for bringing me."

"My pleasure." But he was speaking to her back again.

The sun nursed its way to the horizon. The sky overhead was bathed in color—pink and iridescent gold, violet and baby blue. Jet contrails crisscrossed overhead like lacy white ribbons tying up this special gift of nature.

Renn tacked and weaved his way back to the shoreline. Marlee came to life when they approached his dock, jumped onto the wooden planks and tied off the bow, secured the stern. Together they lashed the sail and secured the mast.

"Do you like garlic on your steak?" he asked as they strolled back to the house.

Her shoes flapped. "Love it. Good protection against vampires."

He reached out and took her hand. "Do you run into many vampires?"

"I'm always amazed at how many bloodsuckers there are in the world—" she curled her fingers in his "—and the television business."

Before long he'd learn what had stirred this note of bitterness that seemed so foreign to her nature; he decided not to push.

While she was freshening up, he removed the steaks from the refrigerator and rubbed them generously with fresh garlic.

"Definitely no vampires around here," Marlee said, joining him. She'd run a comb through her hair, but it still had a windblown appearance. He liked it and the playfulness he saw in her blue eyes.

She accepted the lettuce he'd retrieved from the crisper and the wooden bowl he handed her.

While she tore the romaine into bite-size pieces, he

reached under the island counter and snagged an already open jug of red wine. He poured two glasses and handed her one.

"So what happened today to upset you?"

"Faye called me to her office this afternoon."

Was that the reason she'd asked him to handle a routine matter out of the office? She hadn't said anything about wanting to talk to Marlee. If the VP had a complaint about her, she should have brought it to him first.

"And...?"

"She offered me a new contract."

"She what?"

His movements stalled. Marlee was his subordinate. Faye had no right to make changes in her employment status without consulting him. This wasn't good. His heart began to pound. He felt robbed by the VP's preemptive move, even if it was favorable. He wanted desperately to be a part of Marlee's life, her decisions, her choices. Obviously, Marlee hadn't been offered the anchor position, or she'd be ecstatic, not disheartened.

"Tell me exactly what happened."

He watched her sip her wine almost lethargically, then resumed tearing into the lettuce as she described her private meeting with the station vice president.

His anger mounted, and he knew a confrontation with Faye couldn't be avoided, but it would have to wait. The important person was Marlee. He blamed himself for this mess. The thing he wanted most— getting Marlee the anchor job—had become almost as much an obsession as his need to be with her.

"Do you have an agent?" he asked, when she finished.

She shook her head. "I've thought about getting one, but since my current contract doesn't run out for another nine months, I figured I had time. Any recommendations?"

He didn't answer right away. Instead, he retrieved a fork and jabbed the two potatoes he'd put in the oven. They were done. He turned off the heat, but didn't remove them.

"I have a couple of names I can give you," he said, straightening and facing her. "The ultimate decision will be yours, though, and it doesn't sound like she's giving you much wiggle room."

"None whatsoever. One from column A or one from column B. No substitutions. She was very emphatic."

"Have you decided what you'll do yet?" He didn't want to hear her say she was going to leave, but he had no right to ask her to stay.

She lowered her head and concentrated on the task before her. "I was hoping you might help me think this through."

She was at a critical juncture, one that could change her life, at least professionally, and she'd come to him for advice. He felt a surge of hope, only to have it crash. What right did he have to advise her? He hadn't always made the wisest choices in his own career.

He loaded a bamboo tray with plates and silverware, which she offered to carry, while he handled the steaks and a long cooking fork. The magic light show of sunset wasn't yet complete, so they bathed in its radiance while he attended to the gas grill. She set the glass-topped table, then returned to the kitchen for the salad, potatoes and the trimmings.

Fifteen minutes later they were cutting into juicy medium-rare T-bones. Renn had turned on the patio lights. The night was mild.

"You're a good cook," she noted as she raised a second piece of steak to her mouth.

"We've just about exhausted my repertoire, however. Steaks, chops and an occasional stir-fry. Oh, and spaghetti. I make a mean marinara sauce."

"I'd like to try it sometime."

He splatted a dollop of sour cream on his baked potato, his mind bewitched by the image of her sucking spaghetti between puckered lips.

"How about you?" he asked. "Do much cooking? Besides great pineapple upside-down cake, of course."

"That's baking, not cooking," she corrected him. "Not a whole lot. Like you, a few favorites, but I don't have the time to experiment, and cooking for one... Well, it's not very motivating."

"Would I be correct in assuming your mother doesn't cook?"

Marlee snickered. "We always had a housekeeper-cook when I was growing up. I didn't even learn to bake until college when Clark brought me home to meet his family."

"You were very close to them, weren't you?"

"Audrey is the kind of mother I always wanted, the kind I'd like to be if I ever got married and had kids. Clark was more of a positive male influence in my adult life than Anthony Reid ever was. Dad never came out and said it, but he'd wanted a son, not a daughter. Maybe if they had had another child, a boy, he would have forgiven me for being a girl and the firstborn. Maybe if I'd had brothers and sisters..."

"You wouldn't have been so lonely growing up," Renn finished for her. "I was an only child, too, of career-driven parents. I know what it's like to be an inconvenience that gets in the way of adults' plans."

She assimilated his words. "Something we have in common." She dotted her loaded potato with cracked black pepper. "I'm probably being unfair. My father never mistreated me. In fact, he gave me everything I ever asked for."

"Except genuine affection." He wanted her to know he understood. "So you tried to earn it by doing what you figured a boy would do."

"Athletics come easily and naturally to me," she acknowledged. "I wasn't always the top performer, but I played volleyball and was on the swimming team in school, tennis at the country club, and I learned to ride English-style well enough to compete in three-day events. Isn't horsemanship supposed to be the sport of kings?"

He smiled. "How did you do?"

"Never won higher than fourth place, but I really loved it. Horses and sailing."

"But none of it ever really pleased your father, never made him genuinely proud of you."

She shook her head. "The final straw came when I insisted on attending TUCS. He could afford to send me to Harvard or Yale—or Vassar. That's where my mother went. Why would I choose a regional state school?"

"Why did you?" he asked. "Out of stubbornness?"

"That's what he thought, and I suppose there was an element of rebellion in it, too. But those weren't the main reasons. TUCS has one of the highest-rated schools of journalism in the country.''

''Choosing the best should have pleased him.''

She chuckled. ''Not when I told him I wanted to major in broadcast journalism, specifically sports.''

''I suppose he considered it undignified for a woman. All that sweat and everything.'' He smiled.

She nodded. ''He told me if that was my choice, I was on my own.''

Renn stopped eating. ''He threw you out of the house?''

Her answer was to cut into her steak with vicious determination.

''Marlee, I'm sorry.''

''I should have been devastated.'' She raised her shoulders in a philosophical shrug. ''It was upsetting, I'll admit. But after I got over the shock, I realized I'd been on my own emotionally most of my life. This just confirmed it.''

''What did you do?''

She stabbed another piece of tender beef. ''Moved into the dorms, which I would have done anyway.''

When he shook his head, she added, ''It wasn't as bad as it sounds, Renn. He wasn't driving me out of the house starving and naked. My grandmother had left me a small trust fund. It was enough to live on in reasonable comfort.''

''Still,'' he said, ''it couldn't have been easy.''

''Actually, his washing his hands of me had a kind of liberating effect. I wasn't doing things to please him anymore. I could do what I wanted on my own terms.''

''What about your mother? How did she feel about all this?''

"Embarrassed. Imagine, having a daughter who was attending a public university and studying to report sports on TV. She could hardly hold her head up at her bridge club."

She was mocking, but being abandoned by the people who should have loved her unconditionally had to have hurt like hell.

"I gather Myra was never the cuddly type."

It was a rhetorical statement, which Marlee didn't respond to directly.

"There was a physics major in school who came from a big family," she said a minute later. "Her grandmother knitted her a sweater. It wasn't perfect, and it certainly wasn't stylish. Lorna only wore it around us girls, but I envied her so much. I wanted a sweater just like it, one I could cuddle up in when I was by myself and know I wasn't really alone." She sipped wine. "My mother bought me all the best outfits, the kind that screamed *expensive* and *exclusive,* but they had no soul. Not like a plain, ordinary sweater that was hand-knitted with love."

She shrugged, as if it didn't really make any difference. "How about you? What were your folks like?"

"They were in television. My father was a reporter for the Associated Press in Europe during the Cold War. My mother did fashion reporting. Later they both got into radio and TV commercials, and Mom had a bit part in a soap opera for a while."

"Sound like an interesting life."

"Interesting, yes. Stable, no. I went to six different elementary schools and three high schools. If they held reunions, I wouldn't know which one to attend and probably wouldn't recognize anyone when I got there.''

"Where are your folks now?"

"They divorced when I was fourteen. I lived with Mom during the school year and traveled with Dad during the summers. Mom died a few years ago in a car accident. Dad remarried. Last I heard, he and wife number three—or is it four—were living somewhere in Europe.''

"Yet with all that, you went into the same occupation they did.''

He shrugged self-consciously. "Maybe because it's what I'm most familiar with. I really do like the profession, in spite of the downsides.''

"The downsides,'' she repeated. "Is that why you're not married?''

He scooped out baked potato. "That's one reason.''

She looked at him over the lip of her glass. "What's another?''

He was uncomfortable with her delving into a subject he didn't like to explore, especially with another person. But surprisingly, he felt safe talking to Marlee about it. "I guess I never found the woman I wanted to share the life with, or one I was willing to give it up for.''

"Would you give it up for the right woman?''

He thought the matter over before answering. "If it was the only way for us to be together, yes.''

"Sacrifice,'' she concluded. "Can a person who gives up what he or she truly wants be really happy?''

"I guess it comes down to priorities. If a person gives up what's most important in his life, I don't see how he can be happy. But if he found the other person to be the source of happiness, I think he could give up everything else and still be happy, or maybe even because he gave up so much for her.''

Marlee remained silent for some time.

"What about you?" he asked. "What's the most important thing in your life?"

"Short-term, getting the sports director job."

He smiled. "And long-term?"

"I don't know," she replied a little too glibly. She'd alluded to being a mother a few minutes earlier.

"How about marriage and family?"

"I like the idea, but—"

"You can't see yourself sitting home and knitting sweaters. I know what you mean. This life we've chosen doesn't exactly go hand in hand with good parenting."

"Clark and Audrey made it work," she observed.

He could hear her envy in the quiet statement. Something else they shared.

"But Audrey didn't work in the business," he reminded her.

"That's true."

They let the conversation wander, content for the moment to avoid the subject that had brought her to his house, content to relax in each other's company.

Not until they were loading the dishwasher did he seriously tackle the subject.

"About this new contract...unless you're determined to leave KNCS and go somewhere else," he said, dreading the thought, "you don't have much choice but to sign it. If you don't, you're not only out of the running for the anchor job, you're unemployed."

He hit the switch and listened as the machine began its cycle. "Legally, Faye can't pass on negative information about your job performance to interested employers, but she can still harm your prospects by withholding positive comments. And we both know about unofficial conversations that never get documented." Before Marlee had a chance to voice the objection he could see coming, he added, "I'm not saying it's right, only that it happens...and is something you've got to face."

Marlee conceded the point with a frown and a nod, as she leaned against the kitchen counter.

"The only advantage to refusing to sign is a bigger severance package," he went on. "This is none of my business, but how important is the pay issue?"

"I have some money put aside. Not a lot, but combined with severance pay, it's enough to live on for a year or so."

"And of course you can call on your folks."

"I could, but I won't." The statement brooked no compromise.

Never say never, he was tempted to tell her. Perhaps someday they'd make their peace. For her sake, he hoped they did, but at the moment it didn't appear very likely.

"On the other hand, if you sign the new contract, you're still eligible for the anchor job."

"Come on, Renn. We both know I'm not going to get it, not after this."

"It's not likely, I admit, but until the final selection is made and accepted, there's always a chance. Taggart might screw up big-time, or he could turn down the deal they offer. Don't give up yet."

She ran her tongue along her teeth as she mulled the matter over.

"Also," he continued, "until that happens, you can

apply for other jobs as an active employee of KNCS-TV. Being on the air while you're job hunting has a definite advantage.''

She let out a sigh. ''That's what I was thinking, too. Either way, it looks like I'll be leaving Coyote Springs.''

Friday, April 29

RENN STRODE INTO Faye's office Tuesday morning and parked himself in the chair across from her. He hadn't called ahead or asked for an appointment. He hadn't knocked on her door.

''Why did you offer Marlee a new contract that cut her pay and benefits?'' He leaned back unceremoniously and stretched out his long legs, prepared to stay and listen.

She eyed him critically. ''Budget constraints. You know we've been reviewing our contracts.''

He crossed his arms and stared at her. ''For new employees and when existing employees' contracts are due for renewal.''

Faye tapped her pen on the pile of papers before her. ''Actually, I'm doing her a favor and being quite generous.''

He regarded her askance. ''Really? How's that?''

Faye tossed down her pen, sat back in her throne and hung her hands loosely over the armrests, trying unsuccessfully to mimic his casual posture. ''Her contract is up in nine months. If we choose not to renew it—and given all her screwups, I can assure you we won't—she'll be out the door without any severance. This way she can collect six months' pay without working and spend the time seeking employment elsewhere.''

''Funny, you don't want her here, yet you're offering her a new contract.''

''We're short on people. If she wants to stay around as a reporter—under the close supervision of the sports director—that's her option.''

The sports director she had in mind, of course, was Taggart. ''Yet you told her she'll still be considered for that job.''

Faye raised an eyebrow. ''Have you changed your mind? Are you no longer recommending her for the job?''

''You bet I am.''

She nodded and smiled thinly. ''Then I guess she's still in the running, isn't she?''

This woman was slick and it frustrated the daylight out of him. ''Why didn't you confer with me about this change in employment conditions?''

''You weren't here.''

He glared at her. ''That excuse, Faye, is dishonest and beneath you.''

''I'm getting tired of your personal attacks, Renn.'' She straightened. ''I think you'd better leave.''

He made no move to comply. ''Since you timed this coup while Sal was also away, I assume he doesn't know anything about it, either.''

''Contracts are my responsibility and my prerogative.''

''Hiring the sports director is mine,'' he reminded her. ''Put off Marlee's deadline for signing until he gets back next week.''

''No.''

She'd arranged this move perfectly. Renn had no

doubt she'd gone over this very carefully with the station's attorneys to make sure it was perfectly legal. To hell with ethics. Once the paperwork was signed— either by Marlee accepting the new contract or by Faye giving notice of termination—the deal would be done. Sal could theoretically suspend either document, but he wasn't likely to. If anything, he'd be relieved that decisive action had finally been taken. Case closed.

Renn shook his head. "You're really desperate, aren't you?"

She said nothing, maybe because her jaw was locked.

"I'll be discussing this with Sal when he returns."

"Just remember who you work for, Renn," she advised him calmly.

"Not a chance I'll forget." He climbed to his feet and walked out.

Friday, May 2

MARLEE DIDN'T sign the revised contract until four o'clock on Friday. Keeping Faye guessing was a childish act of defiance, but it afforded her a little satisfaction. Marlee received a simple thank-you and a copy of the new contract.

Renn was waiting for her when she emerged from Faye's office. "Let me treat you to dinner after your broadcast," he said. "We'll go somewhere and have something sinful."

She laughed. She'd been thinking a lot about sinning lately, though it didn't have anything to do with food.

"Haven't got time," she said, "but thanks for the

offer. I'll call out for a sandwich. I need to stay here and work on a few things for the late broadcast.''

''In that case,'' he said easily, ''I'll get takeout for both of us. How about mu shu? The Imperial Garden also has sushi. What do you say?''

She laughed. ''Sounds great.''

Ten minutes after the end of the news hour, they were sitting in Renn's office, his desk covered with a variety of containers. On a separate disposable platter were an assortment of rice cakes.

''I've been thinking a lot the past few days,'' Marlee said, as she used her chopsticks to pick up a curl of pickled ginger.

''About what?''

''Whether I should even stay in this business. The past four months have taught me it's an insecure source of livelihood.''

''No argument there, but then, most jobs these days are unpredictable in the long run. The deciding factor is whether you like what you're doing and if you're good at it.'' He tweezered a braised shrimp. ''I can vouch for the fact that you're good at what you do. Based on that, I'd say you enjoy it, but that's something only you can decide.''

''You used be a newscaster. Do you miss going on the air?''

He lifted his shoulders in a negligent shrug. ''Sometimes, but after ten years I found I wasn't really in love with it anymore. I'm much happier behind the scenes in management.''

She dipped a sushi roll into green wasabi mustard. ''If you weren't in the business, what would you want to do?''

''I've asked myself that a few times. I think I might

like to be an agent, a headhunter for media personalities.''

''So you'd still want to be associated with the industry.''

He nodded. ''I guess it's in my blood, for better or for worse.''

While she sipped her green tea, he wrapped thin rice filo around a piece of chicken and a stalk of green onion.

''Tomorrow is Saturday. Do you have any plans?'' he asked.

She glanced over at him, then smiled. ''Critically important matters like laundry and grocery shopping. The larder is practically bare.''

''Would you like to go sailing with me?''

Her smile broadened.

His pulse accelerated. ''I thought we might go out on the lake for a couple of hours, then fix something at my place.''

''Steak again?''

He couldn't decide if she was teasing him, if she wanted another steak, or if she was saying she didn't.

''Or chicken. Pork chops? Lamb chops? You name it.''

''You cooked last time,'' she finally said, after making him squirm. ''I'll bring the vittles.''

CHAPTER THIRTEEN

MARLEE LAY AWAKE half the night, thinking about her sailing date with Renn the next day. Their relationship had certainly changed over the past three months, from mild hostility to compassion to conspiratorial alliance to a kiss—and now on to something more. The question was how much more. He'd made it clear he wasn't interested in love and marriage—not with her, at least.

She shot up in bed. Love and marriage? Where had that notion come from? If there was one thing they completely agreed on, it was that their profession didn't lend itself to happy children and a contented family life.

She thought, too, about the dilemma she was facing. Hang on and tough it out at KNCS-TV or move on. Fight or flee.

She wasn't happy with the thought of leaving Coyote Springs, though initially she hadn't been thrilled at the prospect of returning to her hometown, either. She could have stayed in Austin and worked her way up, though it would have taken time. The major incentive for rejecting offers from several stations in slightly larger markets had been the opportunity to work with Clark. Now he was gone, yet she was reluctant to relocate. Maybe because Coyote Springs was familiar territory, and Audrey was here. Or maybe she still harbored hopes of getting the sports anchor job. She might even be entertaining a latent wish that her parents would come to appreciate her success.

KNCS-TV was a stepping-stone, she reminded herself, not a destination. She had no desire to homestead and stagnate.

Was that what Clark had done? He could have gone on to much bigger markets, advanced to the national scene, earned several times more money than he was making here. But he'd shunned those opportunities. When KNCS offered him his last contract, he'd already had a better offer from a station in Dallas. She'd asked him why he'd turned it down. His answer had been so prosaic it had stunned and baffled her: he was happy where he was; he was making enough money to provide for the people he loved; Coyote Springs was a good place to bring up a family.

What about ambition? she'd asked. His response had seemed simplistic. He strove every day to do his best. Whether it was in Coyote Springs or Dallas, Atlanta, San Francisco or New York, made no difference. Geography and money weren't important.

She'd loved and respected Clark, but on this issue she had disagreed with him. Moving up, making money, living better, being recognized by a bigger and wider audience were important, at least to her.

Yet now she found herself hesitating about leaving KNCS-TV and Coyote Springs, and she was afraid the reason had nothing to do with her job.

She punched down her pillow, trying to find a position that would allow her to drift off into dreamless slumber. But sleep didn't come. She pictured Renn Davis. In casual clothes. In a tuxedo. In shorts and a tank top. She saw his frown of concentration, his smile of encouragement, the wistful, almost prayerful expression that came into his eyes when he'd bowed his head and kissed her.

She couldn't say the first kiss had caught her completely by surprise. She'd been conscious of him studying her for a while, but she hadn't been prepared for the tingling inside her when his lips met hers. The second kiss had given her time to think, to anticipate. A moan had escaped nevertheless when his mouth brushed hers. But it was the last evening's kiss, and the silky sensation that rippled through her when he'd slid his tongue between her teeth, that was making her restless and conjuring up fantasies of his arms around her, of floating in his grip, of devouring and being devoured by him.

RENN LAY IN BED, his hands clasped behind his head, and wondered what it would be like to come home every evening to a woman who intrigued and fascinated him at every turn. He had almost married once, but his engagement to Pamela had ended in tragedy. A few years later he'd had a live-in girlfriend, but that experiment had lasted hardly a month before he'd craved privacy. He'd concluded he wasn't meant for the married life, even if he could find a woman he loved. He certainly hadn't loved Tina. He'd liked her well enough. He'd enjoyed her company until he felt trapped by it. They'd definitely been compatible in bed, but even there, he'd come to realize, something had been missing. Not sensually, but emotionally.

Which brought him now to Marlee. What made her different? He didn't know. They had things in common. The wrong things. A dysfunctional family background, and a profession that inevitably strained and broke relationships.

He admired her competence, her drive and ambition, her willingness to take chances, but he'd met other people, other women, who fit that pattern. Those same virtues could be said to describe Faye Warren, as well, though the two women were studies in contrasts. What made Marlee Reid so unique that he found himself intrigued by the idea of coming home to her?

He flipped onto his side. Whatever the allure, he had better get over it. Inviting her to go sailing with him had been a mistake. In the loneliness of his bed, his mind and body were turned on by remembrances of the glow of welcome and acceptance he'd glimpsed when he'd bent to kiss her, the soft moan of pleasure when he'd parted her lips, the taste of her and the hot spike of arousal that had resulted when her tongue met his.

He could hear her laughter when they talked, feel long-dormant cravings stirring when she touched him. His mind floated, whirled, when her scent invaded his nostrils.

Pamela had bewitched him, but she'd never kept him tossing and turning in abject torment into the wee hours of the morning the way Marlee did.

What would it be like to come home to Marlee every evening? As the sky in the east tinted with light, he rolled over again and waited for an answer.

HAVING TAKEN so long to finally fall asleep, Marlee rose late, fixed herself a cup of coffee, compiled a list and went grocery shopping. Renn said he liked spaghetti; she decided to make lasagna. She bought the ingredients, assembled the cheese-rich pasta dish and placed it unbaked in the refrigerator. While she did several loads of laundry, she set about her other chores. She'd grown up in a house with servants. Her mother had always considered dusting and mopping beneath her and had never taught her daughter to regard them any other way. Sharing an apartment in college with a girlfriend had changed all that. Remarkably, she found she really didn't mind the minor drudgery. Not that she was about to challenge Heloise or Martha Stewart. Her two-bedroom apartment was neat and clean, but it wasn't immaculate. It was comfortable, but hardly a showplace.

Her thoughts kept revolving around what Renn had said about the instability of the television business. The job was decidedly high stress and extremely competitive, which was part of its allure. Each story brought an adrenaline rush. Was this the big one? The one that would establish her name, make her famous? Even disappointment when it wasn't motivated her to keep charging forward.

The thrill of being in the public eye wasn't all vanity. Well, maybe it was for Taggart, but Marlee saw it as affording her an opportunity to accomplish things she couldn't do in less prominent roles. Look at what Clark had achieved with his celebrity. *Alegre* was a living testament to the goodness of his life. She wanted to have something to leave behind, too. If not children, then something.

She'd dreamed of having kids, once. A part of her still did. But the rational side of her brain said it wasn't likely to happen. Love and marriage weren't compatible with professional success. She didn't imagine her chances of emulating Clark and Audrey were very high, especially since professionally she wanted more than what Coyote Springs and KNCS-TV had to offer.

As she drove out to the lake, her stomach began to growl. She'd grabbed a piece of toast with her second cup of coffee, which obviously wasn't enough. She glanced over at the covered roasting pan of unbaked lasagna on the seat beside her. They wouldn't be digging into it for another three or four hours at least. Had Renn eaten lunch?

She decided to stop off at the Grocery Emporium and pick up snacks they could munch out on the water. Her stomach growled again. If she could wait that long.

In the deli section she purchased paper-thin slices of prosciutto, a round of smoked Gouda, water wafers and a tin of Greek olives. From the produce department she selected black seedless grapes, a bunch of icicle radishes and a couple of plump Anjou pears. On an impulse, she also snagged a bag of salty corn chips and a jar of spicy green salsa. If Renn's tastes were markedly different from hers, she'd soon find out.

Turning into his driveway, she caught a glimpse of him down on his boat. She shut off the engine, retrieved the casserole from the passenger seat and the plastic bag of groceries from the floor, then headed for the back door. She nearly tripped on a garden hose stretched across the redbrick path because her eyes were riveted on Renn climbing out of the car.

He was wearing wine-red shorts and a sapphire-blue T-shirt. The afternoon sun cast tantalizing shadows on his sports attire, emphasized his lean muscles, set off the broad width of his shoulders and the narrowness of his hips. She deposited her burden on the glass-topped patio table and turned back toward the lake. He was trotting toward her, his long legs flexing in the bright sun.

"Hi," he said, slightly out of breath. "I was beginning to worry."

They'd agreed on three o'clock. She'd checked the dashboard clock on her arrival and was pleased to see she was only fifteen minutes off her schedule. Her heart lifted a little to know he'd been worried she might not show up.

"I stopped off to get some nibbles," she explained. The warmth of his smile sent her pulse racing.

"You're a saint." His gaze never left hers. "I think my pantry's down to peanut butter and popcorn." He grinned sheepishly.

"Might make an interesting combination."

He opened the back door and turned to relieve her of the film-covered pan of lasagna. Their fingers touched briefly. She hung on to the grocery bag and followed him into the kitchen.

"Looks great," he said. She assumed he was referring to the casserole in his hands, but his eyes were fixed on her.

"For tonight," she explained, and opened the refrigerator door. She could feel him watching as she bent to rearrange the contents on the middle shelf. "Just put it in there," she said, straightening up.

What's sauce for the gander is sauce for the goose, she decided, and felt a ping of excitement as she studied the compact curve of his narrow buttocks and the cable-hard lines of his muscular thighs when he slipped their dinner into the designated space.

Her words ran together when she began to list the

things she'd bought. He heartily approved of her selections and added them to the chest he'd already stocked with ice and soft drinks.

"No lake wind advisories in the forecast for today," he assured her. They headed toward the dock, the cooler suspended between them. The surface of the water was wrinkled rather than rippled, the air sweet and warm.

Renn had already raised the mast on the catamaran. Marlee stood by, captivated by his strong arms and broad back as he hoisted the sail. An indefinable something she wasn't yet willing to name—was it merely lust?—pulsed inside her with the rhythm of his muscles bunching and releasing, bunching and releasing.

When he turned to face her, she forced herself to tear her eyes away and concentrate on the horizon. The pale hues of early spring had matured to a deeper green. Budding trees and bushes, still shiny leafed, fluttered in the lazy breeze.

Renn tuned in a light-rock station on the radio. They glided away from the dock onto the silvery lake; they drifted in silence with the wind. The sun played over their bodies. He studied her, contemplated the smooth curves of her long legs, the subtly alluring musculature of her arms, the way her shoulders straightened when she was deep in thought.

He caught the light southern breeze. They skimmed along the shorefront, dotted with houses that ranged from opulent brick-and-stone mansions to simple clapboard bungalows. Weekend anglers, dipping their poles for catfish and crappie, waved to them, so did kids and their parents engaged in land and water sports on green lawns and sun-bleached docks.

He enjoyed the sense of freedom sailing gave him and took added pleasure in his view of Marlee in her modest two-piece bathing suit. When she started to apply sunscreen to her arms and legs, he locked the tiller, setting them on a lazy course to nowhere in particular, closed the distance between them and held out his hand for the plastic bottle of lotion.

"I'll do your back," he said, hungry for the feel of her skin under his palm.

She gazed at him. Her tongue swept across her upper lip. "Thanks." She passed the sunscreen to him and spun around.

He stroked her shoulders, the base of her neck, the bare planes of her naked back. He imagined unclasping her top, releasing her breasts, his hands encircling her from behind to caress their heavy warmth.

"Do you want to go swimming?" he asked when he was finished.

She sat down on the edge of the boat and dipped a toe into the water. "It's pretty cold yet."

He wasn't sure even an iceberg could cool the fire inside him.

"Besides," she said. "I'm hungry. Let's eat."

Over the next hour, they nibbled on fruit, hard-cured ham, salty olives, crunchy radishes and washed them all down with chilled bottled water. When she bit into a pear, juice dribbled down her chin. Renn reached out and with the pad of his thumb brushed it away. She clasped his wrist and licked the tip of his finger.

"Sweet," she said.

His breathing hitched, his jaw sagged and his entire body went on red alert. "Come here," he croaked out, patting the bench next to him.

Smiling, she settled beside him. He draped his arm across her shoulders. "We should have gone sailing a long time ago," he murmured, and swiveled enough to brush her lips with his. She angled her head to accommodate him. He deepened the kiss. She responded, her hands coming up and bracketing his jaw.

Whistles and cheers from a passing boat brought them up for air. Neither of them seemed to know what to say, so they did the second best thing. They kissed each other with their eyes.

They'd reached the north end of the lake and had to turn around. He called out that he would be reversing course and would have instructed her to lean out of the way of the heavy sail as it reversed its orientation to the wind, but she'd already grabbed a line and was stretched over the side of the craft to counterbalance the shift in weight. The sweep and glide of the graceful craft, the view of Marlee's strong young body suspended before him took his breath away and sent his testosterone level soaring.

"Where'd you learn to sail?" he asked, when she rejoined him at the tiller, sitting not as close as before, but close enough to make him shaky with the desire to reach out, touch—and taste.

"Right here." She threw back her head so the wind caught her loose hair. "My father's always had boats. He taught me how to swim while I was still a toddler and to waterski when I was in elementary school. It was the only time he ever felt like a daddy to me."

"What changed that?" He didn't care about her father.

She shrugged lethargically. "For a long time I thought I must have done something wrong. Eventually, I realized the flaw was his, not mine."

A rare bit of wisdom, but it didn't make the pain of feeling abandoned any easier to bear. "Does your mother sail?"

She gazed at the placid lake. "Mom's very good at sunbathing and sipping drinks with little umbrellas in them. She prefers to do it on solid ground, however. The yacht they bought may change that, I suppose."

The wind picked up. Marlee laughed with childish delight as they tacked and yawed against the blast.

"Do you want to go in?" he asked, when his house came into view.

"Not unless you do," she shouted back. "This is too much fun."

He agreed. The *Calico* raced past his dock, toward the channel that connected Big Coyote and Little Coyote lakes. They sailed its perimeter and skimmed at full tilt back through the narrow passage. Once returned to the larger body of water, he trimmed the sail and slowed their progress.

The sun was lowering now in the cloudless sky. They'd been out on the water more than four hours. Navigating on the lake at night was no problem. The rising moon was big, full and yellow. Shore lights were plentiful, especially on weekends.

"You must be hungry," he said, his own mouth watering at the thought of the lasagna she'd made.

"A little," she admitted.

The breeze died down almost as quickly as it had sprung up. Their progress slowed.

"Shall I use the kicker?" he asked, referring to the ten-horsepower outboard motor.

"I'm in no hurry," she answered, her voice mellow

and dreamy, probably from the combination of sun and wind.

A speedboat zoomed by, splashing her with a cold plume of water. Her eyes went wide and her belly pulled in, then she crooked a startled smile and shivered. He ducked into the stateroom and retrieved one of the terry-cloth bath sheets he kept there.

She gazed at him over her shoulder as he draped it across her wet skin. He kept his arms around her, leaned over and kissed her softly behind the ear. She nuzzled up to him.

He coaxed her around, still in the circle of his arms and gathered her against him.

"I'll start the engine," he said.

"No." She shook her head. "It's a beautiful night. Let's enjoy it."

"Aren't you cold?" He could feel her pulse racing—almost as fast as his own.

"Not with you holding me."

He dropped anchor, then led her into the small below-deck compartment. It contained a double bed on a low platform of drawers. They'd avoided this shallow chamber earlier, for it served no purpose except for sleeping. But the sun was set. He activated a switch that drew back the canvas covering the glass roof, inviting in the star-filled night.

"You need to get out of that wet suit," he said, sounding serious, probably because he felt as nervous as a teenager on his first date.

Her eyes twinkled in the scant light. "Good idea. I'm afraid I got you all wet, too."

A MOMENT EARLIER she had been shivering; now she was hot all over, especially where his hands touched her shoulder and slowly teased down the straps of her top. She was burning up, yet she could feel the heat emanating from his body. He reached around and unsnapped her halter. She experienced a riff of panic when the damp fabric released her breasts, then an aching surge of pleasure when those hands stroked her pebbled nipples.

She took a step backward, compressed her lips between her teeth and slithered out of her bottom. Kicking it impatiently aside, she stood naked before him.

"You're beautiful," he murmured breathlessly.

He inhaled deeply and pulled his shirt over his head. His chest was lean muscled, his belly rippled.

"Don't stop now." Delight bubbled in her voice.

He met her eyes and smiled. "I'm not sure I could if I wanted to."

He kicked off his canvas deck shoes, sending them flying in different directions. They bounced and clopped somewhere. He stepped forward, caught her chin in his grasp and kissed her hard on the mouth. His free hand roamed the side of her bare torso, down to her hip and up again, finally cupping a breast.

He broke off the kiss, but not his physical contact. With a treacherous smile, he tumbled them both onto the bed. Above her, she saw stars twinkling in the black sky. Closer, she felt Renn's gentle touch, his ravenous mouth as he surveyed her body. She was floating, a gossamer feather on a warm cloud. Desire throbbed. Heat pulsed. Her blood raced.

Her hands journeyed over his shoulders, slid up the back of his neck until her fingers were buried in his hair. He whispered her name and dragged his tongue across her quivering flesh from one nipple to the other. She was molten inside. Hot and steamy. Her need raw and ripe.

He withdrew long enough to remove the last confining vestige of clothing, then groped in a drawer under the mattress for a Mylar packet. Their eyes danced as he knelt suspended over her. He covered her mouth with his. Her fingers raked his hard muscles. Her mind went blissfully blank except for the sensations that possessed her.

She cried out when he entered her, not in pain but in agonizing pleasure. Anticipation gave way to possession. She rose to capture more of him. She indulged. She soared. She savored and wallowed in a shimmering haze of light and darkness. She gasped out his name when the first blinding shower of stars cascaded around her, pulling her in, devouring her and leaving her limp.

Weak and defenseless, she smiled up at him, and the rhythm resumed.

Monday, May 5

AUDREY HAD BEEN pleasantly surprised by Marlee's visit Sunday evening. She couldn't put her finger on it, but there was something different about her, a glow, a radiance. She understood it better when Marlee explained that she'd spent most of the weekend with Renn on his boat. Audrey suspected they'd done more than sail, but she didn't pry. She was simply happy to see her adopted daughter so lighthearted. Which made the news of Marlee signing a new, punitive contract all the more shocking.

Audrey's first thought was to confront Faye with

the unfairness of it, but she quickly dismissed that idea. Faye was the problem, not the solution.

The best person to approach would be the general manager, Sal Bufano.

Monday morning she drove to the television station. She'd always found the place somewhat disappointing, though she'd never told Clark that. It certainly wasn't glamorous. Work spaces tended to be cluttered and shabby, a cross between improvised and worn-out. The sets that appeared pristine and professional on the air didn't have nearly the appeal when seen in person. That, of course, was the illusion of the media and the magic of the theater, which she knew firsthand, having been active in college in the dramatic society. That was where she'd met Clark. They were both trying out for *Brigadoon.* The irony was that she'd gotten a part; Clark hadn't. He'd gone on to make a form of entertainment his career, while she'd abandoned the bright lights altogether.

She missed him and knew she always would, but they'd had twenty-eight good years together, she told herself. Not many women these days could boast that.

The nondescript main entrance was all so familiar, except Clark didn't pop out from behind a desk or partition with a smile on his face to greet her.

"Mrs. Van Pelt," Peggy Faykus said, her eyes wide with surprise at seeing her. She used to be "Audrey."

"Hello, Peggy."

"I...uh...didn't know you were coming in. You cut your hair. Hey, I like it. A lot cooler in the hot weather, too."

She'd had it trimmed, a little more severely than

she'd intended, and the result was hideous. Fortunately, her hair grew fast. "Thanks."

"Can I get you something, coffee?" Peggy asked. "I can make some fresh. Won't take but a couple of minutes."

All this deference was making her feel old, useless. She was getting too much formal politeness lately, probably because it was easier than trying to figure out what to say to a grieving widow.

"No, that's all right," she responded. "Actually, I was hoping to see Mr. Bufano. Is he available, by any chance?"

"He's not in yet, but I expect him any minute."

"If it's all right, I'll wait in the lounge."

The room that employees used for their breaks was square, with a pair of couches and six olive-green, cracked-vinyl armchairs. Vending machines lined one wall. Dog-eared magazines cluttered a scarred, simulated blond-wood metal coffee table. She wasn't sure what color the thin carpet was supposed to be.

She'd hardly read the first letter to the editor in the most recent edition of a newsmagazine, when the general manager appeared in the doorway.

"Audrey, what a pleasant surprise." He approached with outstretched hands. "It's good to see you." He kissed her fleetingly on the cheek. "How have you been?"

"Fine, thanks. I'm sorry I didn't call ahead. If I'm interrupting something, I can come back at a more convenient time."

"Nonsense. Let's go up to my office. We'll be more comfortable there."

As they climbed the stairs, he asked about the kids,

how she was coping. At least he didn't try to ignore Clark's death, as so many people did.

She had been in Sal Bufano's office only once previously, several years earlier. He'd refurbished it since then. New tan leather furniture, maroon-and-gray striped wallpaper and thick forest-green carpet. Very tasteful and masculine. Formal portraits of his wife and two grown sons, one in a navy cadet uniform, added a homey touch.

He offered a choice of beverages. She declined. He waved her to a chair and took his behind the desk.

"Now, what brings you to see me?" he asked brightly.

"I know I have no status here, but I'm concerned about Clark's successor as sports director."

Sal nodded and became more serious. "He's not going to be easy to replace, Audrey. Your husband was an institution. I don't need to tell you that. Everybody loved him."

"I understand you've narrowed your choices to Marlee and Taggart."

"We prefer to promote from within, if at all possible."

"A policy Clark would wholeheartedly approve."

Sal smiled, and Audrey had the impression he didn't know where she was going with this. Clark had liked the GM, respected him as an honest businessman, but he'd also considered him a little dense in some areas.

"What Clark wouldn't have agreed with, Sal, is giving the job to Taggart." She'd considered bringing up Marlee's pay cut but decided that would be interfering with internal policy, which was indisputably none of her business. Better to focus the discussion on public matters, such as the sports anchor.

He leaned back in his leather chair, intertwined his fingers in front of him and studied her. "Why do you say that?"

She had debated the next part very carefully. Marlee was right; short of Wayne Prentice admitting that Taggart had bribed him to sabotage her Friday show, the accusation couldn't be verified. Audrey would be dismissed as a gossip, whose motivation and credibility were suspect. That didn't particularly bother her, but Marlee might also be regarded as the source of the rumor, and that would definitely work against her. Audrey had, therefore, decided on another approach.

"Are you aware of how Taggart tried to undermine Clark? He likes to brag about all the people he knows in the sports community, but my husband had a lot of friends there, too, friends who respected him. Word got back to him about some of the tales Tag was spreading."

Sal's brows drew together. "What kind of tales?"

"Intimations that Clark didn't write his own material, that he had his staff do it for him. Taggart even had the gall to suggest that he furnished Clark with his predictions."

Sal frowned but didn't say anything, making Audrey wonder if he thought the lies might be true.

"Compare his record before Taggart got here, if you don't believe me." She had to keep her voice from becoming shrill.

"Of course I believe you," Sal insisted, disconcerted by her outburst of emotion. "Clark was the most honest man I ever met."

"Taggart also claims he was supposed to get the sports director post when Clark's contract was up two years ago, that it was promised him when he came aboard."

"I'm not aware of any such promise. I certainly didn't make it. We never had any plans to replace Clark," Sal protested, his irritation palpable. "That's nonsense."

"You might want to check with Faye about it. They're pretty tight."

Sal's mouth constricted, but he refrained from making a comment. Audrey wondered if he was aware of their sleeping together.

He shifted uncomfortably on his seat. "Faye has nominated him for the job, Audrey, but as I said, no decision has been reached."

"Who's going to make the final call?"

He could simply tell her it was none of her business, but she didn't think he would.

"As you know, the sports department comes under Renn's supervision," he said, "so the choice is his."

"Subject to Faye's approval."

"This is too big a decision to be made by him alone, especially since he's been here such a short time—less than a year."

"Clark devoted half his life to this station, Sal. I'd hate to see his legacy destroyed. Frankly, I'm afraid if Taggart gets the anchor job, that's exactly what will happen. I'm just a member of the public now, not that I ever had any influence over what went on here," she hastened to add, "but I would like to request one favor from you."

"Name it, and if it's within my power, I'll grant it."

"I can't ask you not to give the job to Taggart or to give it to Marlee, but I do beg you to carefully review the final decision when it's made. Taggart may in fact be the best choice, but please be absolutely certain of it before you offer him the job."

"You have my word," he said.

CHAPTER FOURTEEN

TAGGART CUPPED Faye's breast, but his touch, instead of reassuring, felt somehow threatening.

"I thought you were on my side, sweetheart."

She looked over, catching his profile against the dim light coming in through the bedroom window. The man was rakishly handsome from any angle, making her wonder if it was only his looks, his sexy body, that was his real attraction. He'd charmed her in the beginning, made her laugh and feel young, but lately, every comment sounded laced with sarcasm, every smile camouflage for a sneer. She'd never liked bitterness; it was unproductive, but it seemed the underlying emotion in their relationship. Bitterness and reproach because he was a man dedicated to instant gratification, and he wasn't getting what he wanted right now.

He was ambitious. She understood that. He was counting on her, and that pleased her immensely. What she didn't want to admit was that she needed him. Not professionally. She'd risen to vice president of KNCS-TV on her own merits, by dint of hard work. Some would say by clawing her way to the top. Well, so be it. She could barely remember having been like Marlee Reid, young and idealistic. Ambition soon taught her that very sharp talons were essential to buck the crowd, to make your way in a man's world.

That was Marlee's problem. She was too generous, too accommodating and forgiving. Well, she was about to discover none of that mattered in the real world. She wouldn't be getting the anchor job she wanted so badly, and even if she did, she'd never be able to hang on to it. Maybe, Faye mused, she ought to award her the job, just to see how long she could keep it. It might be a good lesson for the young woman; let her learn early that good girls don't last.

"I am on your side," she said in response to Taggart's complaint, uncomfortable with the direction her thoughts and this discussion were leading.

"What's taking so long, Faye?" He angled himself onto his left side, crooked his elbow on the pillow and propped his head with his hand. He ran his right forefinger between her breasts. "I should have been named to Clark's job by now."

She brushed his hand away. "I told you the station doesn't want to be perceived as acting too precipitously."

"That's crap," he snapped. "You might be able to fool Marlee with that bull, but don't insult me with it. You could have given me the position long ago. Why haven't you? What's the holdup?"

She huffed out a breath. "Because it's not my decision," she explained, not for the first time. "I told you Sal insists on having the final say." And it stuck in her craw.

Mild-mannered Sal Bufano had been livid when he'd summoned her to his office that morning. He hadn't actually raised his voice, but he'd come as close to losing his temper as she'd ever seen him. She knew Renn had gone to talk to him, and she'd been prepared to defend herself from his attack—basically, by pointing out the money she'd saved. What she hadn't anticipated was Audrey Van Pelt's visit just before Renn's. If she had to guess, Faye would say Audrey had been the one who'd convinced Sal to exercise final approval of the selection for sports director.

Had Marlee put Audrey up to it? Faye doubted it. Not directly, at least. But she'd obviously discussed the situation with the older woman. Under other circumstances Faye could have used the breach in business confidentiality against her, but not now. Renn was right. She would just look more desperate, especially when the other person involved was Van Pelt's widow.

To complicate matters even more, Sal said he wanted a decision by the end of the week. That gave her three days to work things out.

"I still don't understand how you managed to lose control," Taggart said. "You're the vice president, for God's sake. You're supposed to be running the place. Even if Bufano does reserve veto power, the final choice will be based on your recommendation. So why don't I have the job?"

She was tempted to say she was doing her best, but it would sound like an excuse, one she wouldn't accept if their roles were reversed.

"Renn refuses to give up on Marlee."

"After everything she's done? God!" He threw himself back against the down pillows and stared up at the ceiling.

Her lips thinned. "Because as much as Marlee

screws up, she also draws in the viewers. If I didn't know better, I'd think the screwups were calculated.''

"Are you sure they aren't?''

She wasn't sure of anything anymore. "It's a dangerous game, if they are. Marlee's bold—'' *the way I used to be,* Faye thought "—but she's also naive and idealistic. She'd never do anything to make herself look bad.''

Taggart snorted. "Let's see. She breaks conference rules by barging into a room full of naked men with a camera—''

"I wish you'd stop harping on that. It's a no-winner. She handled the locker room situation well, apologized to Coach Dreyfus and the team and promised to respect their privacy in the future. Now they're on her side.''

"Yeah, after she'd already gotten a tape of guys in the buff for every woman at the station to ogle over.''

"That really bothers you, doesn't it?'' She blew out a breath, suddenly amused. "Actually, there wasn't that much to ogle.'' She instantly regretted her comment.

"Oh? Been reviewing the uncut version, have you?'' He propped himself up again, a lecherous grin on his face. "You're full of surprises, babe. I didn't know you were into that sort of thing. You should have said something earlier. I have a few feature-length specials tucked away we could really get off on.''

Her jaw tightened. She hadn't been a babe in a long, long time and didn't like being reminded of it. "I'm not interested.''

"No?'' He tilted his head to one side. "Pity.

Maybe another time, when you're in a better mood. There are some interesting positions—''

"No," she shouted.

"Okay." He held up a hand. "Okay. But that still doesn't answer my question. What's taking so long? That fiasco with her tapes being shown out of sequence should have been enough to get her fired on the spot."

"Your little subterfuge backfired." Faye turned her head toward him. "Renn did a focus group and they liked her. They didn't have nearly as many nice things to say about you."

He shot up. "What do you mean?"

"They said your show is all about you, not about sports. You cover the same stuff all the time, football mostly, even when it's out of season, men's sports, and your predictions are too...predictable." She leveled her eyes on him. "You're going to have to do something fresh if you want to compete. Otherwise I won't have much choice but to give the job to Marlee."

His jaw dropped for a second before he caught himself and hardened his attitude. "You'd do that?"

"I have my own position to consider, Tag. I don't think you want to support me in my old age." Damn, she wished she hadn't brought up the subject of age.

"I can be a patient man, Faye. You know that." Taggart ran his hand delicately across her abdomen. "But my tolerance won't last forever."

"Don't threaten me," she growled. "It won't work. Either you let me do things my way, or they don't get done at all. You got that?"

He raised an eyebrow and smiled. "You want to be in charge." His eyes twinkled. "Hey, that's okay with me.'' He spread his arms. ''I'm all yours. Do with me what you want. I'm your love slave.''

She wanted to call him a jerk, to climb off the bed and walk away. She should have, but she didn't. Instead, she scrutinized his rising passion and decided she wanted another sample of it. As she reached her hand forward, a plan was beginning to form in her mind.

Tuesday, May 6

MARLEE WAS WORRIED. She was feeling too good, too euphoric. Renn wasn't the only man she'd made love with since her divorce four years ago, but he was one of the few, and lovemaking—even with her husband—had never been anything like what she'd experienced with Renn. Lying in his arms, sheltered by his warmth and strength, feeling him touch her, become a part of her, was an experience beyond anything she'd ever imagined. Making love with Renn had her breathless and craving for more.

It also left her edgy, self-conscious and unsure of her bearings. Would her co-workers notice a difference in her? Would they laugh behind her back?

She made a huge batch of oatmeal pecan cookies, calculating that snickering with a mouth full of cookie crumbs would be difficult.

Renn wasn't around when she arrived at the station at two o'clock. Just as well. Facing him in the presence of other people wouldn't be easy. She half expected to find a note from him on her desk, but that would have been out of character, and he was wise not to draw attention to their relationship. Still, she was having a hard time concentrating on her work—

until an hour later when she received a call from Maxine to appear in Vice President Warren's office at three o'clock for an interview for the sports director position.

Why would Faye want to interview her? What could she possibly need to know that she didn't already? Maybe it wasn't really an interview at all but notice that they were letting her go. Son of a bitch. They'd manipulated her into a pay cut and a smaller severance package, and now they were going to can her. She muttered a series of unholy words.

Her first impulse was to find Renn. He'd know what was going on.

"Have you seen Renn?" she asked his secretary, trying to hide the desperation clutching her insides.

"He's with Faye and the GM," Trish said. "Heard you're supposed to meet some sort of a board. I sure hope you get the job. We're all keeping our fingers crossed for you."

Board? The note said an interview, not a board. Who would be there? It didn't take a board to give her notice. Maybe she wasn't being fired after all. Despair turned to hope, then plummeted again.

Why such short notice? Her hair was a mess. The yellow pantsuit she'd put on this morning wasn't the most appropriate outfit for a job interview, though it was one of her favorites. The sunshine-bright color made her feel happy and energetic. At the moment, however, she felt only confused and indecisive.

What kind of questions would they ask? She looked at the clock on the wall. Less than forty minutes to prepare. But how? If only Renn were here to bounce questions off, to give her guidance.

She returned to her cubicle and tried to organize

her thoughts. A waste of time. She was a bundle of nerves, a complex of jitters. Okay, if she couldn't quite anticipate the questions—how could they be much different from the ones she'd already answered?—she could at least get her galloping emotions under control. Maybe she should have taken up yoga when her roommate in college had urged her to. Deep breathing exercises. She'd slow her heartbeat that way. She sat in her chair, her back straight, and let her hands dangle over the armrests. She inhaled clear down to her diaphragm and released the air slowly. It didn't do a damn bit of good. She jumped up from the seat and whirled in the narrow space.

Wayne Prentice stuck his head around the corner. "You want the Rangers highlights for five o'clock?"

His gaze was focused somewhere behind her. Wayne avoided eye contact as much as possible since the tape snafu. He'd come to Marlee the following Monday morning, head bowed, and apologized.

"Accepted," she'd said, and walked away. She didn't even ask him why he'd done it or try to confirm that Taggart had put him up to it. Since then their verbal exchanges had been civil but limited exclusively to business, the easy rapport they'd once enjoyed banished. She missed the sense of teamwork and the spirit of friendship that had characterized their former relationship. She didn't doubt the sincerity of his apology; she even felt sorry for him.

"The Rangers. Right," she concurred.

He started to leave. She called him back. "How long is the cut?"

"One minute fifteen."

"You still have the midget soccer footage we took Thursday?"

"Sure."

"Give me thirty seconds of them tangling and kicking a goal, cut the Rangers to forty-five and I'll show the midgets at the end."

"Okay. I…uh…I'll do my best," he mumbled, and disappeared around the partition.

The words echoed in her ears. That was all she could do, too. Her best. Just like Clark. She sat again at her desk, folded her hands in front of her and considered the interview looming before her. If her best wasn't good enough, she'd move on. To where? She'd figure that out when the time came.

RENN WAS FURIOUS. Ever since the problems with tapes getting mangled or mixed up, he'd been showing up later in the day so he could be on hand for the five o'clock broadcast. This morning he'd decided to come in at eight to catch up on paperwork.

Faye arrived at nine, her usual time, but it wasn't until nearly two o'clock that she'd called Renn to her office. She wanted to convene a special board to interview the two candidates for the anchor job and make a decision today. She'd already coordinated it on the phone with Sal Bufano. What had Renn so uptight was the hunch that this was a setup. He wasn't sure how, but he was certain Faye had a trick up her sleeve.

Sal arrived a few minutes later, and the three of them spent the next half hour discussing what they were going to ask. The questions were innocuous enough—a review of histories and achievements. There could hardly be anything they didn't already know. On that basis alone, Marlee should be a shoo-in.

The second part of the grilling would focus on plans for the future. Renn didn't foresee much potential for surprises. KNCS was a small market in a relatively remote part of a big state. Its potential for growth was limited by population and geography. In this arena, Marlee also had an advantage since she was popular in her hometown and knew the inner workings of the station far more intimately that Taggart.

Still, Renn was apprehensive.

He would have liked to coach Marlee, but Faye had been crafty in springing this gambit on short notice, which was another reason he was suspicious. Since the questions were predictable enough, he wondered if she and Taggart had spent the weekend rehearsing his answers. Probably.

He had only a few minutes to pop down to his office and check messages before the interview. He hoped to get a chance to give Marlee an encouraging word, but she was in one of the sound booths, scrambling no doubt to get her five o'clock broadcast ready, and he didn't want to interrupt.

He returned several telephone calls, and before he knew it, had to rush back upstairs. Sal was sipping a fresh cup of coffee, oblivious, it seemed to Renn, to the charade he was about to take part in.

"I've asked Marlee to come in first," Faye announced as she motioned the two men to seats on one side of the long table in the conference room. Yellow legal tablets and sharpened pencils had been placed in front of each of them.

Faye pressed the button of the intercom, asked her secretary to send Marlee in and took her place beside her boss.

Marlee stepped into the room, scanned the arrangement and accepted the single armchair in front of the table. Renn felt as if he were part of a tribunal, an inquisitor instead of an interviewer. He smiled, hoping to reassure her. The nod he received in return was quizzical but not as nervous as he'd anticipated. He wasn't quite sure if she was confident that she'd come out ahead or resigned to the possibility that she wouldn't.

Though Sal held the center chair, Faye was plainly in charge.

"We are familiar with your background, Marlee, but I'd like you to tell us about yourself, about what you've accomplished and what you feel most proud of."

Marlee didn't speak right away. She didn't fumble over words or ramble on about herself. She'd gained considerable poise, Renn realized, in the few short months since Clark's death. Her self-confidence was more authentic now, her ability to cope with adversity more mature.

She began slowly, thoughtfully, reminded them she'd received her bachelor of science degree in broadcast journalism at TUCS, specializing in sports and entertainment, and that her mentor during the past two years had been Clark Van Pelt, the Voice of Coyote Springs. She accounted for her first job in Austin as a producer and outlined what she learned there about writing and editing stories.

"I've never missed a deadline," she said. "Even under the most trying circumstances I've come through with carefully balanced, well-written stories."

She reviewed the type of coverage she'd developed

at KNCS, generously giving credit to Clark for its high quality. "One of the things I'm most proud of," she added, "is the bond I've developed with the community and the support I've been able to give back. I've participated in fund-raisers for *Alegre* and the rehab center, been a guest speaker at charity luncheons and dinners, and I've worked with kids to improve their lives. I'm proud of these contributions to my hometown."

Out of the corner of his eye, Renn saw Sal nod, while Faye remained stoically indifferent.

"Your conduct at the end of the Coyote Springs-San Angelo game was an embarrassment to this station," she said. "It violated conference rules and jeopardized our credentials. It also held us up to public ridicule. How do you respond to that?"

In measured words and phrases, Marlee acknowledged her error in judgment.

"I regret the jeopardy it put us in, and I've apologized to Coach Dreyfus for upsetting him," she said. "But I believe the incident had a positive overall effect. We garnered our highest ratings since Clark's death, and it's at least partially responsible for our continued high numbers. I can assure you, though, that barging into men's locker rooms is not something I plan to do again." She smiled faintly. "The shock value served its purpose. It got people's attention. But I intend to be more discreet in the future. The episode proves, however, that I'm not afraid to take chances, to be bold and aggressive—" she glanced at Renn "—in my pursuit of a good story."

She made brief eye contact with the other two people.

"You asked what I'm most proud of. My interview

with Coach Hillman. I was able to get him to recount how his friend of twenty-five years died tragically but heroically only a few feet from where he was standing. I feel I handled a deeply emotional situation professionally and sympathetically. Our viewers' comments substantiate that claim.''

Sal was somber.

Faye appeared to be unmoved. ''If you were to get the sports director position, Marlee, how would you handle it. Specifically, what changes would you initiate?''

Again, Marlee didn't rush to answer. She pursed her lips and considered the question before responding.

''KNCS is a well-run operation,'' she said, ''appropriately positioned for this market. Clark Van Pelt was a very experienced professional who knew his audience. Like him, I would place emphasis on local rather than national sports, which are amply covered in network programming and ESPN. I'd maintain viewer loyalty and growth by giving people a chance to see their friends, neighbors, children and grandchildren on the air, rather than celebrities they've only heard about. That, I'm convinced, is the key to keeping them tuned in and the best way for us to earn higher advertising revenues.''

Faye thanked and dismissed her.

''I like her,'' Sal said, as soon as the door was closed. ''She's honest and forthright and gives a wholesome impression.''

''Let's keep an open mind,'' Faye murmured. ''We still have another candidate to interview.''

She pressed the button on the intercom, signaling her secretary to call downstairs for Mr. Taggart.

While the three executives waited, Sal prompted Renn about his weekend. "Did you get in any sailing? The weather was perfect for it."

Sal owned a second house on the north bend of Big Coyote Lake. His teenage sons each had jet skis, which they used when they weren't hot-rodding in their late-model sports cars. Sal was an indulgent father, though Renn had to admit after meeting the boys, they were well-mannered and respectful, as well as straight-A students.

"Went out for a few hours Saturday. Sunday was too windy to stay out long."

Renn wondered if Sal or one of his friends had seen him and Marlee and if this might be a subtle way of telling him he needed to be more discreet in socializing with his female subordinate.

"Wish I could have gotten out," he said, "but my wife's brother invited us to Dallas for the weekend. Housewarming for the new place they bought. A damn mansion. So big they've had to hire a housekeeper and full-time groundskeeper."

"Must be nice," Renn remarked, relieved that his question had apparently held no hidden subtext.

Sal snickered. "Unless the bubble bursts."

A tap on the door was followed by Taggart marching to the waiting chair. He greeted everyone and sat without being asked.

Faye began the interview the same way she had with Marlee, by asking him to recount his background.

He didn't exactly slouch in the chair, but he certainly relaxed in it. He mentioned, almost in passing, that he had a bachelor's degree in business administration, then focused on his record as a football player in college, which had resulted in his being picked by the Dallas Cowboys.

"Unfortunately," he said almost cavalierly, "an injury curtailed my professional athletic career, but I was able to make many prominent friends in that and other major national sports. As a result, I have contacts throughout the country who can furnish me with details and inside stories not normally available to even the most seasoned reporters."

He summarized the places he'd been and dropped names like birdseed at a church wedding.

"You asked what I've accomplished since I've been here and what I'm most proud of," he went on. "Professionalism. I've approached this job, not as an analyst at a small station, but as a trained expert on a large scale. I'm proud of that and the awards, both local and national, that I've received."

"You seem to know a lot of people," Renn conceded, "but you have no experience writing or reporting sports events, and you lack the technical skills to edit and produce. How do you propose to overcome those handicaps?"

"The skills you mentioned aren't essential to forward thinking, Renn. It's progressive, innovative leadership—vision—I'll bring to the sports department of KNCS-TV. We're at a crossroads. Business as usual, or break new ground and create something special and daring."

"If you were to assume the role of sports director at KNCS-TV," Faye prompted him, "what changes would you make? What would you do differently?"

"I've given that subject a great deal of thought." He folded his hands in his lap. "I'd make several changes. I'll continue to report local athletic events, not just as a favor to the community, but to promote the considerable talent in our own backyard. I'll also aim our coverage toward a broader market. KNCS-TV today is a local station. My goal is to get our call letters nationally recognized for quality reporting and the talent we discover. I intend to put Coyote Springs, Texas, on the map in the world of sports.

"I've carefully observed the local talent. It's good, and some of it is capable of much more. It's simply a matter of giving the kids the opportunity to be discovered, and that's something I'm uniquely qualified to do—bring in the high-stakes talent scouts, the headhunters who are looking for the next Troy Aikman, the next Magic Johnson, the next Williams sisters." He rested back and balanced his right ankle on his left knee. "That's why I want to syndicate our sportscast. First, by having insightful analysis of national sports. Second, by discovering and touting topnotch local athletes. With syndication will come greater prestige for KNCS-TV and much, much higher revenues. I'm the man who can make it happen, because I have contacts and inside knowledge of the sports world."

Renn didn't miss the subtle expression of satisfaction on Faye's face. The problem was that Sal seemed to be swayed by it, especially the part about higher revenues.

"Why have we never heard of this before?" Renn asked.

"As a matter of fact, I discussed the concept with Clark just before he died. He was very excited about it."

That was news to Renn, a piece of information he

frankly doubted. Clark was no fool. He would have seen through this in a heartbeat.

"He never mentioned it to me," Renn observed.

"As I said, it was right before he died. I guess he didn't have a chance to discuss it with anyone else."

And there was no way of verifying it, which worked to Taggart's advantage.

"Syndication would be a management decision," Renn pointed out.

"And a big step," Taggart agreed. "One I think we need to seriously consider if we want to grow."

"There's no money in the budget for the enormous start-up costs this scheme would incur," Renn pointed out to Sal. "We'd have to hire management consultants, another big expense." He could see, though, that the GM was intrigued by the concept.

Renn quizzed Taggart about personnel changes.

"We have a very experienced workforce here," he responded, undaunted. "Not only do I think they're up to the challenge, I suspect they'll enjoy it."

Not likely, Renn mused. Most people hated having change imposed on them. "What role would Marlee play in this?"

Taggart gave him a casual shrug. "I would hope she'll want to be part of the team. She's a good sports reporter with a faithful following. This will benefit her as well as the station."

An uncharacteristically generous comment, Renn noted. It was also gratuitous. The chances of Marlee hanging around to work for him were zip.

So this was the trap Faye had hatched, a grandiose plan Taggart didn't have a chance of pulling off but that sounded like a magic bullet to success.

CHAPTER FIFTEEN

MARLEE WAS as hyper after her interview as she had been before, but this anxiety was different. She'd done well. Renn had given her one of his little smiles that said he was pleased, and she'd seen Sal nod approvingly several times during her presentation. Faye, of course, had refused to show any emotion, but that was true to form. Marlee didn't delude herself into imagining the VP had actually been persuaded by her arguments. She did like to think, however, that she'd at least rebutted the most damaging arguments against her.

All they had to do now was make the decision. How long would that take? A simple vote. Three people. No chance of a tie. She flopped into her seat. The next hour would tell whether she stayed at KNCS or left, whether she received the promotion she'd been vying for or she marched out the door. If she ended up a free agent, she'd have another decision to make, one that was potentially life altering. Did she want to remain in this business or pursue some other career? She wasn't a quitter. Sportscasting had been her dream for more than ten years. Give it up? What would she do? Where would she go?

She could probably find another job as a reporter, but the idea of not being near Renn brought an ache to her belly. She'd suffered loneliness before, missed people she liked and respected, friends whose company she enjoyed. But Renn was different. What she felt for him was more than friendship. It was—

She refused to consider the word. No, she didn't love him. She was infatuated with him, and, after this past weekend, definitely turned on by him. But lust wasn't the same as love, she reminded herself, no matter how good the sex was.

"Marlee."

Her head shot up. He was standing before her, tall and straight. Her heart began to race, until she saw his face. Then it sank. The news wasn't good. She hadn't gotten the job. Her hands began to tremble.

"I wasn't selected, was I?" Her voice quavered.

He took a step inside just as Quint Randolph passed by, his eyes raking the scene.

"There's no privacy here," Renn said. "Come on down to my office and we'll talk about it."

"What's there to talk about?"

"Please, Marlee. You don't really want to have this conversation here."

He was right. Praise in public, reprimand in private…or give bad news. She exited the tiny cubicle and followed him.

"Sit down." He closed the door behind her.

She wanted to defy him, but her legs were rubbery. She sat.

"First of all, you need to know that Taggart has not been selected. Not yet, at least."

She stared up at him. "But—"

"I voted for you. Faye voted for Tag."

No surprise there. "What about Sal?"

"I thought he was going to be the tiebreaker," Renn said. "Turns out he isn't voting."

"I don't understand." Her head felt light.

"He wants Faye and me to agree on our choice, to reach a consensus. Otherwise, he maintains, we're doomed to failure. He's probably right."

"So what happens now?"

He sat on the corner of the desk. His knee was close enough for her to touch. "For the time being, nothing. He's given us another day to work things out between us. If we can't, he wants us to recruit from outside."

She heard his words, but her mind was too slow to absorb them. "So nothing has changed," she finally mumbled, as if to herself. "Three months have gone by since Clark died, and nothing has changed."

"I'm sorry."

She vaulted out of her seat and began pacing between the desk and the door. Her mind felt swamped, saturated, overflowing with thoughts, memories and feelings. The terrible pain of losing Clark. The guilty grasping at hope that she might get his job. The greedy clinging to Renn's encouragement. Making love to him.

Weak and trembling, she leaned against the back of the door. "I've been a fool. The interview this afternoon was nothing but a sham. You knew from the beginning Faye wasn't going to change her mind. You've been stringing me along." She closed her eyes, as if she could shut out what now seemed so obvious. "You don't really care if I get the job," she said, opening them, seeing him clearly before her. "You just want to make sure Taggart doesn't. You used me."

He'd gotten to his feet and now approached her.

She recoiled, but there was nowhere to go, no escape from all the mistakes she'd made.

"Marlee, you know that isn't true." He reached out to touch her, to hold her in his arms.

"Isn't it?"

He winced at a sharp stab of guilt and stepped back. The truth was he had strung her along *at first,* not completely for the reasons she alleged, but close enough. He'd endorsed her by default, because she was the only alternative to a guy he couldn't abide. If Taggart hadn't been championed by Faye, Renn wouldn't seriously have considered Marlee a viable candidate, except perhaps as a fill-in until a better one came along.

"My initial justification for backing you is beside the point," he said, unwilling to deny her charge. If their relationship was going to continue and succeed, it had to be based on honesty, and that meant owning up to mistakes. His prejudice against women sports reporters had been one of them. Not anymore.

"What's important is that I do want you to be the sports director and anchor."

"No, you don't want Taggart. Those are your only choices. Or were. Now you can get someone else."

"I don't want anyone else." But he could see by the quiver of her lips that she was hurting too much to understand.

"It seems to me," he continued, "you're the one with two choices now. Continue to fight for the job you want and take the chance that you won't get it, or throw in the towel and start looking for employment elsewhere."

He gazed at her, confident of what her answer would be. She'd already proven she was a scrapper.

That feistiness was one of her most endearing qualities. This time he'd support her decision without any
reservations. "So what is it going to be?"

She studied him without responding. That fright-
ened him. He'd expected her to be instantly defiant.

She left his office without answering his question.
Even worse, he didn't know at this point how she felt
about him. They'd spent a glorious weekend together,
one he would never forget, one he wanted to repeat
endlessly.

A stunned minute elapsed before he followed her
to her work space and stuck his head around the partition. She was sitting at her computer, one hand on
the mouse, her attention riveted to the screen.

"Come out to the house tonight after your late
broadcast, and we'll explore the options," he said.
"I'll pick up a bottle of Chianti and that smoked
cheese you like and some fresh fruit. We'll sit under
the stars—"

She shook her head without looking away from the
screen. "I have things to catch up on here, and then
I need to get some sleep."

He wanted to tell her they could catch up on their
sleep together, but he wasn't going to beg. If she
didn't want to spend the night with him, that was her
prerogative. Maybe under the circumstances main-
taining a little distance was a good idea. But that was
being logical. What he was feeling now was a burning
need to hold her, to bury himself in her.

He watched her exit the World Wide Web. She
gathered up scattered notes and shoved them into a
folder, her movements jerky, clumsy. Some of the
papers fell to the floor. He bent to retrieve them at
the same time she did. They nearly butted heads. He

glanced over, about to make a joking remark, when he noticed her eyes were moist.

"Marlee—" He started to reach for her. "Are you all right, sweetheart?"

She froze at the term of endearment, then bounced up stiffly. "I'm fine." She skittered to the door. "I'm on the air in a few minutes. See you tomorrow."

MARLEE MANAGED somehow to pull off her sports-cast without anyone being aware of the turmoil she was in—except Renn. He stood behind the camera-man, watching, supposedly to make sure everything went without a hitch, but she could feel his eyes on her the whole time. Afterward, he complimented her on the story she did about the local kid who'd lost an arm to bone cancer but was still playing tennis. He didn't invite her to his house a second time, though the plea was written in his eyes. She thanked him and moved on to her office, hoping he would trail behind her, hyper at the thought of him reaching out and grasping her arm the way he had that first time she'd shown up at his house, confused, despondent, aching for someone—for him—to console her. This time she wouldn't beg.

He didn't follow, and he didn't hang around for the ten o'clock telecast. She went home alone to an empty house.

She still wasn't sure she believed his protestation that he really thought she had a chance at the anchor job from the beginning. She did remember his advice, though: be aggressive. She'd done just that and had nearly gotten herself fired. Had that been his intent, to prod her into doing something stupid, so he would have a valid reason to drop her from consideration for the promotion? Except…when he could have fired her after the locker room incident, he hadn't. If what he said was true—and rumors bore this out—he'd actually defied Faye by not giving her a written reprimand.

Her problem, she concluded unhappily, was depending too much on other people, guiding her life by their expectations, their standards. She'd spent her early years trying to please her father. In the end, he'd abandoned her. She'd placed her hope and trust in her husband. He'd betrayed her. Clark had been her rock, but he was gone, too.

Renn had urged her to be enterprising. Now it was time to be independent. Maybe she'd been approaching this career choice all wrong, holding on to the wrong dream.

It was after midnight when she sat on her couch at home, booted up her laptop and combed through the listings on the internet of television stations with openings for sportscasters. There weren't many, at least not in markets higher than KNCS. She'd moved down when she'd relocated from Austin. She wasn't about to do that again, even if it meant getting an anchor position in some out-of-the-way place. She wouldn't jump at the first offer that presented itself, either.

A sports reporter job was available in New York. She didn't have a ghost of a chance of getting it, but sending in a tape wouldn't hurt. Two openings existed at stations in the Midwest, one in the South, all of them at small stations. Then she saw the Philadelphia listing. An up market. Apparently, the position had been vacant for almost six months, unless they'd forgotten to remove it from the Web site. She clicked on the e-mail address and sent a short query, identifying herself and asking if the job was still available.

The following day she came to the office early and set about producing a résumé tape. She already had a collection of her best reports, including clips of her filling in as anchor for Clark. To edit and compile a thirty-minute demo and make a half-dozen copies required about three hours.

She was stacking the cassettes on her desk, getting ready to put them into mailers, when Renn appeared.

He took one look and stared openmouthed. "What are you doing?"

She continued addressing a label. "Sending out tapes."

"Why?" He knew the answer of course. What she really heard wasn't the question but the anger in it

"I'm taking your advice." She didn't want a confrontation with him, especially here, but they needed to have this conversation. Maybe she should have accepted his invitation last night to go to his place, except then they would have made love and she would have lost her resolve. It was better this way, she told herself.

He continued to gape at her. She resolved not to feel guilty for doing what she had to do. This career decision was one she had to make alone.

"You said yourself I had two options—stay and waste my energy fighting a losing battle, or move on to greener pastures. Well, I'm moving on."

"You're quitting, just like that?" He sounded outraged.

"Just like that?" she nearly shouted back, temper and frustration boiling to the surface. She lowered her voice. "Do I have to remind you this game has been going on for three months? Yesterday you told me point-blank I wasn't going to get Clark's job. What am I supposed to do, Renn—sit around and be grateful that my pay's been cut and my benefits reduced? I've been played for a sucker, but even this dummy can catch on if you give her enough time and enough hints. I may be a slow learner, but I've finally gotten the message. I don't believe in hanging around where I'm not wanted.''

She didn't understand why her throat burned, why her words sounded strangled. After all, she was being bold and aggressive, enterprising and independent. Wasn't that what he'd advised her? She waited for him to beg her not to go, to say he wanted her.

''The situation isn't hopeless, Marlee,'' he said, his tone firm, yet under it she thought she heard sympathy and imploring. ''We lost the last skirmish, but not the battle, definitely not the war.''

''You didn't lose, Renn. I did. This is my career we're talking about, mine.''

''If you give up now, they win. Faye and Taggart. Is that what you want?''

''It's not what *you* want.''

He pulled back. ''What's that supposed to mean?''

''This hasn't been about me, has it? It's been about you. You don't want to work with Taggart, so you use me as a foil to make sure Faye doesn't get her way.''

Renn's expression went blank. ''Y-you really believe that?'' he stammered.

''What else am I supposed to believe?'' she asked, less sure of herself now than she'd been when she'd asked the question.

He bowed his head and breathed out through his

nose. Silence lingered between them for an uncomfortable interval.

"I'm sorry," he finally said softly.

She didn't know what to say, how to react.

"I'm sorry you've misjudged me, sorry I failed you." He raised his head and met her gaze. "I wish you the best, Marlee. I hope you find what you're looking for. If there's anything I can do to help you, a recommendation…anything…please let me know."

He gave her a perplexed half smile, turned and left.

Thursday, May 8

RENN KEPT telling himself Marlee's departure from KNCS-TV and Coyote Springs was the best thing for both of them. He'd broken his vow not to get emotionally involved with someone in the media. She needed to move on with her career—which, despite his promises, he hadn't been able to advance. What they'd shared had been a pleasant but dangerous interlude that neither of them could afford to pursue. Eventually, he'd put her out of his mind and be able to sleep at night.

Maxine stopped by on her way to lunch. "Here are the latest survey results."

Renn couldn't remember the station vice president's secretary ever delivering the report personally. "Thanks."

She handed him the papers. "Can I talk to you a minute? Privately."

He wondered why she was so nervous. "Sure. Close the door, if you like."

She did. "I'll probably get fired if she finds out

I'm here talking to you, but I don't care. I'm sick of what's going on.''

''You're delivering the latest report on your way to lunch. Sit down, Maxine. What's the problem?''

Still, she seemed momentarily uncertain. ''You know Marlee's been sending out tapes?''

He nodded.

''Faye received a call from a news guy in Philadelphia, Jacobs—''

''Dick Jacobs?'' He was the news director at the network affiliate in Philly. He and Dick went back to their college days and had kept in touch, though Renn hadn't talked to him since arriving at KNCS last summer.

''That's him. Apparently, they've had a sports reporter position posted for some time. Marlee e-mailed him a couple of days ago to find out if it was still available. Before this Jacobs guy answered, he wanted to check her out. I guess you weren't in yet, because Trish transferred the call to Faye.''

Renn felt the hairs on the back of his neck rise. ''And…?''

''I—''

He smiled to reassure her. ''You happened to overhear.''

She lowered her head and bit her lip.

''What did Faye tell him?''

''That Marlee isn't a team player, that she's a publicity hound.'' She frowned, hesitated another moment, then pressed on defiantly. ''That she's more interested in advancing her career than promoting the station. That she had to be reprimanded for unprofessional conduct.''

Renn felt his blood pressure rise. ''That's not true.''

''I just thought you ought to know what she's saying.''

The situation was far worse than he'd imagined. KNCS-TV was devouring its own.

''Thanks, Maxine. I appreciate your coming to me with this. Don't worry about Faye. She won't hear a word about this conversation from me. I'd appreciate it if you didn't tell anybody else, either.''

''I won't. If it were anyone but Marlee, I wouldn't even have told you, but…well…I figured you'd want to know.''

Renn closed the door behind her and put in a call to his old friend. Dick Jacobs confirmed what she'd said: that Faye had given him a very negative report.

''I was hoping she might work out,'' Dick said. ''The slot has been open for months because we need to fill it with a woman or a minority. Haven't gotten any qualified candidates so far. A woman in sports would round out our team very nicely.''

Renn didn't dwell on the irony that she might get the job *because* she was a woman.

''She's good, Dick, so let me set the record straight.''

A quarter of an hour later, he hung up the phone, sat quietly with his hands folded for several minutes, rose to his feet and climbed the stairs to the second floor.

Faye looked up from her desk. ''What is it now?'' she asked impatiently, papers held firmly in her hands. From the frown on her face, they were the survey results Maxine had delivered. Marlee's numbers were holding firm, while Taggart's were steadily declining. An objective observer would conclude the expert analyst wasn't viable as a solo act.

"I want to know why you're not satisfied with Marlee leaving," he said calmly, "why you have to sabotage her reputation with other prospective employers."

She dropped the report on the desk and leaned back in her chair. "I have no idea what you're talking about."

He assumed the seat across from her. "I just spent the last twenty minutes on the phone with an old friend of mine, Dick Jacobs. He asked me to confirm the information you gave him about Marlee. Why did you tell him she was only a passable reporter, that she was reprimanded for unprofessional conduct and that she had been given a pay cut?"

"Because they're all true."

"That's a complete distortion and you know it."

Faye straightened, her gray eyes going battleship dark. "I specifically ordered you to reprimand her in writing for breaking the ten-minute rule and invading the TUCS locker room after the San Angelo game."

"You told me that's what you wanted me to do. You didn't order me to. If you had, I would have refused." He met her unrelenting glare without flinching. "We got damn good ratings out of that incident. I don't believe in punishing people for doing a good job and advancing our interests."

"So you disobeyed me."

"I ignored an unreasonable request." In spite of his resolve to remain dispassionate—how could he possibly where Marlee was concerned—his heart was beginning to pound. "I did counsel her about using due diligence in her reporting, to carefully consider the possible repercussions of her actions, but I did not reprimand her verbally or in writing. If you want to hold that against me,'' he added bluntly, ''go right ahead, but you're a little late. It happened months ago. Now, answer my question—''

''Just a goddamn minute—''

Renn bolted from the seat, swung around and closed the door, none too gently.

''Answer my question.'' He stood over her desk. ''Why are you bad-mouthing Marlee Reid?''

Faye Warren's face froze with shock. No one talked to her that way or challenged her authority.

''I was asked for my opinion of her performance and I responded with what I believed to be the truth.''

''That's a lie,'' he spat out. ''You also broke the law by revealing confidential employee information.''

Shock turned to alarm at his raised voice. Instinctively, she pulled deeper into her well-padded seat.

''She's a damn good reporter,'' Renn nearly shouted. ''You never mentioned to Jacobs that she landed the interview with Hillman, when no one else was able to. That I nominated her for the Affiliated Press Award. That she's been holding down the sports department single-handedly since Clark's death. Or that the only reason she accepted a pay cut was that you threatened her with termination, though you had no legal basis for it. You lied by omission and petty-minded misrepresentation.''

Faye's jaw was jutted forward, her eyes hard and cold. She glared at him and took a deep breath. ''I suggest you leave right now.'' Her voice was raspy with wrath and maybe fear. ''We'll deal with this at another time, when you're in better control of yourself.''

''We'll deal with it now.''

With a shaky hand she started to reach for her telephone, probably to call for help.

''What are you so afraid of, Faye? That your boyfriend will abandon you if you don't give him a job you know full well he's not qualified for? I used to respect you as a smart businesswoman. You didn't get to be vice president of this station by being stupid, but putting your personal interests above those of the company that pays your salary is crazy and unworthy of you.''

She jumped to her feet, her hands bunched into tight fists. ''I'm warning you—''

''You've won, Faye. Why the hell isn't that enough? Marlee's quitting, moving on. You can give your boyfriend the job and watch this place crumble under the weight of his overinflated ego. Why do you have to destroy Marlee's chances of a decent career elsewhere? I don't get it.''

Faye slumped into her chair, her breathing deep and slow. Then her backbone seemed to stiffen.

''Don't be so sanctimonious, Renn,'' she said, straightening up, her tone not intimidated but condescending. ''Do you really think I and the rest of the staff don't know you're sleeping with Marlee? Hypocrisy doesn't become you.''

It was his turn to be stunned.

''You weren't thrilled about her being a sports reporter when you got here, as I recall. Until Clark died you didn't give her the time of day except to criticize, but now that you've gotten into her pants, she's suddenly the best sports reporter in Texas.''

Renn's face grew hot and a murderous rage sent his blood racing. What he and Marlee had shared wasn't some tawdry rumpling of the sheets. The union they had found went far beyond the physical, and he resented this embittered harridan cheapening that experience and the woman he loved. *The woman he loved.* The admission, so long denied, jolted him.

"Who told you that?" he demanded, but the fire in his belly had turned in another direction.

"This is a small town, Renn. You can't go sailing without people seeing you. You can't have someone else's car parked in your driveway all night without neighbors noticing." She tossed him a satisfied smirk before going on.

"You don't like Taggart? Fine. I don't give a damn whether you do or not, but he's got a hell of a lot more vision about where this station can go than your girlfriend does, or than you do, for that matter. So, you see, I have a better reason for backing Taggart than you have for trying to foist an inexperienced reporter on us."

Her mouth curled into a thin-lipped grin. "I advise you to weigh the consequences of a personal attack on me very carefully. There are ethical prohibitions against sleeping with subordinates. If you think you have anything on me, think again. I've violated no rules because Taggart isn't an employee. He's an independent contractor. As for our age difference—" she paused and averted her eyes for a moment before again staring at him "—it would be pretty difficult to convince anyone I hold power over him. Don't you guys usually go for younger women?"

Renn was shaken, but he refused to capitulate.

"I'm giving you fair warning, Faye." He pointed a finger at her. "You continue to spread lies and distortions about Marlee and you'll be sued for slander and defamation of character.''

"Get out," she said in a steady and firm voice, the executive again in charge.

He turned toward the door, then spun around to confront her one last time. "I mean it, Faye. Back off, if you know what's good for you."

Friday, May 9

MARLEE WAS AMAZED on Thursday to receive an e-mail from Philadelphia asking her to overnight a demo tape. Apparently, the news director there was very eager to finally get the sports reporter vacancy filled. He even furnished her a billing number for the courier service. Friday afternoon, Dick Jacobs called her personally to ask if she could possibly come to Philadelphia the following day, Saturday, for an interview.

"When will I be back?" she asked. Everything was happening so fast.

"We'd like you to stay through Monday so you can see our normal weekday operation. You'd fly home Monday night or Tuesday morning. Or, if that isn't possible, we can get you a flight Sunday night."

"I have quite a bit of comp time coming," she said. "I'll check with my boss about taking Monday off."

"Good. I'll have my secretary set up the itinerary and e-mail you the details this afternoon. I was very impressed with your tape, Marlee. I'm looking forward to meeting you in person."

"No problem," Renn said, when she asked him for Monday off. "Take longer if you need to. There's nothing hot going on right now. Quint or Mickey can handle the sports while you're away.''

''Or Taggart,'' she said, with a wry grin.

''Not on your life,'' he retorted humorlessly.

Two hours later she received her round trip e-ticket reservations to Philadelphia, Pennsylvania.

Dick Jacobs met her at the Philadelphia airport Saturday afternoon, drove her directly to the TV station and showed her around. They were joined afterward at a fine old restaurant downtown by his wife and two other members of the staff and their spouses.

Sunday she received a brief tour of the City of Brotherly Love and found it fascinating. Later she observed the weekend news and sports teams produce and deliver their broadcasts. Monday she met with the station manager and owner. The facilities themselves weren't much newer than those in Coyote Springs, but they were bigger and more elaborate. The staff was considerably larger and able to produce programs on a more sophisticated scale than KNCS.

''What do you think of the setup?'' Dick asked Monday evening, as he was driving her to the airport.

''I like it,'' she answered sincerely. ''Your equipment is top of the line, and your people are fantastic, a great team.''

''We're a family here,'' he said proudly, ''and we'd like you to join us.''

Dumbfounded, she stared over at him for several seconds. She hadn't expected an offer this quickly.

''As soon as I saw your tape, I knew you were the person we were looking for,'' Dick continued. ''After meeting you in person, I'm convinced of it. I can see why Renn recommended you so highly.''

Her hand involuntarily tightened on the door handle. "Renn?"

He smiled, his concentration focused on the busy road ahead. "Did I tell you we went to college together?"

"No, you didn't." Renn hadn't mentioned it, either. The news shook her. That they would know each other shouldn't come as a surprise. For all its breadth, the broadcast community was remarkably tight-knit, especially at management levels.

Renn had recommended her. He was sending her away.

The words he'd spoken as he'd stood in her doorway came tumbling back: *I'm sorry you've misjudged me. I'm sorry I failed you. I wish you the best, Marlee. I hope you find what you're looking for. If there's anything I can do to help you, a recommendation...anything...please let me know.*

Oh, Renn.

"You'll want to think it over."

She started. The man behind the wheel was talking to her.

"And of course there are details that'll have to be ironed out, such as your compensation package and buying out your existing contract."

There won't be any flack from that quarter, she was tempted to assure him. Faye wanted her gone...and Renn?

They had no future together. He was right; this wasn't a profession that lent itself to the conventions of love and marriage and a baby carriage. She was a sports reporter. That's all she ever wanted to be, and she was good at it. She'd learned from the best. Getting this offer so quickly, a big step up, proved it.

"I'm interested," she confirmed.

Dick Jacobs pulled up in front of the terminal.

"Good." He reached behind the seat and grabbed his attaché case. "I had a preliminary contract drafted. Here's a copy for you." He withdrew a large manila envelope and handed it to her. "You can study it when you get home, have your agent and attorney look it over, and we'll go from there. I think you'll find the package generous. If you have any questions at all, please don't hesitate to call me. We'd really like you to come aboard."

Marlee felt queasy all the way home, though the flight was smooth and she was normally a good traveler. She was sure she would have been heartsick even if she'd been walking on flat land with a breeze to her back.

She would be leaving Coyote Springs. Saying goodbye to Audrey and the people at KNCS. Saying goodbye to Renn.

CHAPTER SIXTEEN

Tuesday, May 13

WORD FROM Dick Jacobs Tuesday morning that Marlee had left Philadelphia with a contract in hand threw Renn into a tailspin.

"She's perfect, Renn. Pretty, intelligent, quick-witted, and she knows her stuff. The folks here fell in love with her."

Yes, Renn thought, *she's easy to fall in love with.*

He sat at his desk and stared through the open doorway. The sounds of the newsroom drifted in—printers, telephones, police scanners and television sets with their audios turned low. He'd spent all his adult life in this business. It was a world he'd always enjoyed. He'd come to KNCS with high hopes. The fast pace of big cities had tired him. The more relaxed routine of a small town had been very alluring.

What he hadn't anticipated was finding a woman who would capture his heart and make him think of home and family instead of headlines and deadlines.

He wouldn't be having this problem if Marlee hadn't been here and he hadn't become involved with her. He didn't like Taggart, but so what? He'd worked with obnoxious narcissists before. He could have found a way to deal with this pompous ass, too. It was Marlee who'd brought a new dimension to the equation. She'd made him want a life *with* someone rather than a life *in* a business.

He finished his call with Jacobs, hung up the phone and slouched in his chair. All in all, he'd had a good run in the television news business. He hadn't achieved the high ambitions he'd set when he started out, hadn't made the national scene and become a household word, but he wasn't really disappointed. He'd followed his muse and had no regrets. Until now. The one thing he wanted to do, the one goal that mattered—getting Marlee the sports anchor job at KNCS-TV—he'd failed to accomplish. Worse, she'd seen him for what he was, an opportunist.

He turned to the computer at his elbow, pulled up a blank screen and stared for a minute at the cursor blinking in the upper left-hand corner. Then he began to type. He debated with himself about explaining the reasons for his sudden action, but recriminations would accomplish nothing. *For personal reasons.*

He hit the Print key and retrieved two copies, signed one, folded the other and put it in his pocket.

"What's this?" Faye asked, when he dropped it on her desk.

He said nothing, forcing her to read it. "Why?" she demanded angrily. "Because you didn't get your way?"

"Because I don't feel good working here anymore," he stated unemotionally.

"So you're leaving us in the lurch. What about two weeks' notice?"

"I have vacation time accrued. I'm taking it, but I'll still be available if you really need me." Somehow he doubted they would. "We're in a news lull. Whatever may develop, Mickey Grimes is perfectly capable of handling. I recommend him for news director, by the way.'' He paused for a second before going on. ''You've deluded yourself, Faye, into thinking your decisions have been the best for the station, even though they only benefited you and Taggart. I hope this time—''

''Who bought you out from under us?'' she snapped.

He laughed. She couldn't conceive of someone quitting over principles. There was a time when he wouldn't have, either.

''No one,'' he said.

She shook her head, baffled by his abrupt decision, one she no doubt regarded as very foolish.

The silence that ensued lasted only a few seconds, but it was long enough to make them both uncomfortable. She stood up and extended her hand across the desk.

''Good luck, Renn. I wish you well.''

He believed her. Their previous animosity had evaporated.

She walked him to the door. ''What will you do now?''

''Maybe open a consultation service. I haven't decided.''

''Will you stay in the area?''

He shrugged. ''Coyote Springs is a nice town, but it's off the beaten track. I'm not sure how successful a media-focused business can do here. Still, with computers and e-mail, one place is almost as good as another these days.''

She left him at the threshold.

Maxine hung up the phone and eyed him, her mouth slightly open. He extended a hand and said goodbye. She mumbled something and watched him leave. He chuckled on his way downstairs. What were the odds everyone would know he'd just resigned before he even reached the bottom step?

At the foot of the stairs he was greeted by the usual mechanical sounds, but all human voices were stilled and everyone on the news floor was staring at him. He crooked an amused smile and proceeded to his office.

Trish was standing at her desk, her eyes moist. "Is it true? Did you really quit?"

He acknowledged that he had and thanked her for the work she'd done for him.

He was removing pictures and plaques from the wall behind his desk, when Mickey Grimes came into his office.

"I'm sorry Marlee didn't get the sports anchor job," he said. "She deserved it. And I'm glad she got another, better offer."

"How did you know about that?" Renn asked.

Mickey rubbed his jaw. "They wouldn't have flown her there on such short notice if they hadn't been seriously interested. And once they met her, of course they'd want her."

Renn cocked an eyebrow inquiringly.

"Okay," Mickey confessed, with a good-natured chuckle, "a friend of mine works there. I called him a little while ago."

Renn shook his head, but he couldn't help smiling, too.

"Why are you leaving, Renn?"

"It's time for me to move on."

"You've been here less than a year. Are you going to Philly with her?"

Follow her. Should he? She had no reason to want him around, not after the way he'd led her on, then let her down.

"No." He started clearing out his desk of personal effects.

"I wish you'd stay. We really need you around here."

The sentiment was nice to hear, even if it wasn't true. He'd failed, and that inadequacy would forever hang over his head, no matter where he was.

"For what it's worth, I've recommended you as my replacement," he said. "You can probably expect to be moved into the job at least temporarily." He almost advised the newsman not to let the situation drag on the way he'd let it with Marlee, but Mickey was smart enough not to make the same mistake. "It might be a good idea to get yourself an agent to handle the details."

Mickey nodded. "I will. Does Marlee know?"

"I haven't told her yet, but given the grapevine around here, I'll be surprised if she hasn't already gotten the word."

He was on his way out when Taggart came in the front door. The two men studied each other, then the sports analyst smiled and strolled nonchalantly past him. He'd be getting the sports director job now. Renn did an abrupt about-face.

Taggart sat at his desk, feet up, reading a sports magazine. He raised his head when Renn walked in. "Heard you're leaving. Good luck." The words were dismissive.

Renn closed the door. Taggart gave him a critical eye, his expression conveying as much apprehension as curiosity.

Renn lifted the guest chair, turned it around, straddled it in front of the desk and rested his arms across the back.

"You know, Taggart, you're a damn fool."

"Get out of here, Davis." Taggart flipped a page of his magazine. "I don't have time to listen to your sour grapes."

Renn laughed. "Always full of bluster, aren't you? I'll be on my way in a minute, but first I have a few things to say."

Taggart slapped the magazine closed, tossed it on the pile with others and dropped his feet to the floor. "Go ahead. Unburden yourself if it'll make you feel better."

"Congratulations on getting the sports director job."

"I would have gotten it a long time ago if it hadn't been for you."

Forever blaming someone else, Renn mused, unsurprised. "The sad part is that you're going to fall flat on your face."

"You wish." Taggart snorted disdainfully.

"I have to hand it to you. Your syndication idea is a good one. Might work, for anyone but you." Taggart clucked impatiently. "You have no idea what you're up against, do you? You haven't got a clue what it takes to run a sports department, much less motivate people to do what you want them to do because they want to do it." Renn laughed. "Your old friends on the Dallas Cowboys won't be any help. All those coaches and players from coast to coast you claim to know aren't going to do you any good, either. If you weren't so damn vain and lazy, you would have taken Marlee's offer and spent the past three months learning everything you could from her. She knows more about the internal workings of this organization than you'll ever pick up by osmosis.''

Taggart sighed. "You finished?"

"Almost. I'll tell you why your numbers are crashing. People are tired of feeling sorry for you."

Taggart sat bolt upright and slammed his hands flat on the top of his desk. "I don't have to listen to this bull. Get the hell out of here, Davis."

Renn ignored him. "They tolerated you when Clark was around. Now all they see is a pretty-boy has-been who might have had potential once, if he hadn't been injured. But sympathy doesn't last forever. At some point people expect you to produce the goods, and you haven't."

Taggart bounced up from his chair and pointed to the door. "I said, get out."

Renn didn't move except to meet the other man's glare. "Close your mouth and open your ears for a change, Taggart. And sit down."

Taggart paused, stared openmouthed and plopped back down into his seat.

"The truth is, you've blown the best opportunity you ever had. Marlee is a damn good reporter. That's why Philly is grabbing her. She has skills and talents you don't have, the interview with Hillman being a case in point. If you'd had any sense, you would have teamed up with her instead of pushing her out the door."

Renn climbed to his feet but didn't bother to return the chair. "You're a loser, Taggart. You better find someone fast to carry you, because you'll never make it on your own."

WHEN HIS HANDS stopped shaking—Renn was lucky he hadn't punched his lights out—Taggart popped the top on a can of cola from the private stock he kept in the little refrigerator in the corner. Leaning back in his chair, he again propped his feet on the desk. He was glad Davis was leaving. The man was a royal pain in the ass. That crap about people feeling sorry for him was just a load of bull. So his numbers had slipped a little lately. That was only because Marlee had sweet-talked Prentice into destroying his interview with Bill Parcells. The public was blaming him for not coming through, but it wasn't his fault. The bitch was just jealous because the best she could land was a second-rate high school coach, while he got the big boys.

He steepled his hands and touched the tips of his fingers to his lips. Still, Renn might have a point. Instead of kicking Marlee's pretty little butt out the door, maybe he ought to grab it. He smiled to himself. She could be very useful during the transition, and keeping her onboard would show what a generous guy he was. After all, no use breaking in someone new when experience was there for the taking. She knew the technical stuff, and she had the staff eating out of her hands. Why not offer her a partnership? No need to tell her it was only temporary—until he got established.

He'd have to talk Faye into giving her more money than she was making before—enough to match whatever Philly was offering—but the old girl wanted him between her legs bad. She'd do whatever he said and find a way to stretch the budget.

Taggart and Reid. Hmm. Had a nice ring to it. She didn't know as much about sports as he did, naturally, but she did have a pretty face and a sweet body. A lot younger than Faye, too. Yeah, he wouldn't mind working closely with Marlee Reid at all.

He checked his watch. She wasn't due in for another hour. He'd give her time to get over the shock of her boyfriend's abandonment, then he'd approach her. She'd jump at the opportunity to work with him, especially since it would let her show Renn she didn't need him. Taggart adjusted his pants, which had suddenly grown tight. She'd find out what a real man was like.

TWO HOURS BEFORE she was due at the station, Marlee received the call at home from Trish that Renn had quit. She was stunned. Surely his secretary was mistaken. Maybe he only threatened to resign or offered to leave. Even that seemed unreal. He loved his work too much to throw it all away.

She sat in her living room, expecting the phone to ring, waiting for him to explain what he had done and tell her his plans. Twenty minutes went by. An hour. He wasn't going to call. She wasn't important enough to him to let her in on what was going on in his life.

She changed into the kelly-green blouse and tan linen pants suit she'd bought at a shop around the corner from her hotel in Philadelphia. After adding her favorite gold necklace and matching earrings, she stood in front of the mirror. Her hair was long, the way Renn liked it. She'd planned to get it cut but hadn't had time before flying east for her interview. She'd check her schedule at the station and call for an appointment, if not for this afternoon, then for tomorrow and revert back to the shorter style she used to wear. It was easier to care for. Or maybe she wouldn't. She'd received a lot of compliments on her longer hair, here and in Philly.

"He went directly to her office, stormed right in and dropped his resignation on her desk," Maxine confided, as soon as Marlee entered the newsroom. "He closed the door. When he opened it again, Faye wished him good luck like they were old friends, then she returned to her desk."

Trish poured herself a cup of stale coffee. "Did they fight?"

"It wasn't a screaming and shouting match, I can tell you that." Maxine beckoned Trish and Marlee closer. "I tried to listen at the door, but they were talking too low for me to hear. After he left, all Faye said was that she didn't want to be disturbed and closed the door again. Made a couple of phone calls, I know that."

"Probably to her toy boy…and Bufano," Trish commented.

"That's what I figure."

Trish turned to Marlee. "Did Renn tell you what happened?"

She looked up at the clock. "I better get going. I'm on the air at five. See you later."

Marlee checked her office area to see if she had any messages. She didn't.

Wayne poked his nose in. "Some decent coverage on Wimbledon. Quite an upset. Probably good for ninety seconds."

"Thanks."

"You all right?"

Her head shot up. She hadn't realized she'd been downcast. "Did you edit that footage on the TUCS baseball game last night?"

He nodded. "A couple of tight squeeze plays. Tapes are in booth three. Let me know if you want to use either of them."

She wandered down to the editing booth and reviewed his work—he'd done a good job, as usual. She'd just put her finger on the red button to begin her voice-over commentary, when Taggart came in.

"Can I help you?" she asked without paying him much attention. Wayne passed by outside, did a wide-eyed double take and continued on down the hall.

"We need to talk," Taggart said.

She bookmarked the tape, noting the numbers on the digital readout. Cutting it to forty seconds would give her time to show a clip of Wimbledon.

"About what?"

"Us."

She froze the image on the screen and faced the man standing just inside the doorway. "I beg your pardon?"

"You know Davis has left, quit."

Marlee saw Faye Warren walk by and wondered if she was looking for Taggart. Since he had his back to the door, he didn't see her, but she saw him and kept going.

"That means," Taggart went on, "I'm getting the sports director and anchor job."

"Probably."

"Not probably. Definitely."

"I didn't realize a formal announcement had been made yet. Congratulations."

"My promotion's a great opportunity for you, too, babe."

She pulled back and studied him. He was serious. As much as she'd like to tell him to go to hell, curiosity got the better of her. "Really? What kind of opportunity might that be?"

He closed the soundproof door behind him, moved deeper into the tiny room and leaned against a work-table stacked with video tapes. "To team up. You have reporting and technical skills. I have connections and a personal following. Between us we can become the Regis and Kelly of sports. We'll go national, syndicated."

Marlee couldn't believe what she was hearing. Was this guy for real? In spite of everything that had transpired over the past months, he actually thought she'd leap at the chance to team up with him. Three months ago, when she was dull-witted by the pain of Clark's death, before the atmosphere had become so vicious, she might have considered the proposal. But now?

He chuckled. "I've got big ideas, kid. You have great sex appeal and so do I. Between us we're a winning combination. You handle women's sports and the female perspective, and I'll deal with the rest of it. Yeah—" he ran a finger down the side of her arm "—and it doesn't have to stop at the studio door. I can teach you things, sweetheart, that have nothing to do with the small screen. Things that'll make going home from work every day a new adventure."

FAYE WARREN STOOD inside the doorway of the neighboring booth. She'd been baffled, when she'd come downstairs looking for Taggart, to have Wayne Prentice put his finger to his lips and wave her into the tiny cubicle.

"There's something you might want to hear," he said.

She stared at him, then stood in silence as he upped the volume on the control panel to his right.

"Marlee…Ms. Reid turned off the recorder when Mr. Taggart interrupted her dubbing session," the photographer explained, "but she must have forgotten to turn off the mike. I was monitoring her session to make a backup tape. I wanted to make sure—"

Faye motioned him to silence, reached behind him and pressed a Record button. Taggart's voice was coming in loud and clear.

"We can have a good time together, you and me," he said. "You're pretty good at what you do, just inexperienced. I'm good at what I do, too, and I have plans. You want to go on to a bigger market? Believe me, after a couple of years together, the networks will be fighting over us."

"What about Faye Warren?" Marlee asked.

"Don't worry about her." He chuckled. "She's good in the sack. At her age she's grateful, and that makes up for a lot." He chuckled. "I bet you're better."

Faye squeezed her eyes shut as his words burned through her. She opened them a moment later when Taggart laughed.

"Forget Faye," he crooned. "She's in no position to complain. She won't be happy about me abandoning her bed, but she won't jeopardize her precious career and professional reputation by making a public stink about me skipping out on her. Under the steel girdle, she's really a prude. So what do you say?" he asked expectantly.

Silence lingered so long Faye was about to ask Prentice if the equipment was still working. Then she heard Marlee's voice.

"Here's what I say, Mr. Taggart. I'd rather deliver newspapers on a bicycle for the rest of my life than work with you. As for sleeping with you, I'll become a bag lady and live in a Dumpster on the waterfront first."

Faye shuddered out a pent-up breath. Tears threatened, but she held them back by sheer force of will.

"Get out of here, Taggart," Marlee concluded, with more annoyance than anger. "I have work to do."

Faye turned to see Prentice staring at her. She yanked the cassette from the recorder and held it tightly in her hand.

"Is this feed going to any other bay?" she demanded.

"No, ma'am."

She was tempted to ask him to keep his mouth shut, but the request would just make her look desperate. This guy had already betrayed his friend, Marlee. He had no allegiance to her. Besides, things had gone far beyond worrying about her moral reputation.

Bracing herself, she veered around the photographer, opened the door and turned left. She arrived at the neighboring booth just as Taggart was stepping out, his head up, apparently unfazed by Marlee's rejection. He stopped short, color draining from his expensively tanned face.

"F-Faye," he stammered. "What are you doing here?"

"I have it on tape." She held up the small cassette. "You're fired. You have twenty minutes to clear out your desk. If you're not gone in that time, I'll call security. And if you ever show up here again, I'll have you arrested for trespassing."

"I have a contract," he insisted.

"Not in writing you don't. But even if you did, sexual harassment is a serious offense and cause for immediate termination, which I'm exercising."

FAYE HAD ALWAYS prided herself on being able to disguise her emotions in public. Her apparent aloofness was one of the qualities that had helped her climb the executive ladder. Exercising control had never been more difficult, however, than during the thirty seconds it took her to walk from the editing booth to the stairwell. She'd purposely raised her voice for everyone to hear her fire Taggart. Now every eye in the newsroom was trained on her. She wasn't one to blush, thank goodness, but the humiliation she felt had her stomach searing.

Maxine started to ask her something when she entered the VP suite, but it died on her lips. She watched her boss stride into her office and slam the door.

Faye sank heavily into the chair. Her legs trembled uncontrollably. Her breathing hitched. For the first time in twenty years, tears welled up and spilled down her cheeks.

If ever there was a fool…

She'd known all along who and what Taggart was. She'd even been aware of what she was doing to herself, but desperation and the cringing fear of being alone had impelled her to debase herself with a man who was a fraud. What did that make her? And the compromise had all been for nothing, less than nothing. She was as alone as she'd ever been and now she was disgraced.

Swallowing a sob, she stared out the window and willed energy back into her limp body. Once her nerves had settled and the shakes subsided, she went to her private bathroom and freshened up. A quick application of drops erased the telltale pinkness in her eyes.

At her desk, she told Maxine over the intercom to call Marlee and ask her to come up and see her.

She'd actually used the word *ask,* not *tell,* not *order,* not *demand. Ask.* On a muffled chuckle, she realized she was getting soft in her old age.

She'd half expected Taggart to storm into her office, either to demand she retract her termination notice or to offer some sort of lame excuse for his disloyalty. The fact that he didn't appear told her he was gone, which further proved she'd never meant anything to him. But then, she'd known that all along.

Well, that episode of her life was over. If she was lucky, by the time she returned home, all his things would have been removed, all traces of him expunged from her life.

What she had to do now was get on with business. Sal would have to be informed about events, but she had something she had to do first.

After a polite tap, Maxine cracked the door open and peeked inside. "Marlee is here," she announced.

"Send her in."

Marlee entered. She looked neither apologetic nor intimidated by the situation. But then, why should she? She'd conducted herself with honor and dignity, virtues Faye had long since abdicated.

"Please be seated. Maxine, close the door and take a coffee break."

"Yes, ma'am."

"I heard what went on between you two," Faye

said after resuming her accustomed place. "Did you intentionally leave the mike on?"

Marlee shook her head. "I remember turning off the recorder. I must have forgotten—"

Faye believed her. "I'm sorry you had to be subjected to that."

Sympathy softened Marlee's demeanor and her voice. "I'm sorry you did, too."

The sincerity of the statement cut like a knifepoint. She hadn't been very nice to this woman who was young enough to be her daughter. In fact, she'd done everything to thwart her ambitions, yet Marlee had compassion for her pain.

"I offer no excuse or explanation for the way I've treated you, just an apology. Can you accept it?"

"Yes."

Faye nodded her gratitude. "The sports director-anchor position is yours, Marlee, if you still want it."

MARLEE FOUND RENN at his dock bare chested, wearing only running shorts. His hair was tussled, his face unshaven. He'd obviously been working hard, because his skin glistened and the veins in his forearms stood out.

His eyes widened when he saw her strolling down the path. A smile creased his face.

"Congratulations," he called out even before she reached the dock, "on your dilemma. Sports director here or reporter in Philadelphia."

She laughed. "I should have known you'd have heard."

"The grapevine is alive and well. I got a call from Maxine about an hour ago. She said Faye had just sent Taggart packing in front of the whole newsroom.

According to her, people almost cheered when he walked out.''

He set the safety on the sail's winch, leaned against the mast and folded his arms.

"I figured with him gone, Faye would have to do something quick if she wanted to keep the place from completely falling apart. Offering you the anchor slot was the logical move.'' He grinned, pleased with the accuracy of his analysis.

Marlee noted he didn't ask her which choice she'd made. "Getting ready to go out?''

"It's a beautiful day. Care to join me?''

"I'm really not dressed for an afternoon on the water,'' she said. "This suit is much too warm.''

He smiled. "Maybe you should take it off.''

"Good idea.'' She began unbuttoning her blouse.

He muttered something indecipherable when she reached for her belt buckle and unfastened it. He was still goggle eyed when she pulled out her open blouse and dropped her pants, revealing a creamy-white bikini.

He let out a captive breath while his eyes raked over her body. Was it her imagination, or did his shorts fit a little more snugly than they had a minute earlier?

"Uh…let me get the cooler—I think I'm going to be very thirsty on the water.''

"I'll go with you,'' she said, "and drop these clothes off.''

They traipsed up to the house side by side, his eyes flicking over to her. In the kitchen she watched him scoop ice into the chest they'd used in the past. His movements were considerably less fluid than they usually were. He kept sneaking glances at her. Neither of them said a word when he reached into a cupboard, removed a bottle of white wine and put it in the refrigerator.

"Did you bring sunscreen?" he asked.

"Oops, I forgot."

He seemed to have a comment on the tip of his tongue, maybe about her not being so perfectly prepared after all. What he said was, "I have some in the bedroom. I'll get it."

He returned a minute later with the plastic bottle. "I'll help you put it on after we set sail."

"Thanks." She grinned at him. "I'd appreciate that."

Again, she watched his muscles ripple and harden as he worked the crank to lift the sail. His sinewy build seemed more pronounced, more entrancing than she'd remembered. Sexier.

They set course for the middle of the main channel. The wind was light and steady today. They made slow progress. She began to coat her arms and legs with citrus-scented sunscreen.

Renn watched her, then latched the tiller.

"Here—" he held out his hand "—let me do your back."

The lotion was cool on her shoulders and back, but beneath the initial chill she felt the warmth of his palms as they gently worked the unguent into her flesh.

"I've missed you." His breath was close to her ear. "More than I ever thought I could miss anyone."

He kneaded the base of her neck. She luxuriated in the power of his physical contact.

"Have you decided which contract you'll accept?"

His long, powerful fingers tightened and released, sending impulses to hidden regions. "Sort of."

"Holding out for more money, huh? Might as well." His thumbs applied pressure along her spinal column. "You're in an ideal bargaining position—two stations competing for you."

"Money isn't the issue." Her breathing went shallow when his fingers brushed under her arms, mere inches from the sides of her breasts. Her concentration began to falter. "Faye and Dick have both offered generous packages, twice what I was making before, with built-in raises and bonuses."

"Good deal. Since my agency shingle is up, maybe you ought to hire me to conduct the bidding war between them."

"So you're officially in the headhunting business. Any clients yet?"

"A couple."

"Is there nothing that would entice you back to KNCS?" she asked.

He gently rubbed the tender spots below her ears. "I'm content with my decision."

"Pity."

He moved around to face her so fast she could only blink. "Am I missing something?"

She took a deep breath. "The agreement I made with Faye was that I'd accept the sports director position if she would offer you your old job back."

He shook his head. "It would never work. Two people, emotionally involved, working with each other in this business."

"Hmm. I suppose you're right. I guess I'll just have to accept the job in Philly." She started to move away.

He reached out and tangled his fingers in her hair, brought his body in contact with hers, lowered his head and kissed her hard on the mouth. "I can't imagine why you'd want me there."

She had to establish physical separation from him, not because she didn't want to have him touch her, but because she couldn't think straight when he did. "This trip gave me time to think, to put things in perspective, to figure out my priorities."

She settled into the deck chair in the shade of the billowing white sail. "I once asked Clark why he didn't move on to bigger and more lucrative markets when he had so many opportunities to do so. He said because he was happy where he was. He had a good life here, earned enough to support his family comfortably. I didn't understand him then. My job was the most important thing to me. I couldn't understand not aiming higher, not wanting to earn more money and have a bigger audience."

Renn sat across from her, his hand on the tiller.

"Flying back here from Philadelphia, I began to see things differently. The reporter job is great, Renn, a terrific opportunity, one I'm sure Clark would have advised me to take." She scanned the horizon, as if she could see him there. "But I think it would have saddened him, too, because he would have seen that I was chasing after an illusion."

Renn remained silent, listening to her, and that in itself was a source of pleasure.

"You and I talked about sacrifices once, remember? You said as long as you held on to your number one priority in life, everything else was negotiable. Clark's highest priority was doing his best for the people who mattered most to him—his family. It made him happy, and it made them happy, as well. I want that, Renn. I want to be happy by doing my best for other people.''

She got up and sat beside him, gazed into his eyes and placed her hand on his cheek. His skin felt warm under the fine grit of his beard. ''The most important person in my life is you. I want us to be together, Renn. I want us to love each other and have children and share that love with them. I want us to succeed where our parents failed.''

He bracketed her face with his big hands. ''I'll do anything for you, Marlee. Go anywhere.'' He brought his lips to hers. ''I love you.'' He kissed her again. ''Maybe we can work something out,'' he said, when he broke off a third time. ''I have a few ideas I'm exploring.''

''Do you really?'' She smiled, imagining areas she'd like to explore, as well. ''A way for us to stay together?'' She snaked her arms behind his back, rested her cheek on his hard chest and listened to his heartbeat. Sure and steady. ''I don't know, though. I can be a terrible embarrassment.'' She gazed up at him. ''I barge into places where I don't belong, tend to dominate situations, don't take no for an answer.''

He tightened his grip on her, joining them at the hips. ''Would you be willing to take yes for an answer?''

''Depends on the question.''

He arched back and bowed his head to meet her eyes. ''I think we're getting this all backward. What I mean is, will you marry me?''

She thought a moment. ''Okay.''

''Okay?''

''That means yes. I'll marry you.''

EPILOGUE

Saturday, June 21

"STOP FIDGETING," Audrey ordered, as she adjusted the veil on Marlee's head, "unless you want to take your wedding vows looking like a cockeyed sailor."

Glenda snickered. She was wearing a cherry-red knee-length chiffon number, cut low enough to show a marginally modest hint of cleavage. "I'll take care of this," she told Audrey. "Go put on your shoes, or are you planning to be a barefoot matron of honor?"

"I'm not putting them on till the very last minute." Audrey's peach-colored satin dress was set off with a double strand of matched pearls. "And since this happy event is taking place in my own backyard, I reserve the right to kick them off the minute Marlee says 'I do'."

"I'd hold off until Renn says those magic words," Glenda suggested. "Taking them off too soon might jinx things and mean he'll keep her barefoot."

They all laughed.

"And pregnant?" Audrey asked, with a twinkle in her eye.

Marlee blushed. "Not yet, but—"

"That's what yachts and honeymoons are for." Glenda removed the bridal bouquet from the white cardboard box on the edge of the dressing table.

"Speaking of yachts," Audrey commented, "it was very generous of your parents to offer you theirs for your honeymoon."

Marlee clamped down on the temptation to squirm as she gazed into the vanity mirror. She was convinced Glenda had overdone the eye shadow. "Renn insisted we tell them about our engagement in person," she said, and wondered what she had forgotten. "I was just going to send them an announcement of our wedding."

His request was almost as much of a surprise as the reception they'd received. Her parents had acted genuinely pleased with the news and had invited them to spend the following weekend with them on their sloop in Corpus Christi. While the tension Marlee always felt around her mother and father hadn't completely dissolved, she was amazed at how well the four of them had gotten along. The short voyage was the closest she'd felt to being part of a family since she was a little girl—aside from Clark and Audrey, of course.

"Where's the watch?" Marlee asked now, almost in panic.

"Relax." Audrey picked it up from the corner of the dressing table. "It's right here."

The antique gold timepiece was too big for a necklace, so Marlee had elected to wear it as a brooch.

Audrey pinned it on for her. "Ready?"

"FAYE'S DEPARTURE was awfully sudden," Mickey Grimes said, as he tried for the third time to get Renn's bow tie right.

"Let me do that." Sal Bufano elbowed the best man aside.

Mickey exhaled with relief and backed away. "I guess we should have seen it coming...after the way Tag humiliated her."

"Maybe everybody didn't like her—" Sal expertly looped the black tie and adjusted the edges to even them out "—but until Clark's death she was a pretty good vice president."

"I think it's ironic that she asked you," Mickey said to Renn, "to broker her deal with the network."

"Why not?" he shrugged. "In my short-lived career as an agent, I'd already found a job for Wayne out in El Paso. Not on the air like he wanted, but he'll have a better chance there of making the jump."

"He sure screwed up here," Mickey muttered.

Renn nodded. "As far as I'm concerned, he redeemed himself when he called Faye into that editing bay to listen in on Taggart propositioning Marlee."

Mickey removed the boutonniere from the box on the bed and handed it over to the general manager, perfectly content to let him draw his own blood trying to pin it on Renn's tuxedo lapel. "I sure hope Faye likes cold weather. She's not likely to find many hundred-degree days in Alaska."

"Actually, she was looking forward to the change." Renn ran his finger under his stiff white collar. "Turns out she used to be an avid cross-country skier until she came here."

"Ski Texas," Mickey quipped. It was one of the few activities the Lone Star State didn't offer.

"I wish her well," Renn said sincerely. He understood the loneliness he'd glimpsed in her eyes. "By the way," he said to Sal, "I found out from Audrey that the sports-syndication idea was actually Clark's.

He'd been toying with it for a while and finally broached it to Faye the day before the accident.''

Sal shook his head. ''I wondered about that. I didn't think Taggart was smart enough to come up with an ambitious concept like that by himself.

Renn snickered. Maybe the general manager wasn't as oblivious as people thought.

After appraising his handiwork, Sal said, ''Okay, Mr. Vice President,'' referring to Renn's new job at KNCS-TV, ''I think it's time to face the music.''

Mickey hummed ''Here Comes the Bride'' as he opened the sliding-glass door to the backyard, where everyone was waiting.

THE WIND WHIPPED tendrils of her long, blond hair against his face. He brushed them aside, bowed and pressed his lips to the curve of her neck. She raised her shoulder into his touch and smiled.

''It's been a long day,'' he murmured. They'd driven down from Coyote Springs after the wedding, taken the sloop out into the Gulf of Mexico. The longest day of the year was waning.

She leaned against his chest, her vision filled with the golden glow of the setting sun, her entire body warmed by his closeness. ''A wonderful day.''

He turned her in his arms, touched his forehead to hers. ''I love you, Marlee.''

This wasn't the first time he'd said those words today, but they still hadn't lost their magical effect.

''I never dreamed I could feel this happy.''

His hair fluttered in the breeze. His body was warm against her, hard and powerful. She wrapped her arms tightly around his waist.

He brought his mouth down to hers. She opened to him hungrily, aggressively.

The tropical wind filled the jib as they glided farther out in solitude on the undulating sea. An orange moon kissed one horizon as the other faded into darkness. Between them, diamonds twinkled in the black velvet sky.

Her hands stroked his back. He laid his jaw against her temple.

"I pledge with all my heart," he said softly, "with all that I can command, to keep you always as happy as you are today."

"I want us to be a family, Renn. I want children we can love and who will love us in return."

"Then let's see what we can do to bring new life from this joy." He said the words lightly, but they contained a prayer as well as a promise.

Slowly, he began to undress her. His hands trembled as he unbuttoned her blouse; his fingers fumbled. His touch, when it came, was gentle and almost worshipful. Together they slipped his shirt over his head and tossed it aside.

She spread her hands across the firm contours of his chest.

"Shall we go belowdecks?" he asked.

"Here," she said. "Under the stars."

"Heaven."

She laughed. "Close enough."

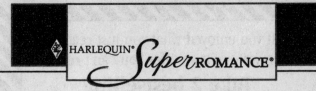

HARLEQUIN *Super*ROMANCE®

A new six-book series from Harlequin Superromance!

THE BIRTH PLACE

**Enchantment, New Mexico, is home to The Birth Place,
a maternity clinic run by the formidable Lydia Kane.
The clinic was started years ago—to make sure the
people of this secluded mountain town had a safe
place to deliver their babies.**

**But some births are shrouded in secrecy and shame.
What happens when a few of those secrets return
to haunt The Birth Place?**

**Coming in October 2003,
Sanctuary by Brenda Novak
(Harlequin Superromance #1158)**

As a teenager, Hope Tanner ran away from a town hidden from the outside
world and ended up at The Birth Place. It became her sanctuary. Now she's
going back there—back to Lydia Kane. And back to Parker Reynolds…

Watch for:
September 2003
***Enchanting Baby* (#1152) by Darlene Graham**
November 2003
***Christmas at Shadow Creek* (#1165) by Roxanne Rustand**
December 2003
***Leaving Enchantment* (#1170) by C.J. Carmichael**

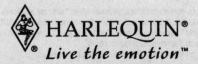

HARLEQUIN®
Live the emotion™

Visit us at www.eHarlequin.com

HSRTBP

If you enjoyed what you just read,
then we've got an offer you can't resist!

Take 2 bestselling love stories FREE!

Plus get a FREE surprise gift!

///////////////////////////////////////

Clip this page and mail it to Harlequin Reader Service®

IN U.S.A.	**IN CANADA**
3010 Walden Ave.	P.O. Box 609
P.O. Box 1867	Fort Erie, Ontario
Buffalo, N.Y. 14240-1867	L2A 5X3

YES! Please send me 2 free Harlequin Superromance® novels and my free surprise gift. After receiving them, if I don't wish to receive anymore, I can return the shipping statement marked cancel. If I don't cancel, I will receive 6 brand-new novels every month, before they're available in stores. In the U.S.A., bill me at the bargain price of $4.47 plus 25¢ shipping and handling per book and applicable sales tax, if any*. In Canada, bill me at the bargain price of $4.99 plus 25¢ shipping and handling per book and applicable taxes**. That's the complete price, and a savings of at least 10% off the cover prices—what a great deal! I understand that accepting the 2 free books and gift places me under no obligation ever to buy any books. I can always return a shipment and cancel at any time. Even if I never buy another book from Harlequin, the 2 free books and gift are mine to keep forever.

135 HDN DNT3
336 HDN DNT4

Name	(PLEASE PRINT)	
Address	Apt.#	
City	State/Prov.	Zip/Postal Code

* Terms and prices subject to change without notice. Sales tax applicable in N.Y.
** Canadian residents will be charged applicable provincial taxes and GST.
   All orders subject to approval. Offer limited to one per household and not valid to
   current Harlequin Superromance® subscribers.
   ® is a registered trademark of Harlequin Enterprises Limited.

An offer you can't afford to refuse!

High-valued coupons for upcoming books

**A sneak peek at Harlequin's newest line—
Harlequin Flipside™**

**Send away for a hardcover by *New York Times*
bestselling author Debbie Macomber**

How can you get all this?

Buy four Harlequin or Silhouette books during
October–December 2003, fill out the form below and send
the form and four proofs of purchase (cash register receipts)
to the address below.

I accept this amazing offer!
Send me a coupon booklet:

Name (PLEASE PRINT)

Address _____ Apt. # _____

City _____ State/Prov. _____ Zip/Postal Code
098 KIN DXHT

Please send this form, along with your cash register receipts
as proofs of purchase, to:

In the U.S.:
Harlequin Coupon Booklet Offer, P.O. Box 9071, Buffalo, NY 14269-9071

In Canada:
Harlequin Coupon Booklet Offer, P.O. Box 609, Fort Erie, Ontario L2A 5X3

**Allow 4–6 weeks for delivery. Offer expires December 31, 2003.
Offer good only while quantities last.**

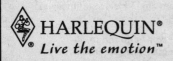

Visit us at www.eHarlequin.com

Q42003

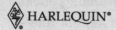

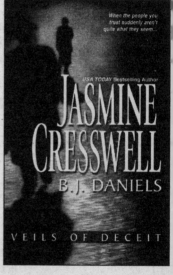

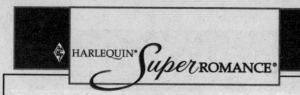

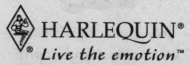